"Don't."

His plea came out in a gravelly whisper, and he kept his eyes closed. But he didn't stop her. Her ire melted into compassion. She knew too well what it was like to fight it as he did now. She'd struggled to keep her physical desire in check from the moment he'd looked into her eyes right after he'd rescued her this morning.

"It's okay, Stanton. Isn't it normal to feel like this with an ex? We're not robots." She shouldn't be standing so close to him, shouldn't tempt fate by touching him at all. Her fingers explored his jaw, stubbled by beard growth, unable to get enough of him. No amount of touch with Stanton would ever be enough. She swayed toward him, unable to stop the desire-fueled momentum that pushed her closer.

"Dom." With no further preamble, Stanton's arms came around her waist and he tugged her flush against him. Air whooshed from her lungs as she felt his full length, including his erection, through their layers of clothing. She let her arms go to his shoulders and met him halfway as his mouth came down on hers.

* * *

The Coltons of Grave Gulch: Falling in love is the most dangerous thing of all...

* * *

If you're on Twitter, tell us what you think of Harlequin Romantic Suspense! #harlequinromsuspense

Dear Reader,

Welcome back to Grave Gulch, Michigan, with Dominique and Stanton's story. As a suspense writer, I had my hands full with all of the bad guys throwing themselves at this intrepid couple, and even I wasn't sure how they'd get out of certain predicaments. What struck me about Dominique and Stanton, however, was how even though they'd parted ways two years ago after a brief but passionate relationship, the bond between them remained stronger than ever. Which makes for the best romantic tension and their pursuit of happily-ever-after while fighting to stay alive all the more intense. Please enjoy this story as much as I did writing it, dearest reader!

I'd love to connect with you. Please find me at my website, gerikrotow.com, and sign up for my newsletter at gerikrotow.com/contact.

Are you on social media? I am, too!

Facebook.com/gerikrotow

Instagram.com/geri_krotow

Happy reading!

Peace,

Geri

COLTON BULLSEYE

Geri Krotow

HARLEQUIN
ROMANTIC
SUSPENSE

Special thanks and acknowledgment are given to Geri Krotow
for her contribution to The Coltons of Grave Gulch miniseries.

Recycling programs
for this product may
not exist in your area.

ISBN-13: 978-1-335-62890-9

Colton Bullseye

Copyright © 2021 by Harlequin Books S.A.

Harlequin Enterprises ULC
22 Adelaide St. West, 40th Floor
Toronto, Ontario M5H 4E3, Canada
www.Harlequin.com

Printed in U.S.A.

Former naval intelligence officer and US Naval Academy graduate **Geri Krotow** draws inspiration from the global situations she's experienced. Geri loves to hear from her readers. You can email her via her website and blog, gerikrotow.com.

Books by Geri Krotow

Harlequin Romantic Suspense

The Coltons of Grave Gulch

Colton Bullseye

Silver Valley PD

Her Christmas Protector
Wedding Takedown
Her Secret Christmas Agent
Secret Agent Under Fire
The Fugitive's Secret Child
Reunion Under Fire
Snowbound with the Secret Agent
Incognito Ex

The Coltons of Mustang Valley

Colton's Deadly Disguise

The Coltons of Roaring Springs

Colton's Mistaken Identity

Visit the Author Profile page at Harlequin.com for more titles.

To my dad, Ed—your love has made all the difference.

Chapter 1

"I am being careful, trust me. It's my job. If I'm not on my toes, I'll never get to the bottom of Charlie's murder. I'm starting with the man who falsely accused him and whose testimony put Charlie behind bars." Dominique de la Vega focused on driving in steadily increasing traffic as she entered downtown Grave Gulch, Michigan. Her morning call to her fraternal twin, Soledad, was over her car's hands-free option.

"I get what you think your job is, sis, but I'm worried. You're pushing your luck too far. If Charlie really was murdered, as you suspect, there are bigger forces at work here than one or two criminals." Soledad's concern made Dominique wish they were speaking face-to-face, so that she could better reassure her sister.

"I'm telling you, Soledad, Charlie was innocent.

And I'm chasing down the best lead since his death, since he was convicted." Ever since she'd started teaching creative writing at the county prison two years ago, Dominique's investigative-reporter instincts had gone into full alert mode. One of her students there, Charlie Hamm, had convinced her that he'd been wrongfully convicted and imprisoned; he'd insisted that the drugs he'd been accused of dealing were never his. He'd claimed the witness who'd testified against him had lied, and that false evidence had been planted, too. When he was found dead from an "apparent prison brawl," she'd wished she'd acted sooner on Charlie's claims of innocence. The least she could do now was dig until she uncovered the truth.

"I get it, Dom. You want justice for Charlie. He was one of your best students and his poetry touched you. He convinced you he's innocent, and I have to agree that it sounds like he was. That's fair. But what kind of justice would it be if you get hurt, or worse? You said this possible lead is about who put Charlie behind bars in the first place?" Interest reflected in Soledad's voice, but Dominique also heard distraction. Her sister was baking up a storm, as usual. As the owner of Dream Bakes bakery, it was her life.

Dominique stopped at a traffic light on Grave Gulch Boulevard in the center of the city and gave herself a heartbeat to answer her perceptive sister. If she told Soledad who she was really interviewing, or where exactly she was going to in Grave Gulch, her sister would relay the information to their father in two seconds flat. He'd flip out when he discovered she was willfully going into a part of town she wasn't familiar with, in the midst of a drug cartel's attempted take-over of their beloved town. If her father had read last night's police blotter in today's *Grave Gulch Gazette*, he'd have figured out that she was going to where drug-related crimes had occurred last night. To complicate matters, there was a serial killer on the loose in Grave Gulch, too, which added to Rigo de la Vega's worries over his family. Dominique appreciated his concern, and while she felt not a little guilty that her actions caused him any angst at all, she wasn't going to stop doing her job. She was in her third decade of life and had ventured into dicey situations all over town and the state for countless stories over the years.

She didn't disagree that any part of Grave Gulch was downright dangerous when it came to ferreting out information from a probable drug dealer and, at the very least, false witness. The particular street she was headed to had seen several serious crimes this past week, all opioid related. As much as GGPD wasn't co-operating with her on this story as she'd like, she felt for them. Every time it looked like the heroin scourge had been tamped down, it popped up again without warning. ODs often happened in clusters, depending on where the dealers were peddling their lethal wares. Dominique had learned long ago that getting the whole story often meant taking risks but getting her dad on board was another matter. Especially difficult to con-vince was her father, Rigo, who was beyond protective of his twin daughters, and always had been.

"Yes, the lede in my story is about Charlie's key accuser. I'm going to get to the bottom of why he lied. Then I hope to tie it into Randall Bowe." She believed Charlie's case was yet another instance of GGPD's forensic scientist deliberately tampering with evidence. "You know he's suspected of planting the false evidence that almost put Everleigh Emerson in jail for murder for good, and several others, right? Thank goodness Everleigh was cleared." She gripped the steering wheel in frustration. "GGPD is in over its head, if you ask me. Now that it's solid truth that Bowe planted false evidence against Everleigh, GGPD has clammed up about the other cases, including Charlie's. It'll be more difficult for me to figure out why Bowe went after Charlie but trust me, I will." Randall Bowe was in her sights, and she wasn't letting up. Charlie's death placed his case at the bottom of the GGPD priority list, as other investigations Bowe deliberately damaged involved the living. It wasn't going to keep Dominique from getting justice for Charlie, though. "Look, sis, I can't give you more information right now. You'll tell Dad." She never could hide her thoughts from her sister.

"Maybe I will, Dominique. You sound like you're already in trouble. Where are you, anyway?" The clang of utensils and aluminum sheets sounded over the connection.

"I'm in Grave Gulch, downtown. I just drove past you. Trust me, I wouldn't walk into a place unprepared, or in a dark alley or anything like that. Plus, it's broad daylight."

"Don't patronize me, sis. We both know that evil knows no time of day or place."

Dominique sighed, wondering why she'd told Soledad about any of this in the first place. Why hadn't she kept their morning connection time simple and allowed her sister to do most of the talking?

You're nervous.

Yeah, she was a little on edge. Going in to find and ask for an interview from the man, according to Charlie, who'd lied to put Charlie behind bars wasn't what she'd consider usual, even for her job. Usually she'd leave the investigation of criminal activity to GGPD. But first Randall Bowe had evaded questioning, and now GGPD was locked down about Bowe's involvement in rigged prosecutions. She had to do something, and that meant going after the false witness. Ever since she'd taught the creative writing and poetry night class for inmates in the county correctional facility, she'd established a bond with the men and women who had found themselves behind bars, rightfully or wrongfully.

She'd listened to those who claimed wrongful imprisonment, agreeing to use her skills as a reporter to investigate what she could, but made no promises. Again, this wasn't her job, it was GGPD's. As she had expected, she found many allegations to be unfounded. When confronted with the facts, most inmates had stopped insisting on their innocence. But not Charlie Hamm. Charlie had always proclaimed his innocence, and had never given up on the hope that he'd be released early, once someone proved his case. He was arrested a year before he'd been arrested again and sent to prison, both times for dealing. Dominique believed his heartfelt admission that he'd deserved the first arrest, and that it had scared him straight. Charlie swore he'd been in the wrong place at the wrong time, trying to help users and dealers break free of the sordid life. He'd been brought up on drug dealing charges with what appeared to be minimal but solid evidence in the form of an eyewitness and a single fingerprint. When the reports of Randall Bowe's alleged evidence tampering began to leak out of GGPD, her reporter senses had tingled. Besides the possibility of a fake witness, evidence against Charlie, in the form of the fingerprint on a suitcase full of opioids, had been handled by none other than Randall Bowe. She knew GGPD was up to its neck in work with the confluence of a serial killer on the loose, the increasingly powerful opioid cartel and the recent kidnapping of a young child who'd been thankfully found safe and sound. All separate incidents. It would be unrealistic to expect GGPD would get answers on Charlie's case with any sensible timeliness.

Charlie had provided her with all of what he knew, and she'd taken copious notes. He'd believed that a cartel kingpin was at the heart of his wrongful imprisonment. When she'd pressed Charlie for names, he'd balked, claimed that "the drug ring in this town is nothing for a lady like you to worry about." Charlie had always maintained that he was in recovery for his own heroin addiction and was a reformed part-time dealer, as well. His goal was to help others and he'd claimed that's all he'd been doing when the event went down that got him in jail this time. Dominique wasn't a novice and knew that addicts were often gifted liars—it was a dark side of the disease. But Charlie was unlike any other addict or dealer-turned-legit she'd ever interviewed. He'd had such a positive outlook, even while imprisoned. If only she'd pushed harder, Charlie might still be here. She still struggled to accept he was gone.

Charlie Hamm had been found dead in his cell from internal bleeding suffered during a prison fight. Some of her students told her that they suspected the fight was staged—Charlie was targeted by the drug cartel's boss because Charlie had specific information pertaining to the drug ring, including the names he never provided her—but they wouldn't tell her more, wouldn't give her one iota of information. They were afraid for their lives, too. Which led her to wonder if Charlie knew the actual kingpin, a name that so far had eluded law enforcement, as far as she knew.

To make matters worse, she'd uncovered facts that made it appear that Grave Gulch PD hadn't done all their homework when Charlie was arrested. Point in case was the faulty evidence, processed at GGPD's small but highly capable forensics lab. Dominique wasn't certain, or convinced, that Randall Bowe's reason for planting the fingerprint against Charlie had anything to do with the cartel. But GGPD wasn't letting her in on their findings, so she had no choice but to follow the drug cartel lead.

Charlie never should have been brought to trial. Her heart ached for him, as much as her fury gnawed at the possibility of his fatal injuries being a premeditated murder. His suspicious death and all he'd told her previously triggered her reporter instincts into rapid-fire, and fueled her quest to solve Charlie's case.

"Please don't go to Dad, Soledad. Not yet. You know that this story is vital not only to my career, but for the *Grave Gulch Gazette*, as well."

"No offense, sister of mine, but I don't give a beaver's butt about the Pulitzer Prize. I want you safe. Alive." More clatters sounded over the connection as Soledad worked. Dominique didn't bother to correct her sister. Sure, she wanted to one day win the coveted journalism award for her paper as much as anyone, but her first allegiance was to the story. The truth. She'd add justice in there but knew that the local courts would handle that part. If she could make sure the bad eggs at GGPD were called out and meted punishment. First she had to get some evidence that Charlie's jail time was for a crime he might never have committed.

"Are you making any of your snickerdoodles today?" Her stomach grumbled at the thought of the buttery cookies, cinnamon baked into their crisp outer edges.

"Remember what I said about patronizing, sis?" Soledad wouldn't be sidelined by Dominique's distraction technique.

"Sorry. Trust me, sis, I'm good. I've got to go, but I'll stop by later if I can." She enjoyed all of the confections her sister created but had to limit herself as her sweet tooth was a serious downfall. As she passed a too-familiar apartment building, the memory of eating hot cinnamon rolls in Stanton Colton's bed flashed in her mind. The deep pang of regret it triggered was immediately followed by frustrated annoyance. She'd split from the dangerously attractive bodyguard two years ago. Ever since she'd taken on Charlie's story, though, Stanton had been occupying more space in her head. Probably because she'd always relished sharing her research with him, getting his perspective as a security expert. Memories of him and their short-lived—but passionate—relationship belonged in the past.

"You sound distracted." Darn Soledad's ability to read her, even over the phone. Dominique got it; she was equally able to sense where Soledad was emotionally, sometimes physically. They definitely had the twin connection.

"I was for a minute. This traffic is nuts. I'm good, though, no worries. I should probably let you go. We both have work to do."

"We sure do. I'm proud of you, sis. But for the record? It's my prerogative to worry about you. Know I love you and nothing is worth any fancy journalism prize." Soledad's sincerity infused Dominique's center with a sense of peace. It wasn't the first time she'd realized how blessed she was to have her sister in her life.

"Love you, too." She disconnected and continued to drive down Main Street, passing all of her favorite haunts, including a used bookstore and nearby coffee shop. Her description of where she was headed hadn't been completely honest. She was well into the east side now, where in a matter of a block the cheery storefronts gave way to run-down buildings and littered sidewalks. Making sure she was as close to the desired cross street as possible, she parallel parked in front of a dilapidated building that had splintered plywood boarded over every window and the door. Still, it was better than driving into the depths of the narrow road she'd have to walk to get to the interview.

Dominique quickly reviewed the address and map on her phone, committing her next steps to memory. Her subject, Johnny Blanchard, was her ticket to the truth. The witness had been difficult to chase down, and he refused to speak to her on her cell phone, opting to leave her messages on the *Gazette*'s landline only. Before Charlie's death she would have thought Blanchard might be slightly paranoid, but her perspective about what was happening in Grave Gulch had changed. The more information she gleaned, the more deadly Charlie's case seemed to have been, from the moment he'd been arrested. The fact that Charlie wouldn't give her names, in his attempt to protect her, was telling.

Grabbing her trusty, purse-size notebook, she locked her wallet in the glove compartment, shoved her favorite bag under a blanket she kept on the back seat and held on to her keys and phone as she exited the car. Once on the street, she pocketed both in her wool cream trench coat. She was grateful for the warmth it gave her on the almost-spring day. April here meant snow and cold temperatures as Lake Michigan slowly woke up from its long winter of freezing conditions.

Her choice of outfit was deliberate. It was important that she looked like her profile photo on the paper's website and her social media, so that Johnny knew it was really her. Otherwise, she'd never get close to Johnny; he'd take off the minute he spied her from the window or peephole of his apartment in this part of Grave Gulch. Which was why she'd opted to not dress down but maintain her preferred style.

Everything she relished about living in Grave Gulch—the large, diverse community with a small-town feel, being able to recognize many faces at her most visited restaurants and coffee shops, the ability to enjoy all four seasons with gusto—faded as she turned off the main street and walked deeper into what could be low-income housing in Anytown, USA.

Except this was her home, and it made her heart ache to see the suffering too many endured on a regular basis. She'd reported ad infinitum on the opioid epidemic's effect in Michigan, but nothing ever prepared her for the harsh separation between the addicted and those who'd either never touched the stuff or were in solid recovery from addiction. Dominique regularly read the published police blotter, and when GGPD hadn't been so shut-down against giving the press case information she'd ask officers for more specifics. Last night two drug deals had been reported on this same street. GGPD had captured one dealer but the other was still at large. The street wasn't abandoned, but the sense that she was being watched hung like a thick wet blanket about her shoulders. It was to be expected; drug dealers were always looking for a new source of income.

How many people had taken this same route to their

eventual death as they sought the fix for their addiction to prescription painkillers?

You can't fix everything. Work on fitting your piece of the puzzle.

Only three more blocks and she'd be where the answers to Charlie Hamm's wrongful conviction, and maybe even his murder, began. A shiver struck her nape and shocked down her spine. Soledad was right; this might be her worst idea yet, coming here alone. Her toes itched for her comfortable and serviceable running shoes. She'd remembered the address, the location on the street grid. But she'd forgotten how quickly a situation could go sour.

You're being ridiculous.

She was. It was the middle of the day and she was here to ask a person a few questions. No need to make a dramatic case out of it. Let the drama stay where it already existed: in Charlie's probable murder.

Dominique breathed in rhythm with her steps as sweat trickled down her back, soaking her blouse under the wool coat. It wasn't one of her usual forest hikes, with hawks, eagles and trees overhead, but only a few blocks.

Only a few more steps. She forced herself to appear confident, without fear. It was only human to be wary when the ravages of several crises saturated Grave Gulch's normally upbeat atmosphere.

You know you fanned the flames unnecessarily.

Admittedly she'd been fired up when she'd used her personal social media to basically threaten the local cartel with retribution for their crimes against Charlie, along with pushing GGPD until all information pertaining to cases Randall Bowe had worked was released. She'd vow to not stop until she had the truth. Her last post had been a bit softer, as she'd promised to seek justice for Charlie and wouldn't stop until she had the entire truth. But the meaning was indisputable.

The address was in her sights. She stepped across a tiny break in the sidewalk, kept going. The interview wouldn't take long if Johnny cooperated.

A big *if.* Interview subjects were notoriously fickle when the stakes were high. Soledad's words haunted her. Was she risking her safety for nothing?

No. Justice was *always* worth fighting for. But she picked up her pace, anxious to get her story and get home.

Stanton Colton used his best security and protection skills to follow Dominique without being detected by the intrepid reporter. Typical of her defiance against what any normal person would consider "too dangerous to go it alone," she was making her way up a street that had appeared on the GGPD's reports from last night.

He had double-checked that he had a weapon both at his waist and ankle before he left his vehicle. He'd parked several spaces behind where Dominique had left her modest SUV on the east side of Grave Gulch. It wasn't the flashiest of cars, and its black paint looked to be covered with an extra layer of dust. He briefly wondered if she was still partial to hiking through the Michigan forests for hours on end. It would explain what looked like long pine needles piled in the corners of her windshield, plus the fresh pollen on the auto's hood. They'd enjoyed hiking the one spring they'd been together. As well as what they'd done before and after the outdoor excursions. Sometimes, during.

Nope. Not going there. Since they'd split two years ago, he'd kept a tight leash on his mind's wanderings regarding Dominique. She'd knocked him to his knees, something no woman before or since had ever done. And he'd promised himself he'd never again be so foolish, leaving his heart that vulnerable to a woman. Fortunately, his workload as CEO of Colton Protection left him little time to worry about being alone.

Dominique picked up her pace and he matched it, careful to stop into doorways or behind battered building corners as needed. He knew it was only a matter of time before she discovered he'd been hired to protect her, but Stanton wasn't ready to come completely clean about the assignment he'd accepted from Rigo de la Vega, Dominique's fortress of a father. Not until he had to. Dominique was in all likelihood going to give him a hard time about protecting her, and while he understood her viewpoint, he also had great respect and compassion for her dad. The man was frustrated by his daughter's refusal to see how her job as an investigative reporter put her life at risk, and he was desperate to keep her safe. Whether Dominique wanted to be protected or not wasn't on Rigo's radar. Rigo's words had been persuasive enough for Stanton to agree to accept the job. He'd reminded himself repeatedly over the past hours that was all this was. An assignment. A contract. It had nothing to do with his and Dominique's past.

Sure, it doesn't.

If he were to be honest with himself, Stanton was curious about where she was headed. He'd scoured the *Grave Gulch Gazette*'s digital archives for her reports from the last six months, which in fact was only a review of what he already knew. He never missed one of her articles. Dominique was a gifted journalist and while his business required mostly the nuts and bolts of crime reports to keep his clients safe, he always appreciated the more human, personal take that Dominique's reporting highlighted. Whether she was covering a crime victim or a high school student who'd been awarded a university scholarship, Dominique put her all into every report.

Stanton hadn't learned anything new from her reports, but when he'd checked out her social media page, his breath had lodged in his chest. Dominique had waved the equivalent of a red cape at the local cartel's kingpin. She hadn't mentioned the cartel or even drug dealing, but had made it clear she was going to uncover "every last criminal" who'd caused Charlie Hamm harm. And taken shots at GGPD, which made his head hurt for his sister, Chief of Police Melissa Colton. Then, as he'd scrolled further, he saw the "anonymous" posts threatening Dominique. He'd bet his professional reputation that the unknown posters were directly connected to the cartel. It made his gut twist to think about the sheer hatred aimed at her.

They'd parted ways two years ago and yet he'd never

been able to let go of his instinct to protect her, to keep her safe. At least, that's what he told himself. If he dug deeper into his emotions, the truth was probably more related to the fact he might still have some remnant of feeling for her.

They were over, though, had been for two years, and he wasn't letting his thoughts wander back into that soul-sucking black hole. At least not during work hours. He had to stay in his lane, which for the foreseeable future was protecting Dominique.

And it was in her best interest to not alert her of his presence just yet. Letting her know he was here, and not leaving her side from here out, would cause a scene and draw the most unwelcome attention. Because no way in Hades was Dominique de la Vega going to accept his services without a fight. She insisted on doing things her way; this much, he'd wager, hadn't changed about his ex.

Her figure swayed with what he'd affectionately told her once was her ability to hypnotize him with a single step. She was clad in dressy wide black pants and a belted, short white trench coat that emphasized her hourglass figure, and he had to consciously work to keep his head in the game. He was here to guard Dominique, keep her safe from the deadbeats who were blasting her social media with vile and vitriol. He might be called to protect her from the kingpin of a major drug cartel operating in Grave Gulch. Not to stare at her ass nor think about how her skin had felt under his fingers.

Reviewing what Rigo had told him, which lined up

with what Stanton had read on her social media posts, infuriated him. She'd put herself at unreasonable risk, and if he had his way, he'd talk her out of pursuing this story. Or at least wait until the dust settled from the blowout that was certain to ensue once she realized he wasn't going anywhere. His gut churned as he followed her, knowing dang well that Dominique was incapable of letting anything go if it involved unearthing the truth.

And then this morning's post. What on earth had possessed Dominique to announce publicly that she was looking for sources and intended to uncover "corruption in the Grave Gulch Police Department"? It was pure madness on her part. Sure, she was a reporter and he was all for her exposés and her investigative journalism. Free press was important. But it was best to leave the riskiest aspects, including anything to do with hardened criminal figures, to law enforcement agencies, or LEA. Let the local, and national as needed, LEAs handle it. Except Dominique seemed convinced that she couldn't trust her local LEA, GGPD. It stuck like a jagged piece of glass in his awareness because he had so many Colton family members who worked at GGPD, including his older sister, Chief of Police Melissa Colton.

Dominique's passion for justice was one of several characteristics that had attracted him to her in the first place. In his current position as her bodyguard, though, it made her a prime target for a bad guy at the top of a local drug ring, as well as a bad cop, or police supporters who misread her motives. The threats facing her were myriad and made his heart pound, his stomach twist. If anyone hurt her—

You've made a mistake.

Yes, accepting this job was pure madness. It would have been smarter to pass this assignment off to one of the half dozen fully trained and capable agents on his payroll. Colton Protection had earned its sterling reputation by protecting high-visibility clients from politicians to judges to A-list Hollywood celebrities. If he didn't get his head completely in the mission, which meant blocking off any thoughts of his previous association with Dominique, he risked blowing their until-now untarnished image.

Rigo made it clear—he's hired you to keep his daughter safe, period.

She turned right and made her way up a side street that wasn't nearly as traversed as the one where they'd parked. He mentally envisioned the side alleys, all memorized. Passing the first side street without a problem, she didn't look over her shoulders once. Dominique seemed to be pretty certain of where she was headed. He scanned the street, approaching the next alley. A hooded figure emerged from behind a large tree and Stanton paused, keeping Dominique in view. The hairs on his nape rose as he saw the man quickly close in on her.

Stanton broke into a jog, then a full run as the figure's hand reached into his pocket.

"Dom, look out!" he yelled at the top of his lungs, but not before he saw the thug grab for Dominique.

Chapter 2

A shout behind her sounded exactly like her name and she halted, frozen in place. No, it couldn't be. It had sounded like a male voice was calling "Dom." Only one man ever called her that and he wasn't here. Not since their breakup.

She pushed forward, quickened her step. Her progress was harshly interrupted by hands that felt like a pair of vise grips on a shoulder and her hair, yanking her backward without warning.

"Ow!" She grunted in surprise, pulled off her feet as though she weighed no more than a bag of flour. Fear drove her to fight like the devil as she was dragged into the alley and then over a threshold, through a door kicked open by the attacker, and shoved into a dark corridor. Her assailant slammed the door closed with his heel as she kicked, twisted and screamed. Anything to gain purchase. Putrid smells of urine and body odor assaulted her and she knew this was a place where people came to use. To die.

"Shut up! Knock it off or you're dead." The thug's hand clamped painfully over her mouth. His voice was low and ugly, and left her with zero thoughts of reasoning him into letting her go. He had her from behind, one beefy arm around her neck, holding her body against his. He smelled like cheap cologne and bubble gum, not much of an improvement over the stench of the building.

She knew she was going to die whether she resisted or not, so she sunk her teeth into the vile-smelling hand. He swore and let go of her mouth, and she sucked in a breath to yell as she tugged away from him. Her scream was cut off by a hard slap to the side of her head. Stars floated in her vision but didn't stop her training and that internal voice that urged her to keep going, to give it all she had. She reverted to the basic hand-to-hand combat techniques she'd learned years ago.

She jutted her elbow back into his gut, which felt like hitting a brick wall, but her stomp on his instep elicited a hiss. Cheered by his discomfort, she did the same with her other leg, taking time to drag her heel down his shin first, then press into his foot with all her might.

He responded by whipping her around and shoving her up against the wall, which forced her head back against the plaster. More stars floated, but not enough to preclude her vision. A mean mug of a man stared at her, his breath foul no matter the huge wad of pink gum he chewed on. Pure menace glowered in his gaze as his hands encircled her throat and he cut off her airway.

Dominique fought for her life, unable to gain enough space to breathe. Using the technique to take her shoulders under his arms and force her arms up to release his proved impossible, as each of his limbs was built like an oak tree. She clawed at his leathery face, kneed his groin repeatedly. He flinched but kept the pressure on her throat. Panic rose and, unable to get his hands off her neck, she gave his head a hard slap.

"You bi—"

An explosive sound, and a burst of light as the door was kicked open. Her attacker let go and Dominique collapsed to the ground, gasping in short breaths as her airway let in precious air. Heavy footsteps sounded, fading through the building.

"Dominique. Look at me."

The voice she'd recognize in her deepest depths of despair broke through her panic and gave her what in the past several minutes had grown dim. Hope.

Stanton had saved her; he was here. With great effort, she turned her head and looked into the deep blue irises that had haunted her every night since their breakup two years ago.

"What the heck are you doing here?" Instead of sounding authoritative and irritated, her words creaked out like a baby frog's first ribbit. Scratchy and weak. "Please tell me you're not stalking me."

He helped her to her feet and put his hands on her head, tilted it to one side and then the other, ran his fingertips over her throat. She batted his inspection away and made to walk out the door of the crusty building. But her wobbling legs betrayed her and if not for his guiding arm, she'd have fallen.

He swore under his breath and pulled her close, encasing her in his arms. It wasn't a bear hug or a greeting, but something to help ground her and convey that she was safe, not alone.

"Stanton, I'm okay. Really." She spoke with the same raspy voice into his shoulder, involuntarily inhaling the spicy masculine scent that was proprietary to Stanton. It was as though his very essence held the elixir for all that ailed her. The bruises that would soon begin to throb, the constant quest to get the best story, to find justice for Charlie. The long lonely nights since they'd broken up.

No.

She pushed against his chest and refused to meet his gaze again. Not yet.

"I'm ready to leave now. By myself. Feel free to finish whatever you came here for. Why are you here, by the way?"

"I believe 'thank you' is a customary response in these situations." His crisp enunciation, the inflection of gentle mocking in his maddening baritone, triggered a waterfall of emotions and memories that she wasn't in any place to handle. Not after being so brutally accosted.

"Sorry, yes, thanks so much. I'm… I'm fine." She lifted her chin but still couldn't meet his knowing gaze. They were on the concrete sidewalk, and the daylight seemed dimmer than it had only minutes earlier. As if they were in a black-and-white movie and the bad guys were all around. She ignored the part about the sexy man who'd saved her life. "I have to talk to—"

"You're not talking to anyone but me until we get out of this godforsaken part of town." He placed her arm through his bent one and urged her forward. "If you can't manage it, be honest." She remembered this tone of his deep voice all too well. Stanton was on a mission. He'd hoist her over his shoulder and carry her out of this derelict neighborhood without a second thought.

"Wait. I can do it myself." She stopped and leaned on him as she took off one, then the other, shoe. "Let's go." Free of the treacherous heels, she still accepted his support but was able to set a much faster pace as they strode toward Main Street. Away from the danger, and her attacker.

Away from finding out who had murdered Charlie Hamm.

"Here's my car." Dominique pulled away from Stanton, but he held tight, keeping her walking past the black SUV. He was concerned not only about her throat and body bruises, but her feet. She'd walked five city blocks in stockings. Or whatever kind of thin socks she wore.

"We're leaving it for now. I'll have one of my agents pick it up later." All he wanted was to get her into his vehicle and get them both out of here. If it was up to Stanton, Dominique wouldn't leave his sight until he'd eliminated the threats against her.

"I only need to get inside it, to take my tote bag. I keep an extra outfit, plus workout gear. I have a pair of running shoes and socks. Let me get them. Then I'll go with you." Her softly mumbled response made the hackles on the back of his neck stand up. She'd been injured worse than he'd been able to assess. Nothing less would explain her agreeing to his direction.

"Where's your bag?"

"Back seat. My wallet's in the glove compartment."

He set her against the trunk of a tree lining the main street while he opened the back door and retrieved her bag, then her wallet. When he straightened, she reached for the strap and he shook his head.

"I've got it. I'm parked here, too." He nodded at his vehicle, a few spots behind hers. "I'll get your car back to you within the afternoon, Dominique. It's the least of your worries right now." He helped her into the passenger seat of his Jeep, specially outfitted for Colton Protection. It was their bulletproof, armored, VIP vehicle. They had another SUV and two similar sedans, but he'd chosen the Jeep for this job. It had the fewest memories of his time with Dominique. Unlike one of the sedans where they'd made love, during that insanely passionate stretch of time they'd dated.

He didn't want any distractions while he was protecting Rigo's daughter.

"What put you here the same time as me, if you're not following me?" Her voice was returning, though if he wasn't bent over her, his ear so close he felt her breath, he didn't think he'd be able to hear her as well.

"My new assignment." He clicked the seat belt in

place for her. "Hang on." He shut her door, walked around the front of the vehicle, doing a 360-degree inspection of the street. Satisfied no one was lurking, ready to follow them, he got into the driver's seat and started the engine.

"Let me guess—your assignment is paid for by one Rigo de la Vega?"

"I haven't even started driving, Dominique." Her brows rose and he hated the sight of smudged lipstick on her cheek, grotesquely elongating her downturned mouth. That bastard had done that to her.

Cursing under his breath, he turned away from the distraction of her face and shifted into gear. He executed a U-turn and headed back toward downtown Grave Gulch. Taking Dominique to safer ground. Anywhere but here.

"Yes, I accepted the job from your father. He's concerned about the threats you've received over your social media posts. He had every reason to be, I'd say."

"He, you—*both* of you—have no right to interfere in my work." Her voice, softened by the attack, didn't hide her outrage. He wished he'd reached her sooner, prevented that rat from laying a single finger on her. Anything to have her be her usual high-energy self. This shell of the woman he knew as strong and invincible frightened him.

She's safe. Focus on keeping her that way.

"Perhaps your work is none of your father's concern, and that's an argument you can take up with him, but you can't tell me you're not grateful that I showed up when I did." Maybe verbal sparring would bring her back from the scare.

She remained silent and he inwardly cursed. Dominique had survived a brutal attack only minutes before, and while he'd argue with her later about his "right" to protect her, he definitely had no business goading her while she was in such a vulnerable state.

Problem was, Dominique didn't do "vulnerable." She was as far from that as any woman he'd ever met, including trained agents.

"You taught me well." Her admission startled him.

"What's that?"

"When you insisted I learn hand-to-hand techniques and defensive maneuvers. All the stuff you taught me? They paid off." He saw her reach for her throat, rub it, in his peripheral vision. "It's true, what you said over and over again. I'd automatically do what I had to, if the time ever came, and it did. I was almost free of him but he was awfully big. I couldn't get his arms to budge once he had a grip."

"I'm glad to hear the training helped. You handled yourself incredibly well, Dominique." His heart had constricted, then pumped with fear, rage and purpose when he saw the thug grab her. He'd been so afraid he wouldn't reach her in time... "Did you hear me shout?"

"I did, but I didn't know it was you. Not at first." Or had she, but she just didn't want to tell him?

"It wouldn't have mattered, as by the time I saw him it was already too late. He came out of nowhere." Stanton hated that he hadn't seen him sooner.

"I feel stupid that I didn't hear or notice him in that alley. I was paying attention to the street."

"I'm sure you were. Don't beat yourself up over this." His choice of words hit him and he grimaced. "I mean—"

"It's okay." She let out a hollow laugh. "I understand what you're saying. I think it'll take me some time to process, is all."

He nodded. "It always does." He turned off the main drag onto a wide boulevard.

"You sure would know. You've been beat up enough times." Dominique's voice held memories that he'd fought so hard to keep behind the mental wall that he never broached. Where their time as a couple resided. How she'd nursed him after an overzealous fan had tried to grab his client, or the time she'd made love to him after work when he thought the agency was taking an economic hit. He needed to stop reviewing the many times they'd made love, but it was difficult to keep the memories at bay when she was right next to him.

"Where are we going? I'm not going to the hospital, Stanton." She looked out the windshield, consternation on her face. He silently thanked heaven that she hadn't noticed their destination until now.

"You're getting checked over." He pulled up to the emergency room entrance of the main city hospital.

"I don't need the ER. I'm fine, really. I didn't lose consciousness, and I can walk. If I'm hurting tomorrow, I'll call my doctor."

"Save it. A thug with hands bigger than my head just tried to squeeze the life out of you. And there's already bruising on your neck." He swallowed. That jerk had come too close to doing permanent, life-taking damage.

She slumped against the seat. "Fine. But you're getting me an oat milk latte after this."

The reminder of her favorite comfort drink should have put his defenses up, reminded him to stay emotionally detached as he protected her. Instead, a tiny sphere of warmth lit, deep inside.

Too close to his heart.

"Here you go." Stanton set the covered paper cup in front of her and she immediately wrapped her hands around it, craving the warmth. After a relatively quick ER visit, he'd made good on her demand and they'd slipped into her favorite café. It was pretty hopping for a midweek morning. She'd noticed a man at the counter, who'd looked at her with unguarded interest when they'd entered, and her first reaction had been to turn and run until she realized why he was staring. She knew she was a sight, had seen her ghastly reflection in the hospital restroom. But she'd settled for simply splashing water on her face and running a hand through her long hair. It required too much effort to fully put herself back together. Thankfully none of the other customers paid her a second glance.

"Thanks for this." She kept her gaze downcast, giving herself imaginary space between her defenses and Stanton's overwhelming presence. It hadn't changed, two years later. At least, not for her. The constant sexual tension still arced between them as if she'd never walked away from him.

"I learned long ago to take your threats seriously. Heaven forbid you don't get a latte when you want it." He took a sip of his green tea, which appeared to be scalding hot as steam rose from the open cup. She knew he preferred to sip his beverages without the plastic cover. Funny, the things she remembered.

"Are you satisfied with what the doctor said?"

"Why wouldn't I be?" The trauma surgeon had been called in to look at her throat X-rays and do a physical exam. She'd told Dominique that she'd heal in time and there was no lasting damage. "The ER doc seemed to know her stuff."

"Some bruises don't show up on X-rays. They can take days, weeks to surface." His mouth was a grim line that underscored his concern.

"Why do I get the feeling you're talking about something other than today's injuries?" She glared at him, or rather, tried to muster the energy to give him the evil eye. Instead she watched his familiar poker face. The only hint of his passion lay in his laser-blue eyes. She swore she saw white-hot sparks in their depths as he considered her.

"I know I'm the last person you want to have to spend any time with, but your father was convincing in his arguments that your life was in danger. I owed it to him, to your family, to take the job."

"Whatever you needed to do, I understand, but I don't have to like it. My sister is the one really responsible for Dad's involvement. I talked to her this morning and I had a feeling she was going to call him."

"Unless you spoke to her about your interview's location before ten o'clock last night, Rigo was ahead of it." Stanton's declaration cut through her wanting to blame Soledad, or Stanton, for her father's overprotective ways. "He told me to start this morning."

"Of course he was on to me sooner. He always is." She sipped her latte, relishing the creaminess of the oat milk, but it did little to soothe her fraught nerves. In all her years as an investigative reporter she'd never faced a life-threatening situation. Criminals, sure. Menacing notes sent to the *Gazette*, meant for her. But not a direct physical assault. That had to be why her hands were still slightly shaking. "And it turns out he was correct. More fool me." Appreciation flowed through her veins as she realized her father had in all likelihood saved her life. As had Stanton.

"You were focused on your job, is all. Getting the story. It's normal for you to dig deep."

She looked at him, ready to see the sarcastic expression on his face. Instead a soft smile played on—

Stop.

"You understand that much, don't you? That my job is my entire focus. It has to be. You never allowed our, um, your personal life to interfere with your job. It's no different for me, Stanton. It has to be all about the story." As her safety would be his single focus as long as she was his assignment. A prescient shiver traveled down her spine and she didn't want to examine the cause. Because the part of her that had never let go of

Stanton, of what they'd shared, was jumping up and down in giddy anticipation.

"I do understand." He didn't elaborate, for which she was grateful. The last thing she needed was any more reminders of how well he'd once known her.

They sat in companionable, or rather, bodyguard-and-person-in-danger silence for several minutes. Stanton had chosen the small bistro table in the corner, away from most of the customers who frequented the busy café. Her eyes took in the familiar surroundings and she tried to allow herself to relax. When her gaze passed over the barista station and she saw the same man staring at her, her back stiffened.

"What is it?" Stanton missed nothing. She wanted to believe it was all about her, but it was why he was such a great security professional. Stanton was an observer and had superb intuition.

"There's a man sitting at the counter, at the far right, who I noticed when we came in. He hasn't moved and has kept his eyes on me the entire time. It could be nothing—"

"There are no coincidences when you're being targeted by a drug kingpin, Dominique." At least he didn't add in the part about how she'd attracted the unwanted scrutiny with her provocative social media posts. And she had the sense that Stanton knew a lot more about why she was a target than he let on.

"Is it the cartel I should be concerned about, or Len Davison the serial killer? What do you know about Charlie Hamm, Stanton? About Randall Bowe's habit of mishandling evidence? Or the drug cartel that's run rampant in Grave Gulch?"

He straightened in his seat, leaned in toward her. It'd be so easy to think he was about to tell her how much he wanted to make love to her again instead of preparing to fill her in on who wanted her dead.

Chapter 3

Stanton avoided giving Dominique an answer right away by checking out the man she was concerned about. He sat at the counter, his eyes on his phone, not looking like he cared an iota about them, or her. But Dominique wasn't about drama or paranoia. If she thought something was odd about the person, he trusted her instincts, even though he knew Dominique was testing him. Or maybe baiting.

She thought he was so busy doing personal protection that he was out of touch with what mattered to her, to the Grave Gulch community. He held back his defensive retorts, reminded himself he had to remain detached. Keeping his peripheral vision on the man of interest, he met her gaze.

"Charlie Hamm was imprisoned two years ago for

dealing opioids, as part of a ten-year sentence. He was killed during a prison fight in the county jail last month. There's been speculation that his death wasn't a result of a random fight but instead a murder. Many in the local community think it's all a big conspiracy theory, though. Several people have been accused of crimes that didn't make sense, and the evidence against them all points back to GGPD's forensic scientist, Randall Bowe. There's a serial killer on the loose, Len Davison. If that's not enough, to swing back to Hamm, Grave Gulch has been slammed by the opioid epidemic, and with so many young victims, scores of families are still grieving. The last thing they want to hear is that a convicted dealer was wrongly incarcerated."

"You've been reading my work." Her eyes sparked and he reminded himself it was from professional pride and not from pleasure that he'd sought out her story. That she wasn't happy about being so close to him.

"I regularly read the local paper, among others. You know that much about me. Like most folks around here, I read the *Grave Gulch Gazette* every day. It's my job to stay on top of events, especially any crime that affects Colton Protection."

She nodded. "That makes sense. Still, it's always reassuring to know someone's reading my words." A grin let him know that no matter how brilliant a journalist she was, no matter how much success the *Grave Gulch Gazette* achieved, Dominique was a humble soul at heart. Her compassion for her fellow citizens had been part of what attracted him to her when they'd met. She'd been researching how well recent parolees integrated back into their community and had fought to find decent employment for a woman she'd first reported on when the woman was still an inmate. He wasn't surprised at all by her interest in another convict's story.

"This story, Dominique. Charlie Hamm, the cartel. Fill me in on what you haven't put in print yet. Do you have the kingpin's name?"

"Okay." She took a deep breath, sat her sore body up straight. "First, I don't have any names. That's one thing Charlie wouldn't give me. Do you remember that I was interested in teaching creative writing and poetry to inmates at the county prison? I followed through with it after, um, we split, and have been volunteering there at night and on weekends ever since. I had Charlie Hamm as one of my students. As you said, he was convicted. But he always proclaimed his innocence. Charlie was different, Stanton. He explained to me that he was put in jail on drummed-up charges by a user he was trying to help. The drug kingpin's honchos got to the witness and threatened him. They wanted Charlie out of the picture—he was making too much of a dent into their profits by referring users, and dealers who used, to the new public rehab that opened four years ago."

"The one halfway between here and Detroit, with costs billed according to economic need?" His agency had protected a handful of clients right after they left rehab, to keep them safe from the cartel, whose spiderweb reach often drew the newly sober back into their addictions.

"Yes. It's provided beds that Grave Gulch's three centers often don't have. At last count the rehab had processed over three thousand addicts. I don't have the statistics about how many have remained sober, but that's three thousand users who otherwise would never have received help. We simply don't have the space to treat them all in our town." The Grave Gulch community had risen to the occasion with public education and health resources. But it was never enough to stop the constant stream of vicious, drug-related crime.

"I thought the follow-up care was a problem, too." One of his agents on staff had a sister who'd been free of heroin for two years. It had required a geographical relocation and thousands of dollars that their parents took out of their retirement funds.

"It is. Most addicts don't want to do—or can't afford to do—the necessary geographical move to get them away from their usual haunts. The dealers certainly don't want to see their prime customers move away. Of course, they'll find more willing users any way they can." She took a sip of her latte. "This is very nice, thank you."

He nodded, ignoring the warmth under his breastbone her gratitude stoked. He always had ridiculous overreactions to Dominique.

"Charlie wrote the most touching poetry while he was in my class. It turns out he left his first wife for his second, in between arrests. The prosecutor used his sudden divorce against him, saying he wasn't to be trusted. He'd been picked up several times for various petty crimes but didn't serve hard time until the dealing charge. Did you realize the only physical evidence against him was a fingerprint on an old suitcase? And the unreliable witness's statement, of course. It was a false charge, in my opinion."

"Which brings us to your obsession with bringing down both the entire drug ring and rooting out corruption in the Grave Gulch PD."

"I don't appreciate the way you said that, Stanton. Is it my passion? Probably. My purpose? Absolutely. When you say 'obsession,' it discounts my motives. I'm not trying to 'bring down' the entire GGPD. And no matter how it looks, I'm not gunning for your sister. Melissa's always done her absolute best as chief. I understand the instinct to shut down discussion with the *Gazette* on a sensitive issue like Randall Bowe. But I'm not giving up on rooting out any bad cops or employees that are working there and have a history of corruption." Her chin jutted and her eyes blazed, resentment enunciating her intent. Had her emotions stayed bottled up deep inside her, the way his bitter disappointment at her rejection was shoved into the moldy basement of his heart?

Crap.

They were back to it, then. "This is where we left off, isn't it." He didn't pose it as a question, as they both knew the answer. Talk after talk, and eventually argument after argument, had led to this. The unscalable wall of discord between them. She never felt he accepted her for who she was. And Dominique had been right—he'd wanted her in a safer occupation, for certain. Since he worked a job that at times brought him face-to-face with his mortality, he had little room to judge Dominique's vocation. But he had a right to care about his girlfriend at the time, the woman he'd thought he wanted to marry, didn't he?

Not according to Dominique, who'd insisted the story always came first.

No matter, as he'd lost her anyway. And to heck with how much of his heart remained sore to this day.

"Stop it, Stanton. No more talk about what's passed between us. That remains in the past. *We're*—" she motioned between them "—over. If you expect me to allow you to follow me and give me your exceptional level of protection—" he didn't miss that she acknowledged his need to provide only the best that he could offer "—then you're going to have to back off trying to keep me away from doing my job. Otherwise I'm going to tell you and my father to shove your intentions—"

"Whoa, no need for cussing, ba—uh, Dominique." *Double dog doo.* He'd almost called her "babe." Letting out a long, extended breath, he flexed and fisted his hands. Wiggled his toes in his shoes. Cleared his mind of the emotions being with Dominique elicited. "Let me rephrase. Your sense of duty to get the story, to clear Charlie Hamm's name, moved you to post your concerns on social media."

"Yes. But lest you think I did that without any forethought, think again." She grinned and his lips twitched in response. "I put my intentions out there on my public profile in hopes of stirring up more witnesses and more sources about what's going on in the police department."

"You had to realize it'd catch the attention of the cartel, Dominique."

"I did. And how do you know it won't inspire a drug ring member to cash it in, give me the story and accept a plea deal, witness protection from law enforcement? I know GGPD's budget has to be stretched to the max right now but I've seen other reporters in similar circumstances get witness security. Melissa strikes me as someone who's all about keeping people safe, even if she won't let me in on the internal investigation." She shook her head. "I'd be further along, frankly, if it wasn't for GGPD. They have messed this case up but good, right from the start, with the either misidentified or clandestinely placed fingerprint."

"Now, wait a minute there. I've read the reports. The police on duty when Charlie's crime, okay, *purported* crime, went down all did their jobs well." His protection service worked in unison with Grave Gulch Police Department. It wasn't just about Melissa being chief, but about the GGPD's professional standing in the community. He kept GGPD informed, and they let him know salient points about cases and persons of interest. The two-way flow of information had allowed him to provide exceptional protection to several high-level political and local celebrity figures who'd found themselves stalked by criminals. Colton Protection had helped GGPD out by taking some of the load around personal security away and keeping intended victims safe while the police did their job to apprehend suspects.

"Maybe they did. But what about Randall Bowe?" She threw the forensic scientist's name out like a tie-breaking card in a poker came. "He's been under scrutiny for messing up evidence on several drug-related crimes. GGPD's apprehension rate was excellent, and they appeared to be making headway against the drug cartel. Until a number of the charges had to be dropped due to lack of evidence or witnesses. Tell me what's going on there, Stanton?"

"I can't tell you anything, Dominique, except that the police are on your, *our*, side. You know this better than I do, since you regularly report on them." He sighed. "I'll concede that there could be one bad cop, maybe two, including Bowe. That doesn't incriminate the entire department, though."

"It most certainly does if no one's trying to find the leaks and get rid of them. I know you're invested in GGPD more than most because of your family ties there."

"It's never as easy as it appears, Dominique."

"Kind of like us, right? We were matched perfectly on most issues, except one." She didn't say it and didn't have to; they both knew she referred to a permanent commitment. "It looked good on paper, made sense that we'd make a good pair, but then when it came down to it we had incompatible goals in life." Her dark eyes blazed with conviction, and color had returned to her cheeks under the bruises. He heard her, saw that she was trying to make a point about why they'd gone their own ways. Mostly agreed. But his mind kept seeing her in his apartment, before the breakup. When she was still his.

What on earth had he been thinking, agreeing to this gig for Rigo?

You still care. Too much.

"Stanton? Are you listening to me?"

Stanton blinked once, twice, and she saw his focus come back on her. He'd drifted, and a pang of regret hit her sideways. It was one of his mannerisms that she'd found both annoying and endearing. A brilliant man, Stanton let his mind run miles ahead of everyone else's, putting together seemingly disparate pieces of information to form a full picture. It made him an excellent personal protection and intelligence professional. And it had made him second to none in bed. She didn't get the impression he was thinking of either, though. More likely he'd been recalling their disagreements, maybe even those last awful few minutes together. Shame hit her as hard as regret had. She'd been so immature, so overwhelmed at the weight of their connection.

"I'm fine, trust me. I heard you. You're juggling a lot of bowling pins, Dominique, that could end up hurting you, be it the cartel or your alleged bad player at GGPD. It's possible that more than one person would want you silenced."

Ouch. He hadn't said anything she didn't already suspect, but the bluntness of his conclusion stung.

"I know." She gave him his point. He was correct. The harsh set of his jaw, covered by its usual shadow of beard growth, was a perfect foil to the light in his eyes and conveyed his confidence. At least he couldn't read her mind as hers drifted. Back to their long hours in bed, how his skin felt against hers. How that light beard had scratched her inner thighs…

Refocus.

She tore her gaze away as a matter of survival. Her eyes scanned over the familiar surroundings of the café and she tried to allow herself to relax, to forget that she was sitting across from the only man she'd ever given her entire heart to. Well, almost. When her gaze passed over the barista station a second time, she saw that the same man she'd seen earlier was still staring at her. Her back stiffened.

"What is it?" Stanton missed nothing. She wanted to believe his heightened perception was all about being with her, but Stanton had superb intuition.

"That man's still there."

"Right. We're leaving. Now." He stood and offered her his hand, which she waved away. Her legs were stronger, the shock having worn off.

She followed him back onto the street, pointedly not looking at the creepy guy at the counter. The fresh albeit chilly wind was refreshing and made her feel more human, less like a stalked opossum.

"I've got to go to the *Gazette* offices. You're going to be bored there." Maybe Stanton would agree to leave her there for the rest of the day, come back for her at close of day. It'd be nerve-racking, working with him next to her. "There's a security guard at the entrance. I'll be safe inside for the afternoon. You know the paper doesn't scrimp on employee safety."

"I do, and it doesn't change my job description, Dominique. No way are you going anywhere without me. And we can't be certain there aren't bad guys staking out the *Gazette*. I've got somewhere else we can go. Come on." Instead of going to his car, parked in front of the café, he put his hand in the small of her back and pointed her to the granite building next to the café. The first several floors were offices, but there were twelve floors of luxury apartments above the commercial spaces.

"I'm not going to your apartment." She halted, refusing to move forward.

"You don't have a choice right now. We need to keep talking about the case, and it's imperative we're not overheard." As he spoke, the man who'd been watching her exited the café and ambled in the opposite direction down the main drag of Grave Gulch, as if he was out for a Sunday stroll. Dominique had her doubts. She looked at Stanton and he was watching the man, too. He pulled out his phone and sent a quick text. When he finished, his gaze was back on her, and there wasn't an iota of compromise in his sapphire irises.

"Let's go."

"Fine." She fell into step with him. "We'll go to the paper after this, then?" She wanted to talk to her boss and fill him in on the most recent events. He deserved more than a text with news that she'd been attacked, needed backstory, no matter how much she'd reassured the senior editor that she was okay.

"Not today." He was resolute. Anger tried to spark in her center but all she felt was resigned. And bone-tired.

Neither spoke as they rode the elevators—first the public one to the tenth floor, then a private, residents-only lift to the penthouse. Memories whirled in her mind the closer they got to Stanton's apartment. When she walked through the familiar sleek doors into the contemporary space, it was impossible to not see every place she and Stanton had made love. On the foyer's tile floor the night after a particularly scary scenario he'd provided protection for, on the sofa that faced a wall of windows that overlooked all of Grave Gulch and to the countryside beyond.

"Let me take your coat." He was behind her, gently easing off her sleeves when she'd wanted to do it herself. "It's okay to accept help, Dom. I know you're hurting. I'd be sore, too, after a brute like that came at me."

She relented and allowed him to slowly ease the garment from her body. He laid it over the end of the sofa and walked to the kitchen, giving her a welcome modicum of privacy. As if he remembered she preferred to work alone, with minimal distraction. The thought of sitting still at her laptop, still in her gym bag, only made her aches hurt more.

"This view only gets better with time, doesn't it?" It was a shallow comment but she wasn't up for deep conversation. Not yet. She needed mental space after coming face-to-face with the memories of her and Stanton. The afternoon sunlight shone on the wooded areas surrounding the medium-sized city, varying shades of green offering hope for warmer spring weather soon. Winter struggled to let go of its hold on Michigan, keeping the mornings and evenings chilly well into May. Trees were a source of strength and peace for

Dominique, and being able to appreciate this unique view on a regular basis had been one of many gifts she'd let go of when she'd left Stanton.

She'd missed this.

"My time to enjoy it gets less and less." He spoke from the kitchen counter. She heard a coffee machine and looked over her shoulder as she timidly sat on the edge of the leather sofa. "We just had coffee and tea."

"You didn't get to finish yours, and I need a shot of espresso. Keeping your insides warm will help you relax, too." He walked back into the room and handed her a pink mug. It had the logo of a local 5K run on it, an annual Grave Gulch fundraiser for breast cancer. It had been hers, something she must have left behind after their breakup. She looked at him, held up the mug.

"I'm surprised you kept this."

"Why? You thought I'd throw everything away? It's a good cup. Keeps my coffee hot the longest."

"There couldn't have been much to toss. I never really moved in here." She sipped and Stanton was right; she needed the warmth.

"No, you didn't." His tone was noncommittal. Why couldn't their relationship feel like that to her? Instead of making all of her emotions churn, with regret's bitter taste heavy on her tongue. "What were we discussing, again? Charlie Hamm?"

He'd thrown her a lifeline and she could have hugged him. No, no, not hug. Nothing that had to do with touching him. In a complete betrayal, her fingertips began to itch as if they'd die from never feeling his hard, smooth skin under them.

"Dominique?"

"Yes, Charlie Hamm. I know that if I can get to the bottom of his conviction, and who the force was behind it, I'll not only get justice for him, but upend the drug cartel that's done its best to decimate Grave Gulch."

"Again, it's imperative to leave the law enforcement to the experts. I'm not discrediting your investigative abilities or saying that your reporting doesn't have serious purpose. On the contrary, everyone needs to be able to understand what we've all been up against since fentanyl hit our streets. A good portion of my business has been protecting people waiting to go into the witness protection program or who don't want to have to lose their identity but the threat level doesn't warrant government-paid protection." He leaned his hands on the counter, his shirtsleeves rolled up and leaving his muscular forearms exposed. "I'm on your side, Dominique. At least as far as getting to the truth is concerned."

"But you're not going to support me going for the jugular. Putting myself back out there, making myself a target."

"There has to be a way to do your job virtually. Can't you call your interview subjects on the phone?"

"Absolutely not. I have to verify all of my sources, and I certainly have to speak face-to-face with the man whose testimony put Charlie behind bars in the first place. Only he can tell me who ordered him to lie on the stand. I have a feeling it'll lead me to the same person who ordered Charlie's murder."

"If indeed the prison fight wasn't incidental."

She shook her head, needing Stanton to believe her, to trust her judgment. "It wasn't like Charlie to get himself in any kind of altercation. He'd had a clean record the entire two years he was in jail. His dream was an early release, on good behavior."

Stanton's cell phone buzzed and he picked it up from the cocktail table, his thumb flicking across the screen. The play of light across his chiseled face mesmerized her. Her stomach flipped and she quickly reminded herself that he was off-limits. Failed previous relationship with him being reason number one, followed by the line of work he was in, and hers. Both were all-consuming, and his was particularly dangerous. Losing him once, no matter that it had been her decision, had been enough. It would be catastrophic to let herself get lost in him again, only for him to be taken out by a madman. Plus, Stanton made it clear that he had zero interest in picking back up with her. Even if he hadn't, she wasn't in the right place or frame of mind for any kind of romantic entanglement with anyone.

A soft groan escaped her bruised lips and she sucked in a breath, hoping he hadn't sensed her subconscious plea for attention from him. His immediate glance in her direction proved he had. Humiliation rushed heat into her face and she pointedly looked out the window, unable to meet his gaze.

"It's a text from Troy. He's on his way over to take your statement." Either Stanton didn't notice her discomfort or chose to ignore it. Instead of relief, disbelief at his words doused her embarrassment.

"Wha—wait a minute! I didn't agree to talk to the

police." Anger fired through her veins, giving her a sense of purpose she hadn't felt since being so brutally assaulted.

Stanton stood up, paced to the panoramic window. It was what he always did when they'd argued. Gave himself space to think.

"You were attacked. I called my cousin the detective when you were getting your X-rays. He agreed to meet you privately, so that you don't have to go into the station. I thought you'd appreciate not facing down every cop in Grave Gulch right now. It's not like you're their favorite reporter at the moment."

"You think I can't take it? I don't care if all of GGPD hates the press. That's not my problem in the least."

"All of GGPD doesn't dislike the *Gazette*, and it's unfair to say that. You have to admit that it's hard to do your job when you're constantly being scrutinized. The *Gazette* hasn't let off GGPD—ever. And it's only gotten worse recently."

"If GGPD would keep the public informed about their internal investigation of Randall Bowe, it might ease a lot of the perceived tensions."

"It's called 'internal' for a reason." He stopped pacing, hands on slim hips, and glared at her. "The world isn't yours to exploit, Dominique."

"Exploit? Excuse me?" She stood up and said a silent thanks that she was able to do so in one steady movement. Her lower back hurt like heck and her shoulders were beginning to throb. She raised her hands in surrender. "I can't do this. Either pay my father back or assign one of your other agents to my case. I'm out."

She moved toward the foyer, needing to be free of the constant nearness of him. His scent, his mannerisms, his voice.

"Dom, wait." At the use of his endearment for her she froze. This was the name he'd shouted earlier, right before the thug had grabbed her. In a moment of danger, he'd called out to her the way he knew she'd recognize it was him. So she'd know she wasn't alone. At some level, he must have known that she still trusted him. She turned back toward him and slowly closed the distance between them, but left several paces as a boundary when she reached the window.

"This isn't working, Stanton. It's not going to. We've been with each other for less than half a day and we're at fisticuffs again." Unwanted tears pooled and she blinked. "I'm not sad. I'm mad."

He ran his fingers through his hair, loosened his silk tie. She'd always appreciated how he insisted on a professional appearance, no matter how dirty his job got. The pale cream fabric highlighted the deep blue of his eyes. The cotton stretched over his broad shoulders, triggering more memories that were best forgotten.

His killer gaze pierced through all of her defenses, reminded her of all she'd lost. Constant stress at how they'd work out their demanding careers, yes. But also, long nights of intimate conversation, soul baring, and of course, lovemaking she'd never forgotten.

He ran his fingers through his hair again. "I'm sorry. There's no need for us to be in each other's face like this. It's my fault. I'm protective of GGPD. It's in my blood. Literally." The reminder of how close he was to his sister triggered a pang of regret in her chest. It was one of the many things she'd found so attractive about Stanton, the way he respected and treasured his family.

"I'm upset and angry that an innocent man went to jail and served time, and while doing so was murdered. And yes, I think there's a dirty cop or GGPD employee behind it, along with the drug kingpin. But I have the highest regard for any man or woman who'd willingly put themselves in harm's way for our protection."

He nodded. "I know. But it's not easy, seeing the headlines day after day in the *Grave Gulch Gazette*. It's exhausting for all involved. And then the rumors that the paper will get acknowledged nationally—no one is against journalism or a local paper being rewarded. But—"

"But not if it makes local authorities, like your sister, look bad." She let the words slip out before she thought, and immediately wished she could take them back. Stanton was offering her an olive branch. His eyes widened slightly but she knew him well enough to know she'd angered him. "Wait, I'm sorry, Stanton. I shouldn't have said that."

"No, you're free to say whatever you want. You always have been." *Zing* right to her emotional solar plexus. He apparently hadn't forgotten their last conversation two years ago, when she'd blithely refused his marriage proposal. It'd been right here, in front of these windows, in the middle of the night after a particularly long round of lovemaking. She only figured it out afterward that he'd been planning it, when she realized he must have bought the ring ahead of time.

But in the moment, they'd both been naked. Sated. Vulnerable. And she hadn't been ready for such a permanent commitment, not yet, but had begged him to stay together until she was. The pain of how he'd shifted gears, told her they weren't on the same page, their relationship wasn't ever going to work, still burned. But so did her attraction to him.

Their gazes met, and in his eyes she saw all she'd lost, all that could have been, and the man he was today.

"I—"

"No." He placed a finger on her lips. As stern and annoyed as his expression was, his touch was gentle. A whisper. "Stop talking, Dominique. Give me a minute here."

Give him a minute? Why did he need time? It wasn't as if he was as unsettled by her closeness as she was by his. He'd given no indication he was. Only then, on closer inspection, did she see how his pulse jumped in an erratic dance at the side of his strong jaw. His pupils were dilated, even with afternoon sunlight streaming into the penthouse. And his breath—he sounded as though he'd run up a flight of stairs as he closed his eyes, presumably to shut out her image.

Clarity hit and her breath hitched. While their minds knew they didn't belong together any longer, their bodies hadn't gotten the text. As if in a trance, her right hand reached up and stroked his cheek.

"Don't." His plea came out in a gravelly whisper, and he kept his eyes closed. But he didn't stop her. Her ire melted into compassion. She knew too well what it was like to fight it as he did now. She'd struggled to keep her physical desire in check from the moment he'd looked into her eyes right after he'd rescued her this morning.

"It's okay, Stanton. Isn't it normal to feel like this with an ex? We're not robots." She shouldn't be standing so close to him, shouldn't tempt fate by touching him at all. Her fingers explored his jaw, stubbled by beard growth, unable to get enough of him. No amount of touch with Stanton would ever be enough. She swayed toward him, unable to stop the desire-fueled momentum that pushed her closer.

"Dom." With no further preamble, Stanton's arms came around her waist and he tugged her flush against him. Air whooshed from her lungs as she felt his full length, including his erection, through their layers of clothing. She let her arms go to his shoulders and met him halfway as his mouth came down on hers.

Chapter 4

Stanton used every ounce of control to not take Dominique here and now, the way he remembered she liked it best, on the sofa. On the same cushion she'd been perched on like an injured bird, still stunned from flying into a window. If not for her earlier scare, he didn't think he'd be able to hold back. She'd recovered enough from her attack to be fully present in this moment, though, as her tongue met his with insistence, her lips pliant and delicious under his. It was as if they'd never stopped kissing since the last time he'd held her like this.

Stanton had never wanted Dominique more than he did in this moment. How had he waited two years to hold her again, to taste her? He shook with need as he held her but refused to manhandle her no matter what he knew—that she loved it when they both gave their sex life all they had to give.

The reminder of that relationship, and why it hadn't lasted, made him lift his head. He stopped the kiss but couldn't keep from devouring her with his gaze.

Her lips were wet, slightly parted, her eyes closed. No matter the bruises, the shadows under her eyes that told him she was working at full tilt on the Charlie Hamm story. Dominique was the most beautiful woman he'd ever known.

"Please, Stanton. Kiss me." Her whisper shot lust through him, and his arousal had to be apparent to her. He moved his hands to either side of her face. Slow. He had to take this slow. Savor it.

"Patience, babe."

He delighted at the moan that escaped her lips. He hovered, making her wait, until he couldn't stand it any longer. She leaned in as he moved in—

A loud buzzer sounded. His doorbell.

"Dang it." He rested his forehead against hers. They were both out of breath.

"Ignore it." Her lips moved to his jawline, down his throat. "We've waited too long for this."

The buzzer rang again and he grasped her hands, removed them from behind his neck. Tried to ignore the disappointment in her gaze. It echoed through his being, too.

"It's Troy. He's here to take your preliminary statement." Frustration rang in his every cell, poised to make love to the woman he'd not been able to forget.

You let her go, man.

He forcefully expelled a breath, moved toward the entrance. It was ironic. He was taking the same steps she had, after he'd proposed, and she'd countered with an offer his pride had been too bruised to consider at the time. He fought to bring his arousal under control. The buzzer rang another two times before he felt confident about opening the door to a trusted colleague and relative.

"Troy. Come on in."

"Hey, man. How have you been?" Troy's boyish face broke into a grin at the sight of his cousin. They shook hands and gave each other a bro hug as he stepped into the apartment. "You've been scarce at the station."

"I know, we've been swamped." It was true. Colton Protection had such an uptick in clients this past month that all of his staff was overworked. "I had to hire two new agents and their vetting took all of my time." And now, Dominique was exclusively his twenty-four seven for the foreseeable future. "Let's go sit down." When he turned and went back into the living room, Dominique was gone. He knew it was probably to the restroom, but seeing the sofa empty made his heartbeat stutter.

You need to take a pause here, dude.

"Is Dominique still here?" Troy sat in an easy chair opposite of the sofa.

"Yes. It's been a rough morning for her, but she's doing okay."

Troy nodded. "Good to hear."

"I'm here." She walked to the kitchen and stood next to the island, helped herself to a tall glass of ice water.

"Nice to see you again, Troy. Can I get you something to drink?"

Stanton should have been the one to offer; it was his apartment, no matter how well Dominique knew her way around it. He hadn't changed it much since the breakup, pouring all of his energy into work. Anything to keep his mind off the memories. He remained in the living room, not wanting to examine how easy it would be to fall back into old routines with her.

"I'm good, thanks." Troy didn't seem surprised by any of this, another surprise. Was he like his entire family, who thought he and Dominique weren't through? He'd never been able to convince his parents, Frank and Italia Colton, that he and Dominique weren't going to reconcile. Now he wondered if they'd seen the parts of him that this morning had revealed. The factions of his heart that hadn't let go, not by a long shot.

"Stanton, do you want anything?" Dang it but she sounded as if she'd never left.

"No, thank you." His teeth ground together.

"Are you sure you're happy to see me, Dominique? Word on the street is that you've got it out for GGPD." Troy kept his smile but Stanton saw the barb for what it was. He'd thrown the same words at Dominique earlier, yet he had the urge to say something to shut Troy down ASAP. Didn't his cousin see that she was bruised, had been through hell today?

"You know you can't trust rumors, Troy." Dominique walked over to the sofa and sat on the end opposite of Stanton. He noticed she'd taken her athletic shoes off. Her one toe looked swollen and he made a mental note to ask her about it later. "Contrary to what seems to be the scuttlebutt, the *Grave Gulch Gazette* doesn't have any issues with GGPD as a whole. Unless you're covering up the truth. We look for the facts in every story, Troy. You know that."

Troy shook his head. "I do, Dominique, but when we have reporters snooping about all the time, it's hard to run a closed investigation. It breeds public distrust, too. Things leak out, factual or not."

"Then open it up. Tell us what we're asking for. Is there a corrupt cop on the force? In addition to Randall Bowe's deliberate mishandling of evidence?"

"You know we can't do that. And you shouldn't accuse someone of a crime unless you're certain."

Dominique and Troy squared off, staring at one another with open challenge. Stanton opened his mouth to cut through the tension, but Dominique spoke before he had to.

"Why don't we focus on you taking my statement for now?" She gave him a smile that didn't meet her dark, troubled eyes. Stanton felt the indecision coming off her. And it got right under his skin. This was why he'd fallen for her years ago.

"Excellent idea. Sorry about goading you, Dominique. But I'm not sorry about sticking up for the good public servants in my department."

"Nor should you be. Unless they're corrupt." Her words and posture remained unshaken but her tone was softer.

"Point taken." Troy's cheeks had reddened. He pulled out his phone, a notebook and pen. "Can you go over your entire morning with me, from when you left your house?"

Dominique complied, leaving no detail out. Stanton looked out the window as she spoke, unable to focus on anything but her voice. He needed to refocus on why he was protecting her in the first place, if he hoped to keep his emotions in check. His arms ached to hold her as she recounted the stunningly brutal attack that could have killed her.

You would have never held her again.

As messed up as he was over coming so close to kissing her again, he knew his inner turmoil was preferable to losing her. He'd already done that once, but knew she was safe and alive, living her life. He'd convinced himself she was free from harm, living in the apartment complex on the edge of town that abutted one of Grave Gulch's nicer suburbs. Her family and especially her twin, Soledad, who lived in the same apartment building, kept close tabs on her. He'd had to believe this, or he wouldn't have been able to let her go so easily two years ago. Recrimination welled again, reminding him that maybe he should have accepted her offer to wait on a marriage commitment. He'd been so stung by her refusal he'd acted before he thought it out, telling her it was either all-in or forget it.

"How exactly did you get the information that led you to your interview subject's address?"

Dominique paused and Stanton's glance strayed from the panoramic view. Her eyebrows drew together and she played with the hem of her blouse, normally tucked in but hanging out since the ER visit. Another sign of how hard all of this was on her, because Dominique was always turned out for work. For life. She rarely fit the description of "disheveled."

"The paper had a voice mail left on the main line, claiming to be Johnny Blanchard, the witness whose testimony helped convict Charlie Hamm. He said he had information I'd be interested in."

"He asked for you by name?" Troy was taking copious notes.

"Yes. Said it was about the Charlie Hamm prison fight." She leaned over and pulled one leg up on the sofa, sitting in the half yoga pose typical of her when she was working on her laptop or involved in a deep conversation. "My boss, the senior editor, gave me the information. I called the number and left a message with my cell number when no one picked up. My work cell, not personal. I have two phones." She shot a glance at both Stanton and Troy, and he thought she wanted to make certain they understood she didn't take her personal safety for granted. "Then he, assuming it was really Blanchard, texted me his address, which I didn't have before."

"Did you follow up with a search of the address?"

"Of course I did, but nothing came up. I wasn't surprised by that, as a lot of witnesses for major crimes go off the grid as far as the internet is concerned after they testify. And this witness had every reason to hide, since he lied on the stand and sent an innocent man to jail."

"You can't be sure of that, can you? Until you interview him and he admits to perjury?" Troy's query wasn't chiding; he appeared genuinely interested.

Stanton wanted to warn his cousin that those were fighting words as far as Dominique was concerned.

"What I'm certain of, Troy, is that the Charlie Hamm I met in my creative writing course that I teach at the prison was a thoughtful, gentle man. He had a reputation for helping druggies on the street, and several sources verify this. From the local food bank to the homeless shelter, to the run-down rehab place at the corner of Main and Fifty-Seventh Street, Charlie was a good player. A positive change agent. You know the rehab I'm talking about, right?"

"Sure do. Had two heroin ODs in front of it last night."

Dominique swore under her breath and Stanton agreed with the sentiment. It never seemed to end, the countless victims of the epidemic. And yet the cartel continued to methodically expand their distribution ring, mixing higher and higher levels of fentanyl into the heroin.

"Both ODs made it, though. Thanks to the Narcan on site, and of course all of our officers carry it."

"Thank goodness." Dominique's evident relief smoothed the lines between her brows. "Did you know Charlie Hamm was the person responsible for getting Narcan into that facility to begin with? The social workers were swamped and he attended the training offered to the community by the rehab on the other side of town. Charlie believed all addicts deserve the same chance to live, to recover, no matter what side of town they came from. Does that sound like the work of a drug dealer to you, Troy?"

"No, it doesn't. But a lot of things don't make sense in Grave Gulch these days. Who knows what a dealer or user is thinking?"

"Charlie Hamm was innocent. Just like Everleigh Emerson was proven innocent, and Len Davison is on the loose because the evidence against him was destroyed. Multiple victims of false evidence and innocent people murdered by Davison. Now that we know that Randall Bowe is officially under suspicion of maligning evidence, all I need is the information pertaining to the fingerprint on the suitcase that sent Charlie to jail, along with proof that the testimony against him was bogus."

"I hope you get it, Dominique, I truly do. I'm all for catching any bad guy, in uniform or out. But I'm here because you were attacked while trying to do your job. It sounded like a classic setup and I wish you had called us before you went to interview your subject."

"If I'd let GGPD know, you would have checked it out and spooked the man." Stanton gave her points for not bringing up her concern over corruption at the department again.

"Which is exactly what's happened. He was scared away, but not by GGPD."

"What?" Stanton and Dominique spoke in unison.

"I took the preliminary information you gave me after the attack, Stanton, and paid my own visit to the area. The witness does indeed live at the address you had, Dominique. He's been there for the last month or so, working hourly at a local café in the kitchen. But he's fled the scene. Two neighbors said he was out in the apartment hallway, told one that he was waiting 'on an appointment.' But when word got out that there was a mugging going down, he took off. No one's heard from him and my bet is he won't risk coming back home for a good while. He might think that whoever went after you would come for him next."

"That sounds like a good assumption." Goose bumps rose on Stanton's forearms. He was glad that she had been correct, but more relieved that Dominique hadn't been hurt worse. The cartel wasn't in the business of scare tactics as much as flat-out murder.

"So it wasn't a setup by the witness, as you've both told me it could have been. My instincts and background work were spot-on. I couldn't have known in advance that I'd be targeted." Dominique's anger reflected in the furrow between her finely shaped brows. His fingertip itched to smooth her concern away. *Careful.* He tried not to frown at his conscience's internal prodding. It was a natural reaction to want to eliminate her stress and she'd had a particularly awful day. He checked his phone. It was only three o'clock. Five hours in her presence and his heart was screaming to take over from his brain.

"Except for your provocative social media posts." Troy held up his hands as if in surrender. "I'm not questioning how you or any other reporter does your business. But if you're going to dig into a case like Charlie Hamm's, it's bigger than any of us sitting here. No question, your interview subject is legit. Johnny Blanchard was the man whose testimony clinched the case against Charlie." Troy spoke with measured neutrality.

"Along with evidence falsified by a GGPD employee." She wasn't holding back any longer.

"If there was any malfeasance by an employee of GGPD, you can be assured we're working to get to the bottom of it, Dominique." Troy glanced up at Stanton. They'd been more like brothers as kids and he recognized the silent plea for a helping hand.

"It's not fair to keep labeling the entire GGPD because of the actions of one, or maybe two, bad players." Stanton repeated what he'd already said to Dominique earlier, hoping that this time she heard him.

"The *Gazette* isn't letting up until we have all the answers, Troy. You can tell the chief that." Dominique's arms crossed in front and he knew it had to hurt to sit like that. He'd bruised his ribs in the past and remembered any movement felt like torture.

"That's fair. It's your job. And I'll pass it to Chief Colton, when I run into her. We're all going pedal to the metal, Dominique."

"Well, then maybe the *Gazette* and GGPD do have something in common, after all."

Stanton silently groaned at Dominique's words. Did she have to throw down all the time?

And did he have to be so turned on every time she did?

"What do you mean she got away?" Pablo Jimenez's eyes were darker than their usual hellish black, and his face was screwed into a menacing scowl. "Your job was to get rid of both of them. Tell me Blanchard is taken care of."

Leo shuffled on his feet, wanting to look anywhere but at his jefe's face. But to look away was certain death.

"It was out of my hands. Blanchard took off before I ever arrived, and as I was about to finish her off, I was interrupted by an undercover cop." He was lying, a bit. Enough. He'd faced the witness and threatened him but he'd slipped away, faster than Leo was on his feet. And Leo had been focused on getting the reporter girl most of all. She'd openly threatened his jefe on the internet.

"What am I paying you for?" A large object, a crystal glass full of hundred-year-old Scotch, flew at him, and he had the sense to remain still, allow the pain to come. Jimenez liked pain, and to avoid the hand-thrown missile only revealed weakness, in the kingpin's view.

"I'm sorry. It won't happen again."

"You're correct, it won't happen again." Jimenez withdrew a long blade from his boot and Leo held his breath, certain he was about to meet *Dios*. "Next time, take more men with you. I want the reporter taken care of, and I should never have trusted that lousy dealer to be Hamm's witness. What good is it if he testified in court but now wants to spill his guts?" Jimenez spat into another crystal goblet, the amber liquid from his tobacco chew both revolting and mesmerizing to Leo. "Take her out, and the man who came to save her. I don't care if he's a cop. This local department refuses to accept who's in charge here. Me. If that doesn't work, we'll go after the reporter's family next."

"Yes, jefe."

No one argued with the jefe, ever. Leo knew his job.

"Go!" Jefe wasn't a patient man.

* * *

If Dominique hadn't felt the air leave the room previously, she'd have known by both Stanton's and Troy's expressions that she'd overstepped.

"I'm not saying we both do the same kind of work. Certainly you're on the streets every day, doing your best to keep Grave Gulch safe." She swallowed, her explanation hanging like the frivolous bunch of words it was. Stanton had returned to staring out the window and Troy looked at her with unabashed annoyance.

Troy stood, pocketed his phone. "I get it. Times are tense in Grave Gulch. It's worse than I've ever seen it. There's a killer roaming loose—I can't confirm if you have the correct name—we have internal issues at GGPD and we were slammed by the heroin epidemic. Not to mention some other cases that are popping up faster than the hungry alligators at the State Fair. Again, all of this is off the record. I don't want to see my words twisted and used as clickbait."

"Off the record. Got it." She wanted to explain how clickbait really worked, that she or any other reporter had no pull when it came to the titles of her articles. Once she sent her work to her editor, it was out of her hands. How much and how it would be published, as well as the headlines. Many times she'd complained to her superiors that she wasn't happy about exactly what Troy had mentioned—a hard-hitting story that had cost her hours, days, months, was all distilled into a misleading banner that ensured the online readers would click through. And that print readers didn't hesitate to buy the paper with their morning coffee. This wasn't a time for explanations, or worse, justification.

"I'll let myself out. Dominique, please come into the station as soon as you can, to file a full police report. I'll file a preliminary one to ensure we keep a lookout for a man matching the description of your attacker. Both of you, stay safe." Troy turned and walked to the door and she sat back down on the sofa, curling her feet under her. It was too hard to keep her guard up any longer. Exhaustion rolled over her but she knew it'd be hours, most likely days, before she enjoyed restful sleep.

"We'll be there within the hour." Stanton nodded at his cousin and watched him exit. Once the door clicked closed, he turned toward her. His eyes—still so startlingly blue—were full of ice shards. "Nice way to win friends and influence people there. I'm sure Troy won't hesitate to give you his next scoop." Stanton's lush mouth pulled up on the left side, his sardonic admonishment unnecessary.

"I messed up. I said as much." She leaned her head back and closed her eyes. If she could get five minutes to herself. "Don't you have work to do, you know, remotely? Where's that laptop you like to spend all your time on?"

"I'm not the same man you knew two years ago." She felt the sofa move as he sat at the opposite end. "I tend to leave work at work when I can. It means I'm at the office for longer hours, but at least by the time I get here, I'm done for the day."

"Except when you work hands-on, like with me."

She blushed at the connotation. "I mean with protecting me. Now you're on the clock twenty-four seven. Seriously, I think you should think about delegating this assignment to one of your agents. Your leadership is needed at the helm of Colton Protection, isn't it?"

"You still think you know what's best for everyone around you. What about you? You're still chasing the Pulitzer like the Holy Grail. How has it worked out for you? You look exhausted to me, and it's not just from today."

She opened her eyes and stood, walked around the room on her sore feet. It was impossible to stay relaxed and quiet when Stanton was so close, and especially when he was grilling her.

"I'm the reporter, Stanton. I'll ask the questions. You know enough about what I'm working on. Let's turn the camera on you. How many more employees has Colton Security gained since—since two years ago?" She was still loath to mention their relationship, and disastrous breakup. Guilt nibbled on her conscience. It'd been brutal, the way she'd looked at Stanton in his naked glory, as he'd told her it was all-in with marriage, or nothing. She'd asked him to reconsider—still remembered the tears pouring down her cheeks—but he'd been adamant. "Marry me or we're through, Dominique." So hurt and confused by his hard line, she'd turned on her heel and gone to the bedroom, gotten dressed, then left. Except for the occasional run-in at a local event she was reporting on, where she did all she could to avoid him, they hadn't spoken since. Until he'd tried to warn her about the attacker this morning.

"Fifteen. Twenty-three employees total, if you count administrative staff. I've opened a second office in Los Angeles that's larger than here and appointed an office manager there. I've no desire to move to California. The occasional commute there is hard enough. But that hasn't changed the smaller staff here, where we have six bodyguards." He spoke in succinct syllables, without any hint of pride. His humility, no matter his incredible success, had drawn her in back then, made her want him all the more.

That was then, this is now.

"Was that the result of saving those big-name actors last year?" She'd read the AP report about a fan sneaking on a movie set, stalking an A-list actor who was guarded by Colton Protection. No one had been hurt, adding to Stanton's firm's stellar reputation.

"Mostly, yes." He sounded impatient and she turned from the window to see him striding across the room toward the kitchen. "I'm hungry. Lunch?"

"No, I don't think I can eat yet. I'd rather go to the station first, get this over with." She shuddered. It wasn't like her to go all vulnerable, but it wasn't every day she got blindsided by a vicious attack. Having to narrate her experience again in the sterile environment of GGPD did not appeal at the moment.

"Try a little something. We could end up waiting a while for someone to take your statement." He pulled salad items out of the refrigerator and set them on the granite counter. "Steak, salmon or chicken with your salad?"

She froze. This was too familiar. They'd fallen into

a routine when they were together. They'd meet here for lunch, or rather, lunch after sex, and then go to her apartment for dinner and often, a sleepover. Stanton had insisted he preferred her bed even though his bed, his apartment, was far more luxurious and accommodating.

"I, uh, whatever you need to get rid of." She'd lied, she was famished. But eating a meal in front of him, in his apartment, seemed so intimate. As if no time had passed, as if they were still together.

Too close.

He raised a brow but continued prepping two salad bowls, topping one with steak and the other salmon. He set hers in front of her at the island and ate his standing up. They shared half a whole grain baguette and he poured a small dish of olive oil for her, smearing his bread with the butter he always left out on his counter, just as his Italian-born mother did in the Colton house. Dominique didn't know where to put the surge of nostalgia that overwhelmed her. Tears pricked and she blinked, faux-coughing to cover it up. He'd remembered that she preferred salmon, olive oil with her bread. It touched something deep inside in the place she didn't allow her thoughts to wander if she could help it.

The place that remained exclusively Stanton's.

Chapter 5

Stanton remained standing on the other side of the counter, eating from his bowl as Dominique at first picked at, then appeared to relish, the meal. He hoped that by shoveling his salad into his mouth he'd avoid further dialogue with her. Any kind of communication with Dominique was lethal to his guard, his heart. As they ate he silently cursed himself for allowing her father to persuade—no, manipulate—him to take the case. But he couldn't lie to himself. Every day of the past two years since they'd been together, he'd scoured not only the news, but the police blotters, the reports, whatever his sister allowed him access to. All in an attempt to ensure no one was coming after Dominique. That she was safe. He'd never stopped worrying about her.

If he dug deeper, he knew it had to do with his regret over forcing the breakup. At seeing the pain etched on her face as she'd comprehended he was ending it. What had he been thinking, throwing a woman like Dominique away?

That worrying about her day and night wasn't your idea of a good time.

"Thank you for this, Stanton. I didn't realize how hungry I was." She picked up the paper towel he'd set down and wiped her mouth, her delicious, dark pink lips glistening with olive oil. Napkins were extra accessories he'd let go after she'd left him.

"I'm glad you finally ate something. You needed to eat before we go to the station." He was about to tell her that he didn't pick salmon just for her, or that the olive oil on the side was something he did for all his guests. But it would be lying. He'd never forgotten what she'd enjoyed, be it a favorite meal or position during their lovemaking.

He missed being with her, sure, but this overwhelming attraction, persistent thrum of his sexual awareness of her had to be from months with zero dates. He'd tried to find someone else…well, kind of.

"Left-swiping on an app is not dating."

His older brother Clarke's sardonic admonishment at a family dinner last weekend echoed in his memory. Clarke was a top PI who often liaised with GGPD and helped Stanton stay in the loop with cases, as appropriate to his protection services agency. His fiancée, Everleigh, had been framed by Bowe for the murder of her cheating husband, so he wanted to see the thug brought down as much as Dominique. But not at the cost of her safety.

Dominique stared at him and he wondered how long he'd drifted for this time. She did this to him. Made him think of things that had nothing to do with the matter at hand. His phone buzzed with a text from Troy. He set down his bowl to read it.

Two thugs hanging out around your building address. Suggest you come up with a different egress than the usual.

Showtime. His mind immediately shifted into bodyguard mode, going over the mental checklist he'd used thousands of times before.

"What is it?"

"Troy's spotted some suspicious-looking jerks hanging around on Main Street in front of the building. We'll go out via the parking garage instead of the lobby."

"They're here? Now?" He watched her chew slowly, swallow. All the time watching him with the eyes that he was still able to read. She'd been turned on earlier, before Troy showed up. He'd do anything to bring that smolder back into her obsidian gaze. After he got her out of here safely. He hated seeing the fear that flickered in her eyes, quickly shut down by her stubbornness.

"Yes. I'm thinking that he couldn't get a photo without letting them know he's on to them, so we don't know if either one is the jerk who attacked you." He didn't bother telling her that cartel thugs were like cockroaches in an apartment. Where there was one...

She speared a cherry tomato. He had to force his glance away from her. No way would he keep his mind on the case, on her dang safety, if he watched her eat. Dominique ate her salad as if she hadn't a concern in the world. Didn't she remember the time they'd turned each other into their own personal salad bar, complete with sexual satisfaction?

"I'm not afraid of him, or any of the bullies Pablo Jimenez wants to throw my way."

"How do you know it's Jimenez?" He'd heard the name mentioned, read it in police reports, but so far no official pronouncement of the identity of the local cartel's kingpin had been made. Not by GGPD or any state law enforcement, and the DEA hadn't come forward with an exact ID yet.

"You're not the only one with connections at GGPD. Not everyone there thinks the media is the devil. I'm convinced it's Jimenez who's calling the shots. I'm going to get to the bottom of all of this. With a little luck, the truth won't give us justice for only Charlie and his family. It'll blow the drug ring wide open."

Her conviction sent a pulse of cold sober fear through him. "Dominique, you're not dealing with a local gang here. From what I know, you're correct. Jimenez is a statewide leader. He works for a network of very powerful men, with international connections." Men who were ruthless when it came to keeping their coffers full of billions brought in by drugs.

"That big network doesn't give a flip about a town

of fewer than forty thousand people in Michigan, for heaven's sake. We're small potatoes for them." She ripped a paper towel from the roll he kept on the counter and wiped her mouth. "It's Jimenez whose pride's been stepped on. He thought he'd get away with silencing Charlie, and now Blanchard. And yes, me. He's not going to stop me."

"You really believe Charlie was murdered by them, right? If that's true, then you have a good idea of how resourceful Jimenez and his gang are. No leads, no witnesses are left behind. You're trying to disrupt that. You're a bug they're going to step on."

"A bug?" Her brow rose, and for the first time in over two years he glimpsed her sense of humor. How he'd missed her low, throaty laugh. How it rumbled across a room, echoed in his chest, wrapped around his heart.

Get a grip, man.

He nodded, scraped his bowl in the sink, rinsed both of their dishes, stacked them in the dishwasher. "A mere pest. Pablo Jimenez doesn't tolerate anyone looking into his business." He knew firsthand, as CP had provided a bodyguard last month for a witness to a fentanyl drug sale by one of Jimenez's guys. Said witness and his former client ended up going into federal protective custody.

"You know something you're not telling me."

"I know a lot of things, Dominique, but they're irrelevant to what we've got to do to get through the next days."

"I won't have this story in a matter of days, Stanton.

Don't kid yourself. It's already taken me weeks to get this far, and I've been doing all the background work on the cartel for the last two years."

Interesting. It was the second time she refused to refer to their breakup. Yet, like him, it seemed she used it as a reference point. He focused on the mission. To dwell on Dominique's motives for anything was a direct road to unnecessary pain. He'd sworn optional misery off after she'd left and he'd taken a long while to glue himself back together.

Are you whole again?

"You ready?" He prepared to leave, but when she straightened, leaned forward, all he saw was the countless times he'd kissed her over this counter. That one time, they'd ended up atop the granite, naked. Did the same mental videos play in her mind?

"Ready for what, Stanton?" She shot him a wary glance that didn't match the way she licked her bottom lip. Yeah, the attraction was still very much mutual. A small consolation when there was nothing they could do about it. Not yet, anyhow.

"We need to leave now if you're going to give your statement before close of business." He glanced at his smartwatch. Hard to believe that in two hours the working day was over for a good portion of Grave Gulch. Not that he worked banker's hours—providing security was a round-the-clock gig. "Get your bag and we'll go now."

"On it." She slid off the island chair but it wasn't with her usual grace. His bones ached for her as she took her time, held the edge of the island for a moment to make sure she had her balance. More telling were her hands, as they still visibly trembled, albeit slightly. He had to give her credit. She'd had a lousy day but was holding up like a champ.

"Let's take the elevator to the parking garage." He'd prefer the stairs but it'd be too hard on her. The door to the utility lift opened and he ushered her inside. It was spacious and bare, normally used by delivery services and the building doorman when a larger piece of mail had to be brought up.

"It would be easier to get into your car on the street. But I get the extra precaution." She moved a stray strand of her inky black hair from her eyes, tucked it behind her ear. A deep blue sapphire earring winked in the bright elevator light. His breath caught. He'd given her the earrings for her December birthday. Right after they'd started dating. He was inexplicably thrilled that she still wore a gift from him. Warmth rushed from his scalp, to his chest, pushed into his groin.

The thug who'd hurt Dom.

He conjured the memory of the man to keep from becoming visibly aroused. It had the desired effect but also reignited his anger, and not a little bit of despair. Would he ever get over her?

Do you really want to know?

The elevator dinged at the building's lowest level and opened to the garage's concrete floor.

He motioned for her to wait as he exited and cleared the area. There were security cameras on his vehicles and he'd checked them from the apartment before they left, on a phone app. The garage was well lit, clean, and there were no signs of bad guys. No matter, he'd feel better once he had Dominique safely in a car and they were en route to the police station.

"Okay, good to go." He held out his hand to her. It was an automatic gesture, but not one he'd do with a typical client. When she slipped hers into his, he vowed to stop overanalyzing himself, his thoughts. A lot of things were different when it came to guarding her. It didn't matter as long as the end result was the same: Dominique remained unharmed.

As they walked toward one of several CP vehicles stored in the parking garage, he allowed the naturalness of being with her sync with his protection skills. The mark of a good bodyguard wasn't how big or badass they were, although that helped. No, it was being able to accept one's surroundings and utilize them to your advantage. As long as Dominique trusted him enough to stay by his side and follow his lead, he'd keep her safe.

"Here." He held open the passenger door of a lowslung sports car and waited as she got in. Dang it, he should have considered her aches and bruises and picked the SUV parked next to it. But he wanted to ensure a quick escape if need be.

"You've improved your transportation means in two years." She spoke as he started the engine and backed out of the space.

"Business expansion." He was half listening as he prepared to egress the garage, his gaze constantly scanning the concrete floor, the walls, the spaces between other vehicles.

"The blacked-out windows are cool."

He drove up two ramps, entered the street-level floor. The exit was in view, onto a one-way, side-access street. Traffic moved along, toward Main Street. The gate arm at the sentry station was down, but was automatic. It would rise as he approached.

"Stanton!" Dominique's scream pierced the air a split second before the gunfire exploded.

"Get down!" His arm reached toward her but then he pulled back when he saw she was already under the dash. He used both hands to maneuver, flooring it through the exit, past the garage tender's booth. Wood splintered as the barrier gate arm broke over the front hood and split in half on the windshield, which thankfully remained intact. Colton Protection had paid dearly for the precautionary extras, including bulletproof windows and double-framed reinforced doors. Still, depending upon the type of bullets flying, "bulletproof" could be a misnomer. He'd had an armored car shot at by tank piercers last month, in the desert between LA and Las Vegas. Their client, a multibillionaire oilman, had remained unharmed, as had the agent assigned, but the car was destroyed.

He drove through the exit, the pings of bullets ricocheting off the car's body filling his ears, and when he heard a definitive crack, he looked at the passenger side to see a long line across the passenger window, with Dominique's head popping up to take a photo with her camera.

"Stay down! What the heck are you thinking?"

"I wanted to get photos of the shooters." Triumph

rang in her voice and he wanted to stop the car and make her see how risky this all was. The impulse rattled him, right in the midst of his automatic motions to keep her safe and his decision to trust her to stay under the dash.

"We don't need photos! We need to get out of here." He turned toward Main Street, clipping two parked cars and a bicycle chained to a lamppost as they sped down the narrow road. The car's extra layers of protection made it take turns a bit wider at times. He ignored the wreckage he left behind as well as he ignored the constant crunch of numbers his accountant fired at him for incidental damages. Colton Protection was insured for any vehicles damaged during the course of duty.

"They're blurry anyway," she grumbled but at least she was slouched down, as safe as she could be at this moment.

A black Porsche cleared the exit behind him and was on his tail almost immediately. The armored car's heft made it an easy target in the short run. Stanton knew Grave Gulch as well as the backyard he'd played in as a boy. He'd lose these jerks with a lot of concentration and a little luck.

Instead of turning left toward the station, he went right, then left down a side alley, turning onto the street that paralleled the main drag. Up and down the side streets, farther and farther away from the center of the city, he kept up the avoidance maneuvers until they were safely on the highway that led out of town, toward Lake Michigan.

"You're circling back, right?" Dominique's query

broke his state of flow—the place his mind went during an op. Where nothing existed except doing whatever it took to keep a client safe. He finally let out a breath and risked a glance at her. Instead of her earlier pallor and the stressed posture, Dominique was the energized version of herself, her enthusiasm contagious. A bark of laughter escaped his parched throat.

"You get off on this, don't you?" The words escaped his mouth and he knew he wasn't over the adrenaline rush either, not by a long shot. It was always a kick in the pants to outwit the bad guys, no matter how many times he did it. But it wouldn't last for long, and he had to stay miles ahead of the cartel clowns.

"If by 'get off' you mean I had something to focus on other than my mind's replay of that loser's paws crushing my throat, yes. Where are we going, Stanton?"

"I'm thinking."

He gripped and released his hands on the wheel a few times, double-, triple- and quadruple-checked the side and rearview mirrors. He'd lost them. For now. He'd never expected Jimenez's outfit knew what his vehicles looked like, where he stored the extras. They wouldn't outwit him again.

"What can I do? I'll call 911."

"Hang on a sec." He used the hands-free phone to call in to GGPD, directly to his sister.

"Chief Melissa Colton." Melissa's warm voice answered with its customary professional clip.

"Melissa. Stanton. We're on speaker and Dominique de la Vega is with me. I called the station number because I'm reporting an attack." He outlined what had happened in the parking garage, and the ensuing pursuit. "Troy expected us to show up at GGPD to file a report. I assume you've heard that Dominique was assaulted this morning on her way to an interview with the trial witness for Charlie Hamm. Witness's name is Johnny Blanchard. Both Dominique and I agree that this is most likely the work of Pablo Jimenez. He's the only one has everything to lose if her story uncovers evidence of witness tampering. We're not heading into the station this afternoon after all. We'll swing in tomorrow, or the next day, whenever it's safe. I'm not messing around with threats from Jimenez."

"That's wise. Troy's filled me in about the attack. I'm sorry, Dominique. Glad Stanton was there to help out. Where are you and Dominique going? To Colton Protection headquarters?"

"No. I can't risk that they knew who I was, what I do. We're going to the lake house."

"Gotcha. Be safe, bro. And Dominique?"

"Hi, Melissa." Dominique's tone was wary.

"My brother's the best in the business. Best listen to him."

The call ended and he continued westward, as though drawn by a beacon.

"That was your sister's friendly way of telling me to stop bothering her police department. And it's pretty clear she still blames me for our breakup and hurting you."

He chose to ignore the reference to them, focused on the case. "Yeah, she's not happy about the *Gazette*'s endless inquiries. But she's as concerned as anyone about the possibility of corruption in GGPD." As chief of police, Melissa had done a fantastic job. Her efforts were currently buffeted by a constant barrage of crime, and the last thing she needed was the local paper questioning the integrity of her force. Stanton felt for his sister, but also hoped she'd get to the bottom of GGPD's bad apple barrel quickly.

"She must be stressed to the max. But still, then why won't she talk to me about it? She's refused every single request for an interview."

"You'll have to take that up with her."

"Please tell me that by the 'lake house,' you don't mean your parents' home." Dread soaked every one of her words.

He couldn't help it; he laughed. A record for him, to find humor during an op. And he'd done it several times with Dominique. "You used to love our weekends out there."

"Sure I did, when your family accepted me as one of their own, and not the traitor I became the minute we split. Answer the question, Stanton." Her icy tone told him she wasn't reminiscing about the times they'd skinny-dipped in the hot tub while the rest of the family slept.

He hesitated. He didn't have to take her to his parents' place. They could go out to his family's cabin, in the remote woods of Michigan's "mitten," but that was at least a five-hour drive on a good day. It was impractical for him, personally, to take her to his parents' place, but it was the best idea he had in terms of her safety.

Frank and Italia kept a very low profile for security reasons, as his father traveled frequently for his job since they'd become empty nesters, leaving his mother alone in the big, rambling home. There certainly was plenty of room at the house, so combined with the optimal security provisions, it was an ideal safe house.

"Stanton?" Annoyance weighed her words.

"Yes. We're going to my parents'."

She huffed sharply in displeasure and he knew if he took his gaze from the road he'd face her ferocious expression, the one that always made him think of a lioness.

"I'm not going. No way. A hotel would be a better idea. You lost the crooks—what does it matter where we hole up until the threat passes? Please tell me you're joking. Just circle back, and let's go to GGPD. You lost the shooters miles ago. I doubt they were able to follow us out of downtown even if you hadn't, with the traffic and construction."

"I'm not messing around here, Dominique. Someone tried to kill you this morning. Do you have any doubts that they meant to kill you? You don't seem to know when to stop. Last month you reported on Tatiana Davison, how her father's a serial killer. Besides digging into Tatiana's private life, how do you think Len Davison took you exposing his daughter like that? But getting yourself in the crosshairs of a serial killer isn't enough. Now you had to stir up the hornet's nest that is this cartel."

"I was doing my job. I am doing my job." She hadn't been thrilled to report on Tatiana, but it was part of her assignment. "But yes, you're right. Those men who shot at us want me dead."

"Right. Jimenez will send in more men the closer you get to the truth. I can't risk keeping you at my place or anywhere in the city."

"What's wrong with my apartment? You know how to drive anywhere without a tail."

"Come on, Dominique. Stop being obtuse. I know how intelligent you are, remember? They already know where you live. We're talking about some very powerful people here. Think about it. If you want this story done right, you need to write it. That requires following leads that will be inconsequential if you're dead. You of all people know the resources a successful drug cartel has at its disposal."

He saw her blanch in his peripheral vision and he wished he could soften the blow for her, but if this was what was needed to make sure she didn't do anything to add to her risk, then so be it.

"I do know their power. They killed Charlie while he was in prison, a place they illegally sent him to."

"There are probably many other victims yet to be discovered. It appears they've infiltrated the legal system."

She nodded, her eyes downcast. "Okay. You've made your point." She sighed, and empathy for her situation yanked at the calm detachment that had taken over from the minute they left his apartment. "I can do this."

He gave a quick glance her way and bit back a laugh—Dominique looked like a victim about to walk the plank and not a grown woman en route to a luxury estate on Lake Michigan.

The more he thought about his decision, the better he felt. His family home was the best place for now. Removed from Grave Gulch, on a rural route, yet fully modern so that Dominique could access Wi-Fi and work. His parents were meticulous with their security, he'd made certain of it, and he'd double-check all of the systems once they arrived. Unless they were directly followed, they wouldn't find Dominique out here.

"You'll be able to hike all you want." He didn't want to examine why it was so important to him for her to have something to look forward to.

"It'd have to be with you, though." Her flat tone stung.

"Don't sound so enthusiastic. But yeah, you're not getting rid of me, not even in the woods." No place was safe until she had her story and GGPD had Pablo Jimenez behind bars, along with his troop of thugs.

"I have no problem with you doing your job. My father's paid you to do it. I'm not happy about being forced to spend time with a man who belittles me and thinks I'm 'obtuse.'"

Crap. He'd let the words fly when all he'd wanted to do was communicate that he knew how intelligent she was.

"I didn't mean it personally."

"Save it, Stanton. I've got to get back to figuring out my next steps. The sooner I get corroborating evidence that Charlie's conviction, and death, were criminally motivated, the sooner GGPD can straighten itself out. And if we're lucky, we'll catch the big one."

He didn't have to ask her what she meant by "the big one." His gut took a nosedive at the stark truth of the danger she'd put herself in. How many journalists were willing to go after criminal mastermind Pablo Jimenez? And why did it have to be Dominique?

Most important, why did he still care too damn much?

Dominique's head pounded and her neck was beyond sore from the roughing up Jimenez's hit man had imparted earlier, but nothing compared to her fury at the way Stanton so easily slipped back into his condescending tone. She knew he didn't mean to sound so dismissive; when it came to security details, he was top in his field, without question. What was easy to see as complete arrogance was in fact his confidence. No one would want anything less from their bodyguard. But as the Michigan countryside whipped by and day turned to twilight, she couldn't stop the sense of complete powerlessness that at once left her despondent and outraged. Not wanting Soledad to worry about her, she texted her, gave her a brief overview of her day. When her sister replied with "hang in there," she wished she was with her now instead of facing her past with Stanton and worrying if she'd live to have a future. Since she didn't do self-pity as a rule, she had to channel her energy into being "ticked off."

There's another way you used to work off your frustration with Stanton.

Heat hit her cheeks as quickly as it pooled in her

midsection, then between her legs. A giggle bubbled up and she forced it back, unwilling to share any of her inner thoughts with him. It was ridiculous. She was being immature at best. Stanton was right: she could have died today, before she found justice for Charlie. The story might have been squashed right there. She kept backup, hard-copy files at the *Grave Gulch Gazette*, but it wouldn't be the same if something happened to her. The reporter who dug up all the evidence and connected the pieces was always the best one to file the story. It was hard enough keeping her enthusiasm up for a story when it was her piece, her passion. Another reporter couldn't be expected to carry the baton for her. Not when the *Gazette* was swamped with countless leads relating to Pablo Jimenez's ring here in Grave Gulch. Charlie's death was just one of too many tragic stories surrounding Jimenez's Michigan operation.

The silence between them grated on her.

"This isn't like us." The words shot out of her mouth and she fidgeted with her seat belt. "One thing we've always been able to do is talk. It doesn't feel right, always trying to cut each other off." Her voice still shook, and it sounded like her voice box had been replaced by a toad's, but the quiet had grown too heavy. They still had another twenty minutes to the Colton lakefront estate, and she didn't want to see his parents for the first time in so long while she and Stanton were at each other's throats.

Italia Colton's intensity was going to be tough enough to cope with. Dominique had no doubt that the family matriarch would question her motives about spending time with Stanton again.

"No, it doesn't feel right. I agree." He shifted in his seat and she realized he might be tired. Where was her compassion? *With Charlie Hamm.*

"It's been a long day for you, too, Stanton."

He shot her a quick, wry glance. "Every day is a long one at Colton Protection. You know that. Your hours are as nuts as mine."

"Yeah. Although I've been thinking about forcing myself to take two full days off each week." She'd committed to one, but then Charlie's death had launched her back into workaholic mode.

His grunt should have been a typical male response, but to her, it was so achingly familiar that tears flooded her vision. Her mind may have let go of Stanton and their connection, but her body, her heart, certainly hadn't.

He chuckled. "The day you take a decent amount of time off to take care of yourself will be—"

He cut himself off, focused on the road. Fear sliced through her. "What is it?" Had he spotted the Porsche again in the rearview mirror? Or another follower?

"Relax. We're safe. Give me a minute." His profile was unreadable in the dusk, no matter that they were driving toward the setting sun. Stanton exited the highway, slowing at the bottom of the ramp to turn right, and followed a local road for a mile or so. Into the entrance of a park where they'd once spent a lot of time hiking, camping and exploring.

"It'll be closed, Stanton." Her voice hitched on his

name and she silently cursed. No need to sound as if she was excited to be alone with him, even if she were willing to admit it to herself.

"I know a back way in. We won't be long." He took a side road, and within a few hundred yards they were on gravel, rocks dinging off the bottom of the chassis.

"This isn't the best car for these dirt roads. Aren't you worried you'll damage it?" She raised her voice over the noise.

"It's more than a typical vehicle, remember?"

Sure enough, the car acted more like a four-wheel drive than a fine-tuned sports car. "I'm impressed."

The dash lights reflected off his white teeth as he smiled. "Here we go." He pulled into what looked like a camping site, except it had one special feature. It was up on a hill and overlooked Lake Michigan, still several miles distant. A full moon rose against the inky blue sky and Dominique didn't think she'd witnessed anything so beautiful in a long while. She had been working too much. And, truth be told, seemed to have lost her desire to seek out the beauty in everything. Since their breakup, her world had turned from an assortment of flavors to vanilla.

Stanton cut the engine and rested his hand on the steering wheel's twelve o'clock position as he stared straight ahead. His body language was clear. This was to be a conversation, pure and simple. She bit her lower lip, chastised herself for wishing they could both let down their guard, be who they used to be.

No. That woman was gone. In her place was a hardened professional who knew how to get a story down.

The Charlie Hamm story could very well give the *Grave Gulch Gazette*, and her, national attention. Nowhere in the mix was getting involved with an ex.

The ex who irrevocably broke your heart.

She waited in the silence, unwilling to guess at his motive for stopping at the romantic spot.

"We need to talk, Dominique, and I didn't want to do it with the distraction of driving. The last thing we deserve, in the middle of all of this, is for my parents to add stress to the situation. I'm still taking you to their home, because I do believe it's the safest place for now, but we should have some ground rules established. The first is always remembering that your life is in danger."

So was her heart.

Chapter 6

"What are your other rules?" Dominique didn't try to hide her sharp tone.

"My parents, especially my mother, are eternal optimists. The minute they see you, they're going to jump to the wrong conclusion." He sighed, looked over his right shoulder at her. "Mom may be a bit, um, overprotective of me. As you know."

"I do." She didn't want to dredge up those first few family dinners that Stanton had brought her to. When Italia asked question after question about her background, her desire for a family, how many children she planned to have. Dominique had never felt good enough for Stanton in those early days. But after several months she'd been accepted as part of the family.

So much so that she'd grieved the loss of the Coltons nearly as much as losing Stanton.

It was your choice.

It had ultimately been her choice to leave, to walk away, in that heated moment two years ago. Stanton had blindsided her with his proposal. And he'd been so stubborn, insisting they be married or nothing. Overwhelmed and gobsmacked by his uncharacteristic unyielding streak, she'd had to walk, hadn't she? Pinpricks of doubt needled her heart as possibilities ran through her mind. If she'd taken just one of Stanton's texts or calls after their hasty breakup, might things have turned out differently? Would he have seen her side, that though she loved him and was willing to commit to him, she hadn't been ready for the white picket fence yet?

"I know my parents are a bit overwhelming, that much hasn't changed."

"So what's your plan, Stanton? I don't want to discuss my story with your parents. I can't, for their safety as well as keeping it under the radar until I have all the facts and witnesses interviewed."

"If they realize I'm working for your dad, and why, they will. Freak. Out." His emphasis caught her attention.

"Why will they freak?"

"They'll try to fix it and want to send both of us overseas or something similar. We don't have time for the distraction, and I don't want to worry them."

"But look at it from their point of view. Why else would you bring me home, though? Except for a job.

They know we're through. I think honesty is the best policy, always." She really didn't see what choice they had but to somewhat level with his parents. Her father knew she was working on a dangerous story. There wasn't a reason to completely hide the truth from the Coltons, but maybe they could soften reality for them a bit. "Why don't we explain that we're working together on a case? Tell them we need to be away from any distractions, and from anyone who might not like what we're researching? You could be providing the security aspect of a story for the *Gazette*, and you picked their place for me to interview you for a couple of hours."

"Hours? First off, we're going to be out here longer than dinner or an overnight."

"What? I thought we were laying low until tonight, when we could go back into the city under the cover of darkness. GGPD is open twenty-four seven." She wanted to continue to protest, but he held up his hand.

"Let me finish. You have got to absolutely be out of sight for the next several days, Dominique. That means no runs into your office, no visiting witnesses for interviews, no moving until I say it's okay. The most we'll do is go into the station tomorrow, but that's it. You can do whatever you need to from the lake house. I'll get your computer equipment brought in, along with clothing and other essentials. But I'm being paid to keep you alive. Are we clear on this part?"

"Do I have a choice? If not you, my father will send out an entire squad of protectors next."

"I'd do the same if I had a daughter. Are we in agreement on my role in your life right now?"

"Yes."

"Back to my parents... This idea I have is going to sound outlandish. I think we should tell them we are exploring a reconciliation, but don't want anyone to see us together. We can say we're only telling them because we trust them—my mother will eat this up—and they will be expected to keep our secret. If we don't reconcile, which we both know we won't, no harm no foul. We'll make it clear that it's not working out, when it's safe for you to move about on your own again."

"We'll be able to have them keep their dignity while ensuring their safety." She interrupted him, warming to the insane idea. And she couldn't ignore the respect she had for him for the sweet gesture. Stanton cared about his parents, his family. He knew what mattered. How many successful entrepreneurs kept their priorities as rock-solid as he had? If she were honest, though, all of Stanton's siblings had their priorities straight. She'd kept tabs on Stanton and his family since the breakup more than she cared to admit. Oldest brother Clarke had fallen in love with Everleigh, even while she was accused—falsely—of being a murderer. Travis had started a family with Tatiana Davison, daughter of none other than serial killer Len Davison. Travis hadn't allowed the sins of Tatiana's father to stop him from seeing Tatiana as her own person, and the woman he wanted to spend the rest of his life with. Melissa and Antonio Ruiz were engaged, planning to start a family soon. A chief of police, under all of the current crime chaos in Grave Gulch, still putting family first.

No wonder Stanton had been eager to settle down

into marriage and family. It was what the Coltons did when they found the one.

It'd be best if she just forgot the latter. She wasn't Stanton's "one" and hadn't been since he'd broken her heart. And now she realized, she'd broken his in return. It was paramount that she kept her own priorities straight for this story. Which meant leveling with his parents as much as possible.

Still, she had misgivings. "There's one thing I'm not happy about." To put it mildly.

"Shoot."

"Wouldn't they expect us to be affectionate in front of them? I'm not up for that, Stanton. I don't have the energy to pretend that much." Her hands shook and she shoved them under her thighs. It wasn't from the cold, and it wasn't from shock any longer. It was 100 percent awareness of his nearness, and how even though the plan was just that, a plan, it reminded her too acutely of the passion they'd once shared. And she was lying, about the pretend part.

"You don't have to pretend. We will make it clear we're simply looking for a place to talk things out, like two adults, without any other distractions. We'll be in separate rooms, so that will be their first clue that we're serious about doing things right."

"What do you mean by that? They never disapproved of us sharing a room before. Did they? Not that I want to share a room now. That's not what I meant." Heat warmed her cheeks for the umpteenth time since he'd walked—no, run—back into her life this morning.

"No, they're open-minded about such things, you

know that. Look, I know this is highly unusual, and I'm asking for more than I deserve here. I get it, trust me. This is for my parents, Dominique. By doing things the 'right' way, I meant differently from how we handled our breakup."

"Oh, you mean the part where you gave me an ultimatum and I had no choice but to leave?" Tears scalded her eyes but she kept her gaze even with his. Let him see the pain. It was about time.

"No, I mean the part where you didn't give me a second chance after you walked out. You didn't answer any of my calls or texts. You blocked me."

"I had a story—"

"Oh, here we go again. It was about the story. I can't help but think your excuse was a convenient way to get away from me. I was too fast, too eager to make us into something we weren't." His voice wasn't bitter, didn't hold the condescending tone. His eyes sparked with something dangerous, and she saw the moonlight reflect in their depths. "Do you ever wonder how things would be now if I hadn't proposed, Dominique? At least not then. If I'd waited. Or agreed to your suggestion on the spot and we'd stayed together, saw how it worked out over time? I never told you this, but what really made me end it was when you first said you weren't ready to commit to marriage, I freaked out. I thought that if I wasn't your husband, I wouldn't be able to ask you to curtail your more dangerous work as needed. The thought of losing you to a story… I could never face that. Do you ever reconsider leaving so abruptly?" His anguish was laid bare. So much in his soft tone, the sensuous way the words rolled off his tongue.

Her body lit with arousal at the soft query, the genuine wonder reflected in his words. "No. I mean, yes, I can imagine but I can't let myself go there." He turned toward her and reached up to stroke her cheek with a finger. Tingles sparked across her skin and down her throat. They were a whisper apart.

"Why not?" He traced her lips with his finger, then leaned in and grazed her mouth with his. She closed her eyes, unable to contain the shots of lust that pooled in all the right places. "Tell me, Dom. Why can't you go there?"

"I can't risk what it could cost me." As she spoke, her body swayed closer, arced toward him. It might be the events of the day, the prospect of pretending to be trying to get back together, or perhaps it was no more than being near Stanton again. No matter the reason, Dominique was done fighting what had ignited in that decrepit building as she stared into Stanton's eyes.

When she saw his lids lower, she reached for him, needing to get to his lips before he did hers again. He had to know she wanted this, no matter what she said. Her arms wrapped around his neck, her fingers digging into his nape. His curls, curls that she knew so well, wound around her fingers as she pulled him in. He cupped her face with exquisite gentleness as he moved in. Their lips met with zero curiosity, as they were already intimately acquainted. The brief kiss in his apartment had confirmed that.

It was the force of her emotions that took her by surprise. All in a simple touch.

Nothing is simple with Stanton.

All of today's pain, yesterday's regrets and tomorrow's worries blew away. Nothing was stronger than this—the bond she shared with Stanton. His hands left her face and his arms went around her waist, his chest surged across the bucket seats and pressed against hers, the friction against her breasts the sexiest sensation she recalled in her thirty years, ever. Stanton's tongue didn't barge into her mouth, or make tentative strokes on her lips, but seemed to join with hers as if they'd never parted, as if being joined together in any way possible was the sole purpose of their existence.

The kiss went on and on, and their hands roamed and roamed. Each caress raised her arousal, and when he gently squeezed her breast she moaned against his lips. How had she survived the last two years without this?

"Dom." His breath, hot against her throat, healing what had been so broken just minutes before, further stoked her need.

"I know." She forced her hands off his neck, allowed them to grasp his shoulders, wander down across his chest. His arms held her, cradled her, and she knew she was safe, secure. Stanton had always been her safe harbor. "I want it, too, Stanton."

His body stilled and she fought to not cry in protest as he lifted his head, his gaze locked on hers.

What had she done?

* * *

Dominique had said she wanted it. Not him, not Stanton, not them as a couple, but *it*.

Dang it all to Hades and back. He couldn't break their eye contact, needing the connection, the reassurance that his attraction, his need, wasn't one-way. Desire made her pupils wide and he felt the strength of her arousal under his fingers as he caressed her collarbone, the way her blood pounded under his fingertips at her pulse points.

"This is what we can't risk, Dominique." He moved away, careful to go slow enough to not hurt her or touch her bruises. He'd been so caught up in the kiss, in her, that he'd forgotten her injuries. He sucked in air, lots of air. "We can't fall back into our physical attraction in front of my parents. It'll get their hopes up too high."

"Is that why you kissed me, to test it out? To see if I still gave you the same thrill?"

Her words drove through him as hard as his lust had, and he rubbed his forehead. "No. I kissed you because, well, it was important we cleared the air." Had he just said that? Did he sound like the biggest jerk to her, too?

"That's fair enough." Her lack of reaction stilled something deep inside him. She straightened her clothing, readjusted her position in the passenger seat. Darkness had fallen and he couldn't see anything through the fogged windows. He started the engine.

At her quick glance he shrugged. "It's getting chilly." It was. Spring was evident in the buds on the trees during the day, but winter held on tight to the night.

"Whatever you need me to do, to keep all of us safe,

I'll do it. Maybe we need to look at this, this kiss, like a bad experiment. We tried it—it's only a path to certain disaster between us, and we won't go there again. I'll go along with your story for your parents. I always liked them, you know." Her countenance was so matter-of-fact it grated on him as he struggled to contain his emotions.

"As they did you." He replied before his grudging admission would stir up more memories. "I'm glad we're in agreement, then."

"Wait, there's one more thing." She put her hand on his forearm, stopped him from shifting into gear. "If we're really clearing the air, let me say this. I didn't thank you for today. Thank you, Stanton. You saved my life. I admit I thought it was only an attempt to scare me, to warn me. But after getting shot at in the parking garage, I realize you're right. Pablo Jimenez has to be behind it all, and he wants me dead. Thank you for seeing what I couldn't. And for saving me a second time."

Her eyes, pools of sincerity, tugged at that same spot in his chest that he was doing his best to keep under wraps, far from the reach of any silly dreams about the two of them. He glanced away before he did something stupid like kiss her again. "It's my job, Dominique. One your father is paying me handsomely for."

If only he could remember this. Before he let his guard down and Dominique got hurt, or worse.

The lake house came into view only on the last turn of the driveway, emerging from the tall maples and pines as if from a dream. Her stomach flipped. She'd missed this so much, what had once become her retreat from the often harsh pace of her career. Had she been naive to think it could last forever? Or had she confused her feelings for Stanton with convenience?

Her severe self-examination would have to wait. As she got out of the car and joined Stanton for the short walk to the front door, she breathed in the lake air, let it soothe her agitation. The scent of wet grass and early spring filled her with a sense of peace, if only for a millisecond.

His tall form was a comfort no matter that they'd agreed to keep the careful physical boundaries between them. It was always like this around him. She felt at once safe and threatened. Secure in his larger-than-life warmth, afraid of what her feelings for him could do to her carefully constructed peace of mind. She focused on her surroundings, the lake air laden with the scent of whatever was cooking for dinner inside the house. Gravel and seashells—the tiny kind unique to the Great Lakes—crunched under her feet. It was as satisfying as hearing pine cones crush under her hiking boots.

"Do they know we're coming?" She hadn't heard him call his parents all day. He could have sent a text, though.

"No. You know my family. There's bound to be at least one of us kids showing up at any time. They'll be thrilled to see us." He hadn't spoken for the rest of the drive, after the park. After that kiss—

"Are you ready for this, Dominique?" He stopped under the porch light and the soft glow made his dark curls almost blue in the night, which made her think of his eyes, how they could devour her as good as his hands, his lips.

Stop.

"Yes, of course." She had a story to finish and this was another step toward it. Staying alive, getting the statements she needed from all sides, compiling all the information. Whatever it took.

Are you willing to risk your heart?

"Okay, then. Let's do it." He rang the doorbell, punched in a code as he did. He motioned for her to step in first and she walked into the foyer. The video doorbell had at least revealed it was Stanton, and probably her, as well.

"We're back in here!" Italia's musical voice reached them from the spot Dominique always thought of her in, when she allowed herself to dwell on her memories of Stanton's family. They walked forward, across the polished floors, into the large, colorful kitchen. Italia rose from the island, her short brown bob the perfect foil for her bright green eyes. Frank's motions mirrored his wife of forty years as he stood to greet his son. Half-empty wineglasses, water goblets and plates of broiled salmon and rice signaled they'd interrupted the couple's dinner.

"Mom, Dad." Stanton kissed his mother on both cheeks, in true Italian fashion. Italia had immigrated to the States after falling in love with a certain Michiganian, Frank, forty-one years ago. Dominique had the numbers and dates memorized. She couldn't help it; her mind had a yen for numbers. And they'd celebrated an anniversary with his parents years before.

As Italia kissed Stanton back, her gaze strayed to his guest, and her eyes widened when they met Dominique's. "Dominique, *bella*, how wonderful!" Italia didn't miss a beat as she walked over to Dominique and gave her an equally warm welcome. Frank Colton followed with his usual bear hug, and Dominique tried to ignore the guilt that dug its claws into her conscience. She'd never asked Stanton how his parents had taken the breakup, never reached out to them to say goodbye. Belatedly she realized that at least a handwritten note would have been a nice gesture. Grave Gulch wasn't that big a place, and anything to ease otherwise awkward run-ins couldn't hurt. Fortunately she'd only seen them from afar at large charity or sporting events.

"Italia, Frank, it's wonderful to see you both again." The warmth in her voice wasn't forced. In fact, it came from a deep well of longing she'd been unaware of until she walked back into this kitchen, smelled the fresh rosemary that Italia grew, along with other pots of herbs on the massive marble countertop. Frank, a shipping executive, had personally seen to the shipment of Carrara marble from Italy for his wife.

"What brings you here? Both of you? Have you eaten?" Italia fired the questions as she pulled Ravello ceramic plates from the deep drawers under the counter, placed them on the island next to hers and Frank's. "I've got more salmon, and oh, Stanton, your favorite dessert is in the cupboard."

"That sounds great, Mom."

"Can I take your coat?" Frank stood in front of her and she shrugged out of her coat as smoothly as she could without making herself wince. Her discomfort was as much from her bruises as the reality that no matter how nice and cozy this seemed, she was now a guest in the Colton family home. When she and Stanton had been together, she'd hung her coat in the front closet, next to Frank's and Italia's.

"Thank you."

"Here, come sit." Italia patted the seat next to her and gave Dominique her classic "you wouldn't dare mess with an Italian mother" look. Dominique complied, and Stanton slid into the seat on her other side. Was that a smile he was keeping to a minimum? "So tell me, Dominique. What have you been up to?"

Italia may as well have asked how many lovers she'd taken since walking away from her beloved son. Dominique sat up straight and forged ahead. "Nothing any different. I'm wrapped up in several stories but one has taken all of my time as of late."

"Dominique's going to get a Pulitzer for the story she's working on now, if it all goes well." Stanton's praise made her start, and she twisted around to him.

"That's not true, and, well…" She gave him a look that his parents couldn't see. *What are you doing?* He grinned.

"You've always been modest." Italia didn't miss a beat. "Stanton, tell us why you haven't been out here for over three weeks."

It was Dominique's turn to stifle a laugh.

"What your mother means is that we've missed

you, and we're certain that Colton Protection has been busy with all of the recent local activity. I imagine the drug issue will keep you busy for a long while, unfortunately." Frank's smooth baritone was familiar—Stanton had his father's voice.

"Not to mention the movie premiere." Italia laughed. "I'm happy to say that I've scored an invite to the Italian movie they're streaming at the theater next weekend." Italia loved any reason to dress up, and she wore evening wear well. Which reminded her of how well Stanton wore a tux. She stifled a groan. *Focus on dinner.*

"That's great, Mom." Stanton helped himself to creamed spinach, homemade dinner rolls and salmon. Dominique did the same, suddenly hungry, no matter that she'd already had salmon at lunch today. The Coltons enjoyed their fish and seafood. It felt good to not be so anxious that food turned her stomach.

"I bet you'll have a blast at the party, Italia."

"I'm sure I will. I was invited to provide artwork for the social beforehand, and it'll be on display at the charity silent auction, too, which is always nice for my business. It might not be the big-time, but it's close enough for me." Italia sipped her wine. "Did you know I saw Sophia Loren once, when I was a girl? My mother took me to Napoli, to the Teatro San Carlo. It was the opening of *Carmen.* Sophia and Carlo Ponti were in the box closest to the stage. They waved right at us." Italia's verve was invigorating, and with longing Dominique realized how much she'd missed her, and Stanton's family. Italia was one of a kind, an artist. Frank's success in steel had paralleled hers. Italia had a larger-than-life personality and charmed everyone she met.

"I'm sure they waved right at you, Ma." Stanton spoke around a large mouthful of food.

"Manners, Stanton." Italia reached around the back of Dominique and playfully swatted at her son's nape. Frank's chuckle resonated through the large room.

Italia clicked her tongue. "Don't be such a slob around your *fidanzata*, son." Her casual use of the Italian word for *girlfriend* or *fiancée* sliced through the easygoing mood.

Dominique's hand froze midway between her plate and mouth, the creamed spinach suspended in unison with her shock. *Here we go.*

"Um…" Stanton chewed, wiped his mouth with the crisp white napkin that Italia seemed to have an endless supply of and sucked down half of his water goblet. "We're, ah… Dominique and I are not back together. We, we've decided to see if we can work on being good friends again." Stanton's voice shook the tiniest bit, but Dominique didn't miss it. Judging by Italia's sharp intake of breath, neither did she. Frank remained silent, always the steady rudder for Italia's enthusiasm and at times, over-the-top emotions.

"I'm so sorry we barged in on your dinner. It's delicious." A change of subject was in order.

"We're just happy that you joined us, Dominique." Frank rose from his end of the island and took his plate to the sink. "You two were awfully close for a while there. I understand that things don't always work out as we hope, and I'm glad you've got a chance to salvage a friendship from your time together."

Dominique blinked. Frank wasn't one for false praise, or overt sentiment. He took things in stride, like when Travis decided to start his own business with Colton Plastics, breaking from the other siblings in their law enforcement or security fields. Italia overflowed with enough emotion for the entire town of Grave Gulch, not to mention her family.

"Thanks, Dad." Stanton had recovered his composure and she looked at him. He met her gaze with a warm smile, made to look as though they were really seeking to become good friends again. His eyes told her the truth. They'd managed to get through dinner, and his parents appeared to have accepted their explanation at face value. But not for one minute should she forget why she was here. She was hiding from potential assassins, and in the midst of a story that did, in fact, have Pulitzer Prize potential.

Funny how the possibility of global attention mattered little since this morning's events. It had to be the shock of the assault, and the shooting in the garage. It couldn't be because she was painfully aware of all she'd lost and left behind. How ironic to figure out what really mattered to her when Pablo Jimenez would do all he could to kill her.

Chapter 7

The next morning, Dominique lay wide-awake in the guest bedroom from dawn onward. The lake's view was just out the window, but she wasn't interested in looking at the sunrise, or reminiscing over how she and Stanton had made good use of his parents' dock, swimming naked on more than one occasion.

She'd brought Jimenez's wrath to the Colton home, and she had to get out of here. It was one thing to put herself on the line for a story, and Stanton had willingly agreed to protect her. But Frank and Italia didn't deserve this. They had to leave before the cartel found her again.

She left the bedroom to find Stanton and tell him they had to leave ASAP. The clothes his mother had loaned her, a loose sweatshirt and yoga pants that belonged to his younger sister, fit fine and were, in fact, far more comfortable than her usual work clothes. But she had only her high-heeled boots or her sneakers, no slippers, so she padded to the kitchen in stockinged feet. Her feet were still sore from running in her trouser socks on the street yesterday.

Stanton sat at the island, his laptop open, steaming mug of coffee in hand. His hair was sleep-rumpled and he hadn't shaved yet. An old college sweatshirt was stretched across his torso, the logo long faded. He didn't look up at first as her steps were silent on the polished wood floor. She paused. It couldn't hurt to soak in this glimpse of what she'd turned down, could it? Not that she had regrets. They'd made the right decision. Hadn't they?

It was being back here, all the time together yesterday, not to mention the life-and-death situation of her almost strangulation, that was making nostalgia tug on her heartstrings.

"Good morning." She walked in as he looked up, helped herself to coffee from the half-full carafe.

"Morning. How did you sleep?"

"Okay. How long have you been up?"

He grunted. "Since four. I had paperwork to catch up on so it was a good time to do it."

"Are your parents out walking?"

"No. In fact, they're gone."

"What do you mean, 'gone'?"

"They left a note. Apparently they left late last night, after we'd crashed. They're flying out to San Francisco together for one of Dad's business meetings. Said they didn't want us to have to worry about anyone intruding on our 'reconciliation.'" He made air quotes with lanky fingers. "But I think the real deal is that Dad had the business commitment and Mom decided to join him at the last minute. She can't help her matchmaking tendencies."

"Oh."

"You look like the wind's gone out of your sails."

"I was just about to tell you that we needed to leave. I can't live with the fact I've put a target on this house."

"You haven't done anything. Jimenez is the bad guy. If he finds you here, you're not alone. I'm here and I'll protect you. No one's getting to you. Trust me."

"I do trust you. You're the top in your business."

"But?" He was picking up on her worry.

"You said yourself that the cartel has limitless resources. How are you going to protect us against an arsenal that's likely to arrive with his hired criminals?"

"We have backup, Dominique. It's called the Grave Gulch Police Department. Add in the FBI as the cartel operates across state lines, and the Drug Enforcement Administration. Not to mention the state troopers."

She watched his expression become more animated as he spoke. Stanton's passion stemmed from his childhood obsession with law enforcement. He'd often spoken at length about it to her. Two of his three siblings had gone into law enforcement, too, no doubt inspired by the tragic unsolved murder of their Aunt Amanda. It provided the impetus for what Dominique suspected was a Colton genetic trait: to serve and protect. Stanton had picked personal security and protection instead of police work after college, when he'd discovered his real talent was working one-on-one with clients and security systems.

"What?" He paused, tilted his head.

"You are so into your job. It's a good thing, don't worry. I forgot how much you deal with on a daily basis."

"No reason for you to remember any of that." He sipped his coffee and stood up. "Are you hungry?"

She decided to stop fighting him, fighting her every instinct to disagree with him on each issue that came up. "I am. But you made lunch yesterday. My turn to cook."

He shook his head. "Naw. Why don't you tell me about Charlie Hamm, and your story, who you need to still interview? The sooner we get your piece filed, the better."

"Okay. You're absolutely right." Dominique took one of the stools and watched him as he made them bacon cheese omelets. Bacon had always been irresistible to her. But Stanton was cooking it because it was in the Colton refrigerator, not for a personal reason like the fact that it was her kryptonite.

He did a mock grab at his heart. "Whoa—you're admitting I'm right?" His grin was playful and she smiled back.

"Where to start? First, I already told you, Charlie was my student in the county jail. His poetry was exceptional. I have copies of his poems you can read if you want. They're incredible. Working with him led me to listen to him and I wrote down all of it. How he believed fake evidence had been planted in the form of one of his fingerprints on a suitcase that held drugs. How all of the witnesses that could have testified that he wasn't a pusher, that he was helping local addicts and dealers get off the stuff, somehow disappeared when it came time for the trial. And of course, Johnny Blanchard, whose testimony put Charlie behind bars. Charlie believed that Blanchard was paid off and/or threatened by the cartel. As for the fingerprint on the case with over one hundred thousand dollars in opioids, I can't help but think Randall Bowe had everything to do with that. We don't even know that it was Charlie's fingerprint, as all we had, all the court accepted as evidence, was a statement from Randall that the print was Charlie's. It's as if the entire system let him down. But I think it was more a chain of bad guys who turned at Jimenez's pressure."

He whipped the eggs while the bacon sizzled in his mother's extra-large cast-iron frying pan. "The fingerprint report should be easy enough to dispute. If Randall doesn't have a digital scan of the actual print saved, it boils down to his word. And right now, his word isn't holding a lot of water."

"But he's still on the police force!" Anger made her cheeks red and her eyes flash.

"Actually, Melissa told me he's been furloughed until the investigation is complete. There's a possibility of another corrupt cop, too. But you didn't hear that from me."

"I'm sorry, Stanton. That's awful for Melissa, and

the entire department. But it's about time some progress was made on the internal investigation. I hope for GGPD's sake it's resolved quickly." It would be a win to have the evidence against Charlie stricken, too. One step closer to justice for him.

"I don't disagree. By the way, how are your feet doing? I noticed yesterday that your toes were swollen."

She grinned. "I did make a mess of them when we were in the East Side. They're fine, thank you. Wearing socks and sneakers for a while will help."

"You like to wear dress shoes for work, though."

"Since we won't be going into town much, I'll be happy to stay in socks, maybe hiking boots when I can get into the woods. Speaking of which, can we go to my apartment to get some of my clothing, my cosmetics?"

"I'm working on it. Our first priority is to get you into the station."

For the rest of their breakfast she made notes on her phone of all she hoped to accomplish today with the story. And ignored as much as possible how very comfortable it was to be with Stanton in the morning.

It was as dangerous to her well-being as being hunted by a criminal.

They were both introspective on the drive back into Grave Gulch. Stanton tried to think of something he could talk to her about, but his head was wrapped around keeping her under the cartel's radar. He'd gotten intel via Troy that GGPD had determined that the local heroin kingpin was indeed Pablo Jimenez. He passed the information to Dominique.

"Thanks for letting me know." Appreciation, rather than the sarcasm he'd expected—and she'd be entirely in her rights to express—laced her words.

"You already had it figured out."

"I was almost certain, but having law enforcement validation is always welcome. Despite what you might think, I always value official information."

"I don't think that at all. I know you, or knew you, pretty well. And you me. I know that you respect law enforcement. That's why it's been so hard to hear you throw accusations at GGPD, warranted or not. Plus, my family has so many connections to GGPD."

"I get it, Stanton, I do. You help the local police by protecting civilians, taking the onus off them. I shouldn't have been so harsh with Troy yesterday. Or you. We all want the same thing—justice."

"I appreciate that, and Troy didn't take anything you said personally. You were there—it was smoothed out before he left. And another thing. Please understand that I respect your work, Dominique. I always have." Even when he resented the time it cost them, how many nights had been lost to her being buried in research or hunting down leads. He'd had the same issue with committing time to their relationship, as protecting people was almost always a twenty-four-seven gig. He sighed. It had been easy to blame Dominique's stubbornness for their breakup, but he had to cast equal blame on his own workaholic tendencies, too.

"I know that I have your respect, deep down. It's easy to ignore it, though, when I'm looking for ammunition when we disagree on an issue." Her brows were raised and the frank assessment was another thing he missed so much. Only she could be brutally honest with him.

He laughed, and after a heartbeat, Dominique joined in.

"You've always been honest with me. So let me be frank about my concerns over the cartel that's taken over Grave Gulch." He hated to douse the warmth of their shared humor so quickly, but they were nearing town. "I've come face-to-face with Jimenez's guys while protecting a client. It kills me to say this, but they're close to invincible. They have unlimited resources—by that I mean money they spend on everything from private investigators to weapons to assassins. They don't limit their assignments to cartel members, or drug dealers, only."

He'd guarded a celebrity earlier this year who'd drawn the ire of the cartel. Stanton had had to use everything at his disposal, all of the resources of Colton Protection and his law enforcement contacts, to keep the star safe until she was able to finish her testimony to the court. Three members of the cartel had been convicted, but Jimenez remained at large, unscathed. He was an expert at keeping his hands clean.

"Right, I've figured out pretty much the same about their business dealings. They hire out the jobs that they can without tipping off law enforcement. I've had to read up on cartel activity ever since I became a reporter. It's constantly changing, and fentanyl has really turned what we thought we knew about the drug trade on its head." Exasperation edged her sigh. "I shouldn't have posted that challenge on social media. I knew better. It's brought the danger too close to those I care most about."

"You wanted a timely resolution to something that's plagued this town for too long." He surprised himself with his response, surprised how easy it was to see Dominique's point of view. It'd always been like this with her, with *them*. They fit each other like a favorite winter sweater. "I'm glad I can be here for you now, even if you wouldn't have chosen me as your bodyguard."

"I'm glad you're here, too." She didn't look at him but he risked a glance to see her profile was set in resolute determination. Poised to get to the truth, no matter the personal cost.

"Is there anything more you want me to get from your place?" She'd finally agreed to let him be the one to go to her apartment and had already texted him a list of essentials. He was inexplicably relieved that he'd been able to convince her that she needed to stay away from her usual haunts. There was no fighting the ties that still bound him to her. She wasn't just another client. He was thankful for her business at GGPD—he knew she'd be safe there while he ran over to her place.

"I can't think of anything else. I appreciate you doing this, Stanton. If you feel weird about it at all, I can ask Soledad to meet you there, and she can pack up my stuff." Her tone was so professional, her ability to detach from their previous relationship so surgical, he wanted to stop the car and remind her of the depth of what they shared, by kissing her.

That would be the stupidest thing he'd done since giving in last night. *Giving in? Or instigating?*

"There's nothing weird about facilitating a client's safety." Two could play at emotional detachment. No matter that for him, it was an impossible feat.

"I suppose not. You do whatever you have to for your clients, always have. No matter how it ended between us, I've always respected your sense of duty. And I know I'm giving you a hard time now because I want the freedom to research this piece without the shackles of caution. But that's not an option with this cartel after me, is it?"

"No." They entered the downtown area and he stopped at a light. "Speaking of which, now that we're definite about Pablo Jimenez, do you know more about him you haven't told me?"

Her profile was classic, with high cheekbones and long lashes, her curtain of silky hair caught up in a low ponytail. He lov—*appreciated*—her beauty no matter what she wore, whether or not she had makeup on. This morning she'd gone barefaced. It was hard to keep from reaching out, touching her cheek, her throat. His fingers knew every inch of her skin by heart. She'd dressed in the same clothes as yesterday but somehow still appeared fresh.

She shook her head. "I'd like more information on Jimenez for my story, but my priority has been getting to the witnesses who can verify Charlie's wrongful imprisonment, along with others whose lives have been ruined by similar tactics. It's finally official, then. Jimenez is the one who sent the strangler to find me."

"Jimenez must be reading your social media, Dominique. I noticed you didn't tag your location but we're dealing with smart crooks. I hate to admit it, since it's my job to keep you safe, but given enough time, they'll find you wherever you are. You can't provoke him anymore, not while I'm in charge of your safety. It's as reckless as showing up to a gunfight without a weapon."

"Good thing I agree with you on this point. Otherwise we'd get into another argument, Stanton. Remember our old motto that we each do our respective jobs and stay out of the other's?"

"The problem with that is that you're my job right now."

Her eyes narrowed but he couldn't engage in a staredown as the light changed. He thought he caught a low growl and hid his smile. No matter what, he got Dominique. They were exceptional at pushing each other's buttons.

He pulled into the station and parked in the only empty spot on the modest lot.

"They're always busy," she murmured to herself.

"Grave Gulch is a decent-sized place."

"With big problems." She reached for the door handle and he leaned over and placed his hand on her arm.

"Wait. Always wait for me to open the door."

She turned to him. "I'm sorry. I forgot." Her breath hitched, lips parted, her tongue flashing behind her white teeth. He breathed in her scent, free from her designer perfume; he had the gift of smelling her unique scent of sultry sweetness that he associated with waking up in bed together. Her eyes shone with a question he wasn't willing to answer, and she sure as heck wasn't verbalizing. They were too close. The space between them was several inches but it was as if she were pressed up against him again, and he was about to kiss her full lips.

"I'll be right there." He turned and let himself out of the car before he did something catastrophic. The worst part was that for those intense seconds he'd been thinking nothing about her security and only about what they'd lost. Thrown away.

But regrets weren't part of this security detail. Only keeping her alive was.

Dominique couldn't recall a time she'd seen GGPD so busy. It wasn't as if it was ever quiet here. It took longer than usual to find an officer who could take her report. After she'd gotten past reception, Stanton had left for her apartment. It should feel freeing to be away from his constant scrutiny. Next to him she always had the sense that while he was alert to any threats, he didn't miss the smallest reaction on her part. Yet instead of relief, all that was left in his absence was a forlorn emptiness. How could this be? She'd done just fine without him for two years, and after only twenty-four hours, she was dependent on him?

It's because your life has been upended. First getting jumped, then shot at. It'll pass.

She was asked to wait in the break area, where she helped herself to a cup of tea and scanned her emails and texts. A quick search in databases subscribed to by the *Gazette* confirmed what Stanton already told her about Pablo Jimenez and the cartel. They'd been poisoning Grave Gulch for months, leading up to the current onslaught of opioid-related crimes and circumstances in her beloved town. Stanton's DEA source also verified that her social media posts about GGPD corruption, her declaration to seek justice for Charlie's death, had triggered a reaction. Pablo Jimenez prided himself on having ironclad control over illicit drug flow into Michigan and remaining anonymous locally—until now. Dominique's overt inquests into the cartel and its connections had hit a sore spot. Jimenez must have slipped up with his communications or whereabouts. The report she read indicated that his sloppiness had allowed DEA agents to ascertain his identity.

But Jimenez was still at large. Drugs remained on the street, and citizens of Grave Gulch were dying from fentanyl overdoses. There weren't enough police or EMTs to get to every OD in time, with Narcan.

As further fuel in an already combustible scenario, separate social media accounts were calling for an inquest into GGPD activity pertaining to forensic evidence. No wonder Stanton was protective of his sister.

"Dominique. Long time no see." As if conjured by her thoughts, GGPD Chief Melissa Colton spoke from a few feet away. Dominique put her phone in her coat pocket and stood. She quelled her nerves with a deep breath. Melissa wasn't about to engage in girl talk with her.

"Chief Colton. I'm here to see an officer, file a report."

Melissa nodded. "I know why you're here. You can file it in a bit. Come with me first." She turned and led the way to her office, a modest space with enough room for her desk and two chairs. "Have a seat."

Sharp blue eyes the same color as Stanton's focused on her. "You always go for the tough stories, don't you?" Melissa's slight grin eased the accusation, but not by much.

"It's my job. People deserve to know the truth. You still haven't released any information about the other cases Randall Bowe tampered with. Drew Orr almost got away with murder before you shot him dead in self-defense. Fritz Emerson's death was first blamed on Everleigh, who could have spent years in jail if no one pursued it. Don't you think the very citizens you protect deserve to know how they were ripped off? How innocent people went to jail and criminals got off? Some may still remain behind bars for all we know."

Melissa leaned forward in her chair, her hands folded on the desk. "You know me well enough, Dominique. Better than any reporter at the *Gazette*, in fact. We're conducting our own internal investigation and you have to trust me that any officer or employee of my department will face the appropriate consequences if we uncover wrongdoing."

"Stop with the formal talk you give all the media outlets. We're talking about lives, Melissa."

"My department works at *saving* lives each and every day." Melissa wasn't budging and Dominique didn't expect or want her to. What she wanted was answers.

"You weren't there for Charlie Hamm."

"Since when is grilling my sister part of your

story?" Stanton entered the room and sat in the chair next to her.

"She's just doing her job. And who invited you in here, brother?" Melissa's eyes didn't hold scorn or contempt for Dominique or her profession, as she'd faced with the rare cop over the years. Instead, Grave Gulch's chief of police looked flat-out exhausted. Compassion welled for Melissa, not as Stanton's sister, nor as the police chief, but as a woman trying to do the right thing against what looked like impossible odds. Dominique knew how draining tracking a serial killer and a kingpin must be, in addition to investigating Randall Bowe. No one was immune to the taxing fight against the tsunami of a crime wave, including Melissa.

"As long as I'm assigned to guard Dominique, you get me, too. We're a package deal until we catch Jimenez."

"Mom seems to think you two are reconciling." Curiosity lit sparks in Melissa's eyes.

"Hey, please don't tell them that I'm actually protecting her. I told them that we needed space to figure things out, to repair our friendship. I don't want them worrying. You know Dad. He'll have us on a plane to Europe in no time if he finds out."

"Dominique's become a target, and it won't be private for long. I can't keep our parents from finding out, Stanton. Neither can you."

"They might not see the papers for a few days. They were gone this morning when we got up. Mom went with Dad on a business trip to California."

Melissa nodded. "They like to escape from it all a

few times a year. So you're staying out at the lake house for the duration?" She cast her speculative glance on Dominique, who nodded.

"I don't have a choice. Stanton thinks it's the safest place for now, and since your parents left I feel better about being there. The last thing I want to do is attract the cartel to them or any other innocent bystander. This makes my desire to wrap this up all the more urgent, Melissa. I'm sure you feel the same. Which is why I need your help here. With each passing day I'm not getting any closer to proving how Charlie was wrongfully imprisoned. All I'm asking from you is for a chance to look at Bowe's records. Or at least Charlie's evidence file." Dominique knew it was futile but she had to ask. It was her job.

"I'm sorry, but until our internal review is complete, I don't have anything to tell you. Now let's get on with why I sat you down." Melissa's expression was full of concern. "Your social media posts triggered a hit being put out on you."

"We know."

"We figured that out."

Both she and Stanton replied in unison.

Melissa's brows arched. "Well done, you two. Stanton, you read the DEA report?"

"I did. And no, I didn't tell Dominique everything." He turned to her, a question in his eyes.

"I have my sources." She laughed. "The Associated Press published the news this morning."

Melissa grinned. "There's the woman I know."

Dominique smiled back, until she remembered how

and when Melissa knew her. Back when she and Stanton were together. As much as her reporting duties brought her over to GGPD to track down stories, she rarely ran into Melissa. But when she'd been with Stanton, she and Melissa had hit it off and gone out for a couple of girls' nights. Their budding friendship had wilted after the breakup, mostly because Dominique had avoided not only Stanton but his entire family. Another regret she'd ignored until now.

"I just want the truth to come out, Melissa. *Chief.*" She smiled, wanting the chief to have no doubt that she respected her position.

Melissa nodded. "I get that. And I also get that Pablo Jimenez isn't going to rest until he thinks you're no longer a threat. To someone like him, that'll be when you're dead."

"I've already figured that out. Yesterday was a game changer." Did she have to spell it out again? Melissa knew she was here to file the incident reports with Stanton for both of the attempted killings.

"It's important that we're all on the same page here. That includes you, Stanton. Neither of you are to go rogue on this story. I want to know exactly who you're going to interview and when. I need to know your whereabouts at all times, Dominique. I'm not interested in curtailing your story. In fact, I relish your eventual publication of the truth. I need your help to break these bastards wide open. I also don't want you dead."

"I appreciate that."

"Don't you agree that it would be better for Dominique to lay low, ease up on the story, until after

Jimenez is caught? DEA is closing in." Stanton's interjection made Dominique's teeth grind.

Melissa shook her head. "DEA's not getting the critical intel fast enough. None of us are. Figuring out the kingpin's identity is one thing, a break for us. He messed up, but he'll know that he did. He'll assume there's a good chance we're on to him. That'll only drive him further underground, make him more determined to strike out and prove his power." Melissa looked at her clasped hands, then at her brother. "Let me ask you something, Stanton. If Dominique was a male reporter, would you expect her to ease off?"

Dominique remembered why she and Melissa had become easy friends in the first place. They were both driven women who knew how to do whatever it took to get a job done. And Melissa never balked at dishing out guff to her brother, which frankly delighted Dominique.

"If I were assigned to protect him, yes, I'd ask him to stop whatever was causing the greatest risk." Stanton's quick reply was expected, but Dominique heard the slight tone of defensiveness and looked at him. He was staring at his sister, his jaw stubbornly set.

Melissa's soft smirk revealed that she didn't believe her brother's lame reply, either.

"He's right, Melissa. It's his job to keep me alive, so of course he had to try to convince me to stop agitating Jimenez. Which of course I'm not going to do. But Stanton's actually listened to me pore over the story details I have so far, helped me sift through them." Dominique's unexpected defense of Stanton came from somewhere deep inside. For some reason, she wanted Stanton to know that she appreciated his concern not just for her, but for her story, as well.

"Did he?" Melissa's brow arched but she didn't say anything further as she stood and nodded at them. "I can see Officer Colton headed this way. Give Jillian your report, and then you're free to go. Go ahead and press forward with your interviews, Dominique, but stop back in here after each one if at all possible. I don't want to risk passing information over cell phone lines that can be intercepted by the cartel. We'll combine your information with ours. Please, both of you, be extra careful. This is the most dangerous criminal we've seen in Grave Gulch for a long time. Maybe ever."

As they left the chief's office, Dominique allowed the gravity of Melissa's assessment to settle over her. So far she'd lost two battles: finding the truth about Charlie, and having to spend each waking second next to the one man she'd ever loved. And not let him back inside her heart.

Dangerous times, indeed.

surrounded everything. His shirt was torn. His shoes—
Trial run was out. Randall supported the TTI landscape—

"It'll be fine, she," she murmured to herself.

Rafe noticed that Dominique wasn't on the porch yet.
There was something about something. She told him to
wait for the all clear, he'd do it in his own time.

"Ready?" he asked, but he was already sharing his
rights. Rafe fastened his own seatbelt.

Everything else would be fine.

He shot a glance at the man in the Stetson as Rafe
climbed out. He stood to block the door—but then again
the case was too close to touch it with a barge pole.
The way to go about her best, he wasn't going to disagree,
wouldn't try his best. Still if it was necessary, disagree,
would not agree, but they'd go about it with him, then

Chapter 8

"You'll let me do the talking, right?" Dominique
waited to get out of the car after he'd turned the engine
off. They sat on a residential street on the outskirts of
Grave Gulch, in front of the house where the family
of another one of Randall Bowe's wrongly imprisoned
suspects lived.

"Of course. I'm nothing more than your shadow."
Unless circumstances dictated otherwise, but he wasn't
going into it again with her.

"Okay. Thanks again for getting my clothes." She'd
changed into a caramel turtleneck and dressy dark
jeans. He noticed that she kept the sneakers instead of
fancier shoes and knew that her feet were giving her
more trouble than she admitted. Just as the bruises
on her throat were. They'd appeared dark and angry

against her skin when he glimpsed them this morning in his parents' kitchen. She tugged at the high collar. "I thought it'd be best to not scare my interview subject."

He smiled. "Good call."

They walked up the narrow walkway that split the tiny front yard and climbed steep concrete steps to a stoop where Dominique rang the doorbell. It buzzed inside, immediately followed by the ferocious barking of several dogs.

"Stand back." He tugged on her wrist and didn't stop until she was even with him in the middle of the steps.

"I love dogs." She grumbled under her breath just as the door opened. A petite young woman with bright fuchsia hair that matched her fuzzy sweater greeted them. Two large rottweilers sat on either side of her, snarls matching their laser-focused eyes.

"I'm Dominique de la Vega from the *Grave Gulch Gazette*. I'm here to see Beverly Lubinski."

"I know. We're waiting for you. Are you afraid of dogs?" The girl moved, motioned to the animals.

"Not at—"

"It's best if the dogs are restrained for the duration of the interview." Stanton's statement immediately drew Dominique's wrath-of-the-goddess glance but her aggravation was the least of his worries. He couldn't focus on keeping her safe with two burly canine bodyguards in the same room. Dogs were great; he wished he had time in his life to have one. But he'd learned early on in the security business to always eliminate whatever distractions possible.

"Okay, no problem." The girl took each dog by its

spiked collar. "Come on, boys. To your crates. Mom! That reporter is here." They watched through the screen door as she disappeared into the house with the "boys," until an older woman with short, spiky silver hair appeared in the threshold.

"Dominique?"

"Yes. You must be Beverly?"

"I am. Sorry about that. Our boys are sweet but loud. Come on in."

Stanton was tempted to enter first, to protect Dominique in case the "boys" escaped their crates, but then she'd be vulnerable to any danger from the street. He kept his hand on the small of her back, let her know he was right there.

They settled in a shabby but clean living room. The younger woman returned and sat next to her mother and held her hand. Stanton noticed their matching dragonfly tattoos on the top of each hand.

"I'll get right to the point, Beverly, and…"

"Trina. I'm the daughter. Daniel Lubinski is my father and he's in jail because of a scumbag cop at GGPD."

"That's enough, Trina." Beverly shot them both an apologetic glance. "She has every right to be angry and she's not wrong about the police department, but I don't like her being so disrespectful to law enforcement."

Stanton clenched his teeth and struggled to stay silent. It wasn't his place to interject. He wanted to right their misconceptions, tell them he knew firsthand how hard GGPD worked, including its chief, his sister.

"I understand your concerns, Trina. To be frank, I

have them, too. It's why I'm here. I hope I'm able to help uncover what's going on in the department." Dominique handled them so professionally that Stanton took note. "I also want to reassure you that most of GGPD is top-notch. They're working 'round the clock on the cartel issue and will get to the bottom of any mishandled cases. If there's a bad cop or employee, they will be unearthed and face justice. Why don't we start with you telling me about Daniel and how he ended up in police custody?"

Beverly took a deep breath before she began. "My husband, Daniel, was working on the East Side, doing whatever work he could find. He's a contractor, electrician and plumber. One of the places he was helping renovate for public housing seemed to have a lot of drug deals going on from all appearances."

"By 'place,' what do you mean, exactly?"

"It was an apartment building, next to that center. Now, let me tell you something. My Daniel has never, ever done drugs. He had a problem with booze years ago, but he's been a chip-carrying member of AA ever since, sober for twenty years."

"Since I was born," Trina added.

Dominique took notes on her laptop, her fingers flying. Stanton was mesmerized by how she appeared so relaxed while he knew her mind was racing with the facts of this story.

"Go on."

"I got a call at work—I'm a school nurse—saying that he'd been arrested for drug possession and dealing. I thought it was a joke. I mean, no one believed it.

All his AA friends that we've met are certain he was framed, too."

"Why do you think he was framed?"

"He came home one day and confided that he'd seen a man, dressed in fancy clothes, different than the other shady characters there. He didn't get the impression the man was a user, but maybe some higher up with the folks he'd seen selling stuff. The dealers all acted scared around him, and he always traveled with five or six bodyguard types."

"Did Daniel ever tell you what he meant by 'stuff'?"

"Yes. Packets of white powder. Sometimes several to the same person. The day he witnessed what he thinks landed him in jail, to keep him quiet, the woman selling the drugs got knocked around by the man in charge. He hit her hard in the face, made her bleed. Daniel was installing lights in the hallway and shouted so that they'd leave her be. By the time he got down from his ladder, everyone had left the scene. Except..." Beverly shuddered and Trina's grip on her mother's hand visibly tightened.

"Except?" Dominique's prompts were soft yet firm, just the right tone to convey her confidence in her interviewee.

"When he got to the end of the hallway by the back door, where the deal was going down and the woman got beaten, they were all gone...except one of the body-guards, who looked at Daniel and made a slit-throat gesture." Beverly demonstrated by using her finger like she was drawing a knife across her neck. "He thought he was going to be killed right then and there. He was so shook-up."

"Why didn't he call the police?"

"That's just it. He did. An officer came out here and took a report. But he didn't leave us with a copy of the report, so we doubt it was ever filed."

"What was his name?"

"I think it was Bixman or something like that. He was in civilian clothes and Daniel said he flashed his badge so fast he never caught the number or name exactly." Beverly shook her head. "It doesn't matter. The next day Daniel was arrested in the middle of wiring an apartment."

"And he was charged with possession?"

"And dealing." Beverly took a tissue from a purple print box on the coffee table. "They found enough heroin cut with fentanyl in his toolbox and jacket pockets to charge him with the intent to deal."

"But if your husband wasn't really using, or dealing, then he never touched the packets."

"No, he didn't. But GGPD said his prints were all over the plastic bags."

Dominique's gaze met Stanton's and he knew her thoughts. *Randall Bowe.* He had to be at the bottom of this. Had he been paid off by the drug cartel to plant the evidence? And who was the mystery cop who'd interviewed Daniel Lubinski? It sounded like someone posing as police, which would be a felony.

Dominique shut her laptop and leaned forward, placed her hands on top of Beverly's and Trina's. Stanton felt like an intruder on a girl-power meeting, but he didn't at all feel excluded. Dominique had a way of making others always feel part of the team. He'd missed being on her team.

"I can't thank you enough for being so honest with me. And I promise that I'm going to use the power of my pen to write a story that will help bring down the cartel. As I said earlier, please know that GGPD is not made of all bad players. They're working hard on this."

Beverly nodded. "I know. But understand that I had to take care of my family. Daniel told me that he and Charlie Hamm had become friends in prison due to the fact they both wanted to stay sober. Plus, Charlie had some of the same issues as Daniel." Her gaze sparked with regret, sorrow. "They both strayed from their marriages. Charlie's wife left him for cheating, and I decided to stay with Daniel, to work it out. It's part of the reality of being in the midst of the addiction and disease." She offered a brave smile. "They also figured out that they were both victims of the same bad players, whoever they were. I've retained an excellent attorney, who's close to getting Daniel out. Turns out the evidence was highly circumstantial, because he'd left his jacket in the building overnight, and the toolbox, too. Someone broke into the locked building and planted the drugs. And his fingerprints could have been planted, according to our lawyer."

Stanton knew about Charlie's wife leaving, as it was in the file Dominique had on him and had allowed him to read.

"Did Daniel ever say if he and Charlie thought there

were more people in the county jail who were wrongfully imprisoned?"

"No. He only told me about Charlie after we found out about his death. Daniel doesn't like to talk about any of it. Says it's for the best, that as long as we're safe—" she cast a glance at Trina "—that's all that matters."

Dominique nodded, then stood, her gaze seeking Stanton's. Was it his imagination, or was she looking at him as though he was not only on her team, but a full-fledged partner?

Back at the station, Dominique shared a small table in the break room with Stanton and was grateful for his ear.

"Now do you get my reasons for being so upset with how slowly things are going with the internal investigation?"

The muscle on the side of his jaw jumped and he took a swig of his coffee. She noted that he had his own mug with the Colton Protection logo on it. In fact, there was an entire shelf of the mugs in the cabinet above the counter. "I do. And do you 'get' how concerned I am about my family, especially my sister? She's got the weight of all of this on her shoulders. Besides, it's not your place to delve into an internal GGPD investigation. I don't have to tell you this."

"I know. But I'm not letting up."

"Hey, you two. Want to follow me?" Troy nodded toward his tiny office just off the break area. Once in his office, she and Stanton sank onto a cracked faux leather sofa and faced Troy across his desk. Stacks of files, two computers and a printer crowded the room. Yet Troy seemed in charge, confident, if a bit tired.

With a start she realized that every single officer appeared to need at least a nap if not a long rest. Like her, they'd been fighting against time. The longer the corrupt cop and/or employee went unidentified, the greater chance of misfortune falling upon Daniel and any other wrongfully imprisoned people.

"I won't take any more of your time than I need to, but Melissa told us, told me, to report back after every interview."

"Shoot." Troy leaned back as she began to share. She relayed what they'd learned, with emphasis on the description of the man "dressed in fancy clothes" and the possibility of wrongful evidence. As professional a setting as it was, as rapt as Troy's attention was, it was impossible for her to shake how Stanton's nearness affected her. He radiated complete confidence in her abilities, which she was certain helped with Troy's attentiveness.

"What do you think, Troy?" She waited for him to answer instead of prodding him with her opinion and requests for Daniel Lubinski's case evidence file.

"Thank you for telling me all of this. Even though Chief asked you to come back after each interview, you didn't have to provide all of the details. I, and the entire department, appreciate it. We'll add all the facts you collected to our data board in the ops room. Have you by any chance been able to get in touch with the witness in Charlie's case? The one you were going to meet yesterday, Johnny Blanchard?"

She shook her head. "No. I've tried to text and call, with no luck. He's not answering. I'm actually surprised he hasn't blocked me yet."

"You didn't mention that to me," Stanton cut in, and she heard his irritation.

"I can't weigh you down with every tiny aspect of my work. It's difficult enough that you've been roped into this case as deeply as you have." She spoke before she thought about Troy sitting there, watching their interaction. And was that light in Stanton's eyes not disapproval for her work, but…pride?

"You can work that out between the two of you later, but Dominique, I'm with Stanton as far as safety goes. The more you tell him, the more he can anticipate Jimenez's next moves. We all have to be hypervigilant."

"I know." Now to see if Troy would be as stubborn as Melissa. "Do you have anything new on Randall Bowe? I'm not looking for confidential information, Troy, but I need you to throw me a bone here."

He shook his head and she felt Stanton stiffen beside her.

"I can't talk about internal ops, Dominique."

"Come on, Troy," Stanton wheedled. "What would it hurt you to at least confirm that Randall committed wrongdoing or that you suspect he did? At least let Dominique look at Charlie's evidence file." Stanton's support made her insides warm. If she wasn't careful, she'd believe they were more than just a professional team.

"I'm sorry, but I can't comment on an active investigation. Both of you know the rules." Troy's expression was as grim as his reply. Her heart sank but she held on to her purpose—to clear Charlie. There were other avenues she hadn't been down yet, such as talking to Charlie's lawyer. The attorney had refused to see her when she'd reached out last week, but perhaps when she explained what had happened to her, how they'd identified the man responsible for Charlie's incarceration and in all probability his death, he'd do the right thing.

"You know she's right, Troy." Stanton stood up, but not before Dominique grasped his forearm.

"It's okay, Stanton. I get it. We have to play by the rules."

Troy's phone buzzed and his face turned to stone as he read a text. He looked up at first Dominique, then Stanton. "I've got to go, folks. Do you mind going to the ops room and giving the officer on duty the information you've told me?"

"Not at all." But Troy was already out the door, leaving her alone with Stanton. The door shut behind him and the room felt incredibly small. Especially since there were no windows, and mere inches between her and Stanton.

"Since when did you decide I'm on the winning side?"

Stanton's brow rose. "I never said you weren't. My request is that you ask yourself if this story is worth your life. Because that's what's at stake, Dominique. Your life. You're uncovering insects with each rock you turn over and they're getting uglier as you get closer to the truth."

"You're here to make sure I keep my life. Unless my dad told you to try to talk me out of following this lead?"

Stanton's mouth lifted in a one-sided grin. "No, he didn't suggest that."

Heat made its way from her center to her cheeks, then rushed back to her sensitive parts. "Do not tell me that he said you should try to distract me in other ways."

"It's no secret that he was upset at our breakup."

"How do you know that?" She'd never discussed the end of their relationship in detail with anyone but Soledad, and even her twin didn't know the depths of her sorrow and grief over the end of her time with Stanton.

"He called me right after you told your sister we'd split."

"Did he?" She tried to feel angry, betrayed, but it was impossible with her father. Rigo de la Vega loved his family and was incredibly protective. For all the right reasons. "Of course he did. He never questioned me on it, and this explains why. What on earth did he say to you?"

Stanton's expression shut down. "That's between Rigo and me."

"You never mentioned it."

"When could I have? You shut me out of your life the minute you walked out my apartment door."

"I did, didn't I?" What had she been thinking? Her mind raced for one solid reason she should have left him, his heart in his hands, that spring day. Remorse swirled in her gut, self-recrimination close on its heels. "I was rash in the moment. I thought about coming back to talk things over, but we'd said so much." Too much.

"We'd only cracked the tip of the iceberg, Dom." At the pet name her gaze collided with his and the latent heat between them flared. Her nipples tightened under the cashmere turtleneck and she grasped the edge of Troy's desk. It was wrong to indulge in her attraction to Stanton in the very police department she'd complained about. Yet she couldn't look away, nor turn away from the pull of his nearness. When his lids flickered, and she knew he saw her arousal, she did some exploration of her own and saw that he was rock-hard under his dress trousers.

"Stanton." Funny how a name, whispered in the right octave, could betray her deepest longings.

Stanton's reply wasn't verbal. He reached for her and hauled her up against him, and she met him halfway. She was beyond ready for his kiss and didn't hold back. They both knew this was a stolen moment, that Troy could walk back through that door at any moment.

It only made the kiss all the more delicious.

Stanton let his mouth plunder hers, and thrilled as she explored his. He felt every stroke of her tongue, wished to Hades and back that they were anywhere but here in his cousin's office.

Troy's office.

He pulled back, his lips throbbing from the sudden

lack of contact with hers. As if they were one whenever they were together, kissing or not.

She stared at her hands as they rested on his chest, both of them breathing audibly. "Wow."

"Yeah. 'Wow.'" He placed his forehead on hers. "It's not wrong, but it's not right in this place." He lifted her chin with his finger and waited for her to look at him. A man could live forever in her gaze.

"This has got to stop. We're adults." She offered a small smile.

"I can agree to waiting until we're alone and in a safer space to take this any further."

She pushed against him, took a step back. Ran her fingers through her hair. His own itched to follow suit. "You're right. No, we can't do this, not here." And if she were smart, not anywhere. "Let's get to the operations center and give them a copy of my interview." Along with taking notes, she'd recorded it, with signed permission from Mrs. Lubinski.

"Right." He opened the office door and checked the corridor before he stepped out. GGPD or no, he couldn't trust anyone else to have her safety as a priority. He felt like he was coming out of his skin at the thought of a cop-gone-bad on the force. The forensics expert was one thing, and more than enough to put him on edge. "Okay, let's go."

They walked next to one another down the corridor. Voices reached them from a room to the left, and Dominique put her arm in front of him, forcing both of them to stop. Her eyes widened as she comprehended what he was hearing, too.

"What's so important that you're this upset, Chief?" Troy's whisper carried into the hallway.

"Desiree called me and she's positive she just saw Randall Bowe lurking in Grave Gulch Park." Melissa wasn't whispering but Stanton had to strain to hear her lowered voice.

"In broad daylight?" Troy's disbelief was evident. "No way."

"Yes, 'way.' He was in a blue ski cap, tight to his head, which hid his hair, and he had a fake mustache on. She said it was definitely Randall. She's a sketch artist. If anyone can ID someone in disguise, it's Desiree." Melissa was convinced.

"I'll get someone out to the park ASAP."

Dominique looked at Stanton, her eyes wide. They had to get out of here before Melissa or Troy knew they'd overheard their exchange.

"What are you two doing out here?" Too late. Troy stared at them.

"We overheard everything, Troy. I'm going to Grave Gulch Park with you." Dominique spoke with her usual gutsy determination.

"You had no business snooping on police business, either of you." Troy's voice shook. Stanton hadn't seen him this angry since he'd lost in a family game of Thanksgiving Day football. Which, to be fair, some of the cousins had cheated at to win. "I wouldn't expect this from you." His anger was all for Stanton.

"Hey, the door was wide-open. We all know that Randall Bowe is on the loose. You've got WANTED posters up all over Grave Gulch. You can't tell us anything about your internal investigation, and yet you expect innocent citizens to report if they've seen him. That's putting civilians at risk, Troy. And the longer you keep us from the truth, you keep Dominique at risk, too."

Troy had the integrity to admit the truth. "I'm sorry. We're as worried as you are about the cartel's next move. Who they'll target next."

"You think Bowe was paid off by the cartel, by Jimenez, don't you?" Dominique never missed a chance to get an answer. But he didn't agree with her on this. In fact, he doubted Bowe had any tie-in with the cartel. Whatever Randall Bowe was up to was his own insanity. The cartel didn't need someone in GGPD to help out their cases, anyhow. They preferred to handle everything with threats and death.

"What I think is immaterial. My objective is to capture Bowe and you're both in my way." Troy looked at the floor, in deep thought. When he glanced up again he looked at Dominique. "You can have the news scoop that Bowe's been spotted in the park. Go ahead and release the description of his disguise—blue ski cap, mustache. We've already got a sketch coming in from Desiree within minutes. Feel free to publish it. Now, let's both get some work done." Troy strode off, and Dominique quickly punched in a number on her phone. He listened as she reported what she knew to her editor. When she disconnected, she smiled.

"What's so funny?"

"Not funny. Happy. We're this much closer to getting to the bottom of all this."

"Okay."

She playfully punched his upper arm. "Come on, you're excited. I can tell. Your first big scoop."

He grunted, unwilling to give her the broad smile that tugged at his lips. This was dangerous territory for him. If he allowed himself to let go and enjoy the sunshine that was Dominique, he faced certain extinction when she again disappeared from his life.

Stanton didn't have another heart to shatter.

Chapter 9

It took no more than ten minutes to make certain the operations team had all the pertinent details from her interview with the Lubinskis. Dominique was relieved to leave the station because she wanted to get to the *Gazette* and finish filing her article, as well as brief her editor on what she'd found out to date. Stanton was waiting for her in the break room and she walked toward it, eager to be near him. Or the sense of safety he gave her.

Stop hiding from it. You're loving spending time with him again.

She was, but had to constantly remind herself that they weren't a couple, there was no chance of a reconciliation and Stanton would be gone from her life as quickly as she could say, "Pablo Jimenez is under arrest."

"Dominique." Melissa called to her from inside her office and dread filled her stomach. *Here it comes.* First Troy had chewed her out for eavesdropping earlier; now Melissa was going to have her turn.

"Chief Colton." She entered the room.

"Stop it. I'm always Melissa to you. Where's my brother?"

"He's waiting for me in the break room."

Melissa nodded. "Please don't feel you need to call me 'chief' when we're alone. In front of the officers, sure, but you'll always be family to me, Dominique."

"I appreciate that. I've missed our girl talks."

"As have I. Any chance that you and Stanton are going to make a go of it again?"

"Absolutely not. This is all business. My father hired him to protect me."

Melissa laughed. "I'll bet you were thrilled by that."

Dominique felt a knot of tension in her shoulders go. "Yes, it was a surprise. Let's leave it at that."

"I trust that Troy steered you clear of going to Grave Gulch Park with him. It's too dangerous."

"He did, but he was generous enough to give me the scoop on Bowe's sighting."

Melissa nodded. "I've no problem with that. While I still can't give you any information about our internal investigation, I want you to know that it's perfectly okay for you to interview one of Bowe's lab assistants who still works here. I can't let you interview Bonnie Stadler, yet." Dominique knew that Stadler was fired during the Everleigh Emerson case, and now wondered if she'd been let go over the wrongdoings of Bowe.

"Also, one of our rookies, CSI Jillian Colton, wants to talk to you about her misgivings over Bowe."

"I thought GGPD can't tell me anything about the investigation?"

"We can't, but an individual cop can tell you about their personal experiences. Is that clear?" Melissa wasn't going to spoon-feed her any further. Dominique got it.

"Gotcha. I'll find both of them before I leave the station, if that's all right."

"Absolutely. Jillian's down in the bullpen. Her desk is smack-dab in the middle. You'll find the lab assistant in Forensics, probably at his desk this time of day as he's got reports to file."

"Thank you."

Finally, a chance to get some answers.

Bowe's most junior lab assistant expressed concern about his boss's erratic behavior over the past several months. But he couldn't give Dominique any more information yet, not until the GGPD's internal investigation was finished. Plus it was clear that Bonnie Stadler, the assistant who'd been fired, would know more. This assistant was barely a step above intern. It was as if Melissa had sent her on a wild-goose chase to keep her busy, to prevent her from digging too deeply into GGPD workings. Frustrated, she trudged over to Jillian's desk.

Jillian's demeanor was professional and she seemed eager to talk to Dominique, but again, her loyalty was to GGPD.

"I don't have a ton of information to give you, because as I'm sure Chief Colton told you, we can't talk specifics about the internal investigation. But suffice it to say that I was gaslighted by Randall Bowe on several occasions, with more than one case. As a rookie it's important that I don't mess up the most basic parts of any case, and yet Bowe gave me the wrong information and in one case lost all of the evidence I'd collected during a drug bust."

"Didn't you have a forensics team with you?"

Jillian shook her head, her bright eyes cloudy with anger. "No. It was a short-notice incident. I was on foot patrol on the East Side, on Main Street. If we need to go on side streets, we have to either be in a cruiser or call for backup. Anyway, I received a call about an OD. I rushed to the scene, in front of an old building, and was able to revive the addict with Narcan. She gave me several packets of heroin—I tested it with the kit the backup unit brought—and I was careful to bag it all as evidence. I'd hoped we'd get the dealer's prints on it. But Bowe said the bags didn't have prints, which I found odd as the victim wasn't wearing gloves and at least her prints would have been on the bags."

"Anything else?"

Jillian shrugged. "To be honest, it's all a mess right now. There's the cartel that you're looking at, and we have a serial killer on the loose. We've had three women go missing from Grave Gulch over the past five years, as I'm sure you know. With Len Davison out there still, these disappearances could be linked to him. Our forensics lab is the backbone of many of our cases, and to have it swamped with a backlog, without a senior scientist and with our best assistant fired, is not helping matters."

Dominique did know about the missing, but the opioid epidemic had "disappeared" many, many people nationwide.

"About how Bowe 'gaslighted' you—"

"Jillian, I need you with me now." Troy stood at Jillian's desk and he gave a cursory nod to Dominique. In that one gesture he also expressed that police business trumped journalism.

Jillian shot her an apologetic glance. "Sorry, Dominique."

Disappointment roiled in her gut but she offered a smile. "I get it. Can I call you later?"

"Yes. I'm happy to finish this later."

"Jillian." Troy was already at the other side of the bullpen.

"Coming!"

Dominique tapped a reminder into her phone so that she'd remember to call Jillian later this evening, or early tomorrow morning. So many developments were snowballing into one complicated, layered story.

She found Stanton in the break room, an empty mug next to his open laptop. Engrossed in his work, he didn't stir as she approached.

"I'm done for now. I would like to go to the *Gazette* offices before we head back to the lake house."

He looked up and she thought she'd braced herself for eye contact, but there was no use pretending. It was impossible to prepare herself for the immediate flood of warmth that rocked her every dang time he looked at her.

"Sure thing. Did you get everything you wanted?" He must have seen the shadow of disappointment in her eyes.

"No, not by a long shot. Cop business takes precedence over my story, though." She watched him pack up his computer, rinse out his mug and place it on the drying board next to the break room sink. He turned and faced her.

"You'll have all night to work if you need to, in a safer spot than downtown Grave Gulch." His bodyguard expression was back: lips pressed together in determination, eyes scanning the room as they left.

"I admit I'm looking forward to chilling out at your folks' place again."

"We're going to do more than relax, babe." His words, low and spoken next to her ear, sent tiny thrills of arousal across her skin. If she were sane she'd insist they go back to her apartment, or his, instead of the remote lake house.

Like it would make a difference.

"Mmm." She signed out at the reception desk and pushed through the exit door, sensing his nearness as they walked out into the pale golden sunshine. This time of day was her favorite, as was the season. Nothing like a late spring afternoon—

The sound of gunfire erupted in her ears.

"Get down!" Stanton's command was her only warning before she was thrown to the ground, her body squashed by a solid heavy weight. *Stanton.* They'd been shot at.

A scream echoed and she realized it was hers.

"It's okay, Dom. I've got you. Stay down." He shifted, a knee on either side of her. "Three uniforms are in pursuit."

Footsteps running, more gunfire. An engine's roar and wheels screeching filled the air.

"Stay here." She did as he ordered, completely trusting him. It was difficult trying to catch her breath while face down on the graveled lot, but she was still here, alive. As was Stanton.

"Okay." His hands were on her, helping her up. As soon as she was on her feet she turned to find comfort against his broad chest. Until she saw the bright red stain on his suit's upper sleeve.

"Oh no, Stanton, you've been shot!"

"Have I?" His brows drew together and he looked where she stared, held his arm up. "It's a graze. Never felt it, trust me."

"How can you be so sure? Stanton, you're bleeding! That is more than a graze."

"She's right, Stanton. You need to let her drive you to the ER, or one of our officers will take you." Melissa stood next to them.

"Did you catch the shooter?" Dominique was at a disadvantage; she'd not seen the attacker or the police officers who'd come immediately to her defense and Stanton's. She sent up a silent prayer that they'd be safe as they chased down the shooter.

"No, but we've got a unit in pursuit. We'll get to

the bottom of it soon enough, but I think we all know who's in all probability responsible." Melissa's blue eyes sparked with anger. "We're getting too close for Jimenez's comfort."

Dominique found no sense of accomplishment in the pronouncement. Not when Stanton had just taken a bullet in all likelihood intended for her. She swore she could feel her bones rattling at the thought of how close she'd come to losing him. Again. And it wasn't his job that was to blame, but a story she'd insisted on pursuing. Charlie Hamm's justice was a priority, but maybe Soledad was right. Was it worth putting the one man she'd ever loved at risk?

"I'm driving to the hospital, no arguments." She held out her hand and Stanton reluctantly dropped his keys in her palm.

"Only to keep you happy, and because the hospital is nearby." He accepted a large gauze pad from the receptionist who'd brought out a first aid kit, and pressed it to his upper arm. "Let's get this over with. All they're going to do is wash out the graze, trust me."

"You need to go for our insurance purposes, since you were shot on police property." Melissa's displeasure at the fact was evident in her stern reply.

"Roger. On our way."

"Thank you, Chief. And please thank the officers who responded." Gratitude engulfed Dominique and she blinked back sudden tears.

"It's our job."

As she made sure Stanton got into the passenger side and buckled, then took the driver's seat, Melissa's words echoed in her mind. Protection and apprehension were GGPD's job. Getting the dirt on Jimenez and his cartel, whatever it took to clear Charlie Hamm, was hers.

"Don't make any funny moves," Stanton chided her as she drove out of the lot and proceeded to the ER, also downtown. "I'm a little sore."

"You mean like the ones you taught me?" When they were together he'd taken her out to a defensive driving school and taught her some very basic maneuvers.

"Good to know that you remember something useful from our time together."

She bit her tongue from retorting that she remembered more than he'd imagined, including how he'd always made her feel so important, so special. The issue wasn't her memory, but how she'd ever forgotten how good it felt to be next to Stanton.

Stanton was glad to be home earlier than normal from work. Correction, he was happy to be at his parents' estate with Dominique safely inside, away from the targets that Jimenez's men kept placing on her. He thanked the stars above that he'd been standing where he had and that the thug had been a poor shot. His injury was a bit more than a graze, and he'd been sent home without any stitches, but just a simple bandage that he was instructed to change twice a day for the next few days. The doc's instructions to take it easy were easily swatted away in the ER, when the adrenaline still surged through his system.

Now that he was back at the lake house, he was becoming more aware of the soreness that he knew from experience might bother him for the next several days. He had to ignore it, because he had a job to finish: to keep Dominique alive. No matter how much he repeated it to himself, he couldn't erase the kiss they'd shared in his cousin's office this afternoon. His body thirsted for her touch. That had never eased no matter how much time grew between when they'd been together and now.

"Can I get you anything?" Dominique spoke from the kitchen, where she was putting away the groceries they'd picked up for the weekend. He'd tried to help but she insisted he sit down for a bit.

"You."

He heard a pause in her movements and smiled to himself. There was nothing like the thrill of catching her off guard. It wasn't often when the woman you cared about broke her reserve, not if she was as intelligent and focused as Dominique.

Had he just admitted to himself that he still cared for her?

"What?" She stood at the end of the sofa he was stretched out on, contemplating him with wariness.

He laughed. "I meant I want you to take a break, too. Have a seat." He pointed to the large white easy chair with the woven throw tossed over the back. It was usually Italia's spot when she and Frank spent their nights inside during the cold months.

She perched on the edge of the cushion and looked over her shoulder out the window to the lake below. The house was perched on a high bluff but protected from Lake Michigan's worst gales by the surrounding trees. "It's still as beautiful as I remember. It must be hard for your parents to leave when they travel."

He pushed himself up and leaned against the back of the sofa, his feet on the coffee table. "They certainly love it here, but I know they also cherish the freedom to travel. Dad's business has been successful and they've raised all four of us. It's their time to enjoy life."

"They know how to live, don't they? They could have chosen to leave the area like many do, heading south to warmer weather, or back to Italy, to be with your mother's family. But they've picked Michigan."

"Yes, I'd have to say they've found their paradise." He didn't want to talk about his parents or his siblings. It was a rare gift to be alone with Dominique and he wasn't a fool. He knew that this might be the last time they'd be so close, without interruption. As long as Jimenez's thugs didn't find them here, they were safe for tonight. And they had the entire night in front of them.

"When do you think you'll want dinner?" She looked at the clock that hung over the kitchen's back counter. "It's almost six."

"Any time that works for you." He really wanted to eat yesterday and skip straight to where he hoped they'd spend the night. In his bed. Well, in what was now the guest bedroom, formerly his childhood bedroom. He'd left home for college at eighteen and when he'd returned to Grave Gulch he'd been eager to start his own life downtown, with his security protection business. It had been the right move for him but he still had nostalgia for this house. It meant a lot to him to have Dominique here, whether forever or just tonight.

Stick to thinking it's only tonight, bud. Far safer.

"I'll get it going in about twenty minutes. It won't take long." She stood and stretched. "I'd love a walk on the deck and yard, down to the steps. Do I have your permission to go?"

She stood with the glittering lake as a backdrop, the trees on either side budding, the small new leaves appearing like little golden green birds on the branches. Dominique faced him, her skin flushed over her cheeks, making the sparkles in her obsidian eyes look like diamonds. Her persimmon-red lips were slightly parted, revealing a glimpse of her white teeth. Unable to keep his gaze on her face alone, he took in her full breasts, her small waist, the enticing flare of her hips.

When he looked back up into her eyes, they'd narrowed. But not in displeasure or disgust. Dominique knew what he wanted, and she wanted it, too. But one thing about her he'd never forgotten was how she had a love-hate relationship with seduction. So often she'd stop their flirting, the tug and release of tension, by kissing him deeply, her tongue communicating their mutual need in a most effective manner.

If he was going to follow through with his desire and leave here with his heart intact, he had to remember to keep his cool. Take it slow. To remember that what drove them apart two years ago hadn't changed. Dominique was all about her career, and he couldn't be married to someone he had to worry about each and every second of every day. It was what kept him from succumbing to his baser desire, which would have already found him hauling her over his shoulder and taking her back to his bedroom, sore arm be damned.

"Stanton? Can I go outside?"

"Sorry. I'm a little tired after all the shootout drama." He made it a point to shrug as if he hadn't just made love to her with his eyes. "Sure, you're safe out here. The security cameras are all working and I'll see you the whole time. Stay up here, though—no wandering down to the beach. The tide's high and a storm is brewing."

"There isn't time for that. We still need to eat. I won't be long." She grabbed the blanket off the chair and wrapped it around her shoulders. At the door, he saw her face reflected in the glass right before she slid open the door and stepped into the night. The confusion and, if he were lucky, disappointment on her expression allowed him to hold back and not follow her, warm her with his kisses in the chilly spring evening.

The night sky was visible through the trees and above the lake. Dominique shivered against the cold and wrapped the blanket tighter. Disappointment swam in her gut, but it wasn't because Stanton hadn't followed her, or asked her to stay inside longer. Or to sit next to him. Or to kiss him again.

Face it. The words he'd murmured in her ear in Troy's GGPD office had been nothing more than whispers in the heat of the moment. Even if he'd meant them, that was before he'd been shot. He'd had plenty of time to remember why they were spending so much time together, that it had nothing to do with intention on either of their parts. It was a job for him, and a means to an end for her.

In truth they'd never wanted the same thing, had they? Stanton wanted a woman to spend his life with, one without such a risky job. Not all of her stories involved dangerous situations, but enough of them did. Too many for Stanton. And even if she'd rethought her desire to put off having children, it wouldn't be enough for Stanton. She'd always know he was worried about her, and she'd be frightened every time the phone rang at odd hours when he was out on a protection contract.

She looked up at the stars, remembering again how much she loved this vantage point. Frank and Italia had left the back patio lanterns as motion detectors, timed only for after they retired for the evening, so that they could come out here and see the stars with minimal light pollution. Stanton's parents had lived a dream romance, staying together for over forty years, raising four incredible children, and contributing to the community in a real way. Both donated their time and talents often. Italia's art was a familiar sight at local charity auctions, and Frank's shipping company, at which he was an executive, provided scholarship funds to Grave Gulch High School graduates. Italia's charity work had inspired Dominique to volunteer at the Grave Gulch prison, teaching her creative writing class, right after the breakup.

Dominique knew Frank and Italia's relationship had had its ups and downs; Italia had been quick to tell her that during one of the many weekends she'd spent out here with Stanton. As if Stanton's mother wanted to convey that Dominique shouldn't expect life with her son to always be perfect.

A stab of regret melded with realization. Had she been so focused on perfection—in her job, her relationship with Stanton—that she'd missed out on what mattered? Had she overlooked what Italia had tried to tell her? Soledad had warned her to not throw out the baby with the bathwater, but she'd thought her twin was more concerned about her settling down than anything else. And she'd thought she'd find someone else who wouldn't pressure her into marriage so soon. Stanton's proposal had seemed impetuous and innocent enough, but she knew him, knew his family. Children and a lot of sacrifices she wasn't willing to make were part of the deal. Weren't they?

She shook her head and closed her eyes, gave herself a moment to soak in the trees, the lake, the star-splattered sky. Nature had always given her peace and she didn't think the term "forest bathing" was so farfetched. As if the trees heard her, a softer breeze swept down, and she heard the gentle scrape of branches against each other. It was the closest thing to lighting a candle and sending up a prayer, and right now, her spirit needed it.

Because when it involved Stanton, she couldn't trust her instinct. There were too many layers of emotion, so much complicated history between them. Yet as she stood in the quiet night, the one thought that kept circling her brain seemed to slip down to her heart.

Maybe it's okay to enjoy the moment, whatever it brings.

Chapter 10

Stanton made certain Dominique was back inside before he went to his room. He took his time, needing things to be perfect for her. He'd bought some of his own supplies and had them rung up while Dominique was still picking out produce. The candles were her favorite scent—jasmine.

He knew he was a hopeless romantic. His family never ceased teasing him about how he'd wooed women through college, always insisting on bringing flowers to a date. But his father had set a good example. Frank Colton never took his wife for granted, not that Italia would let him. Not for the first time Stanton thought about how much he and Dominique seemed to parrot his parents' relationship; they both were two strong-willed people with their own lives and careers, finding common ground.

But it had blown apart all because he'd let his emotions drive the boat that day he'd ridiculously proposed to her. Her refusal, his pain, followed by her hasty departure, had left a hole in his heart, and from what she'd admitted and how she'd reacted these past few days, Dominique had experienced her share of heartache and regret, too.

Tonight could be a way for them to leave one another with a lasting, loving memory. He wasn't the same foolish man he'd been two years ago. He knew this wasn't the start of anything with Dominique. But he did want a better ending with the one woman who'd ever stolen his heart. He only hoped she'd accept this last gift from him.

"I'm not used to someone else cooking for me."

Dominique tried to keep her cool as she made their meal. With Stanton sitting at his parents' kitchen island, his enigmatic charisma sucked her in deeper with each moment they spent together. He'd been correct about his bullet wound; it was nothing more than a graze. It didn't matter to Dominique because as far as she was concerned, he'd taken a bullet for her. Had he not reacted as quickly as he had, getting her to the ground, she might not be here. A shiver ran through her at the thought, and she focused on mixing roasted garlic into butter.

"I'm waving the BS flag on that one. Your mother cooks for you whenever you visit."

"Which, if you heard her giving me grief last night, hasn't been in a while."

She smeared a baguette cut crosswise with the mixture. "Your parents understand that their kids have their own lives."

"Yours don't?"

"Please." She raised her brow. "You're living proof that my father can't stay out of my life." Satisfied with the garlic bread, she turned the state-of-the-art oven's broiler on, slid the bread onto a sheet and then under the blue flames. "I love my father, he's the best. And in this case, he was right to trust his fatherly instincts. It's unfortunate that I've worried him, yet again. This isn't the first time he's worried about a story I'm working on." And reason number one she'd thought she didn't want her own family, at least not children. She never wanted them to feel stifled by her overprotectiveness, or to not go after their dreams because of what they thought were her wishes.

"I think once you become a parent, that's it. There's no longer a way of ever turning the spigot off. A parent's love is unconditional." He sounded wistful and she took a long look at him. He sat with his uninjured arm on the granite top, his gaze flitting from the basketball game on the elevated, muted television in the far corner of the kitchen, to her, to the meal she prepared. In this moment it was impossible to remember all the reasons she'd convinced herself they'd split. Before she said something stupid, she grabbed the salad greens and began chopping. A buzzer sounded and she pulled the bread out, its top perfectly browned.

"That smells incredible."

"At least I didn't burn it this time." The time she'd charred garlic bread in her apartment had been one for the record books.

"Yeah, we don't want the Grave Gulch FD showing up out here tonight."

"I was mortified, in case I never admitted it back then."

"It was the first time you made dinner for me."

"I'm surprised you ever let me cook for you again." She placed the salad aside and tended to the shellfish she had steaming on the stove top. "We're just about ready here."

"Bring it." Cioppino, an Italian seafood dish of broth over mussels, clams, octopus and scallops, was their main course. When they'd stopped at the small grocery on the way here, there had been a plethora of fresh shellfish and she'd impulsively decided to prepare the recipe she remembered as Stanton's favorite. They'd both agreed that they were together for only as long as it took her to get her story, or GGPD to arrest Pablo Jimenez, eliminating the threat to her life. What would it matter to make the same meal they'd enjoyed several times when they'd dated?

"I've set the table." She'd helped herself to Italia's bounty of cheerily printed table linens while Stanton had showered.

"We could have eaten at the island."

"Are you that into the basketball game?"

"No, not at all. I didn't want you to go to all of this trouble. But I do appreciate it."

She set the food on the table along with a carafe of sparkling water. "I thought you might pass on the wine if your wound is bothering you."

"You'd be correct. I'm pretty sure I won't need any anti-inflammatories, unless this scrape surprises me and starts aching in the middle of the night. Besides, you know I don't drink on duty. Don't let it stop you, though."

"I'm good." She wanted to remain alert, too. "I honestly don't know what was scarier—being directly attacked by that thug or the gunshots. The bullets came from nowhere."

"Only one made contact, and barely at that. This looks amazing, Dominique. You've outdone yourself. Thank you." They sat across from one another.

"You're welcome. It's the least I can do, now that you took a bullet for me."

He grimaced. "Please. Your storytelling abilities are evident."

She laughed. "I don't write fiction, only the truth, backed up with facts. You definitely took the fire today and saved both of our lives."

"Why don't we declare the dinner table a cartel-free zone for now? We both deserve a quiet meal to regroup."

"Works for me."

They dug in. Dominique was grateful for the meal to focus on, instead of her resolve against allowing her attraction to Stanton to overtake her common sense. He'd promised more when he'd kissed her in Troy's office earlier, but since he'd been shot between then and now, she figured he'd forgotten. It was for the best; neither of them needed anything to take them away from their main missions. His to protect her and hers to finish the story.

No matter the keen stabs of disappointment that peppered an otherwise enjoyable meal with her bodyguard ex.

Stanton had lied. His arm hurt like hell, and it was a combination of the minor bullet wound and how he'd landed on it when he'd covered Dominique from the gunfire. He'd had to convince her to stay out of the exam with the ER doctor and thank goodness he had. The doc had told him to take it easy and use ibuprofen regularly for the next several days. As a former collegiate athlete, Stanton was familiar with muscle pain. What wasn't familiar was having to hide it from someone else. He didn't want Dominique worried. She'd been through more in the last two days than probably her entire life, no matter her tough reporter facade.

The last thing he wanted was for her to think they shouldn't finish what they'd started in Troy's office earlier. He didn't give a fig's tree about his arm and needed to make sure Dominique didn't think it precluded him from being able to make good on his promise.

Not a good idea, man. Not if you want to keep yourself together after she's gone again.

"You're awfully quiet. Is the cioppino that bad?"

He grinned. "Not at all—it's beyond compare. Don't tell my mother, but yours is my favorite."

"Really?" Her tone suggested total disbelief and he waited until she looked at him.

"Really. After you left, the one thing I regretted most was that you hadn't written your recipe down for me." He maintained a straight face until her nonplussed expression yielded to narrowed eyes and a smirk.

"You are still such a jerk." She laughed and tossed her napkin at him.

"Whoa!" He feinted a dodge and inadvertently slammed his injured arm on the solid maple table's edge. *Ouch.*

"You okay? Oh, Stanton, did you hit your wound?" Her mirth changed to concern tinged with a healthy dose of annoyance.

"Stop saying 'wound' like I have a life-threatening injury."

She let out a sigh and reached over to retrieve her napkin. He took the opportunity to grasp her hand.

"Stanton…" She said his name like a prayer. Tugged her hand, but he held tight as he stood up and leaned across the table.

"How do you want this, Dominique? Messy and full of crushed shellfish, or in my bed?"

She gasped, and he let the fullness of his arousal hit him at the sight of her pupils dilating under the chandelier that hung over the table. He pulled her hand to his face, keeping their faces inches apart, and stroked the inside of her wrist, her palm, with his tongue.

"No, wait." Breathless, she tugged her hand from his grasp and this time he let go. The seconds it took her to walk around the end of the table and stop next to him felt like eternity. She didn't touch him, didn't move, but stared up at him. "If we do this, it will change everything." Her eyes beseeched him but he didn't know what she was asking. What had he missed?

"It doesn't have to. It can make things better." He balled his hands into fists to keep from reaching for her before she was ready. This had to be entirely her choice.

"How?" She kept staring at him, and he saw her eyes move as if she was absorbing every inch of his face. Her skin, smooth as silk, highlighted the dark curtain of hair that flowed over her shoulders like inky black liquid. He'd never met anyone more beautiful.

"We can make a new ending for ourselves." He thought it was the most brilliant thing he'd ever thought of. Except for the pit in his gut that told him he didn't want anything to do with "ending" what he and Dominique shared.

Her lips lifted into a small smile. "I'd like that. A different last memory."

"So you're in?" Waiting for her to answer took all his strength.

"Yes, Stanton. I'm in." Only when her hands touched his shoulders, her arms wound around his neck, did he let go.

"This first time isn't going to take very long." He sounded like a Neanderthal and felt more primal as all he could think of was joining together with this woman in the most fundamental way possible. Their lips met without preamble and they progressed to tongues, touching each other's most erotic places and loud groans. When she grasped his length and stroked him through his suit pants, he tore his mouth from hers.

"My bedroom. Now."

"No, here. I can't wait." She hooked a leg over his hip, using the table edge for balance as she moved her pelvis against his. When she nipped at his lower lip, he had no choice but to acquiesce. He'd promised himself to let her do whatever she wanted, however she wanted, to him. Stanton was a man of his word.

Dominique's rational thought fled the minute Stanton challenged her over the dining room table. It wasn't a choice to go to him, to begin what had been brewing not for the past two days as she'd told herself, but for the last two years. Her entire life, it seemed.

Now she was balanced over him, totally trusting that this was the next right thing to do. Make love to Stanton.

His hands grasped her buttocks and pulled her more snugly against him as he leaned against the table, taking both their weight. The table didn't budge and she sent up a silent thanks for the furniture, heavy and strong. Like Stanton. His erection pressed into her softest place and she thought she'd go insane if she didn't find release with this man, in his arms.

"Kiss me." He compelled her to lower her mouth on his, her hands helping her balance by grasping his shoulders. She lost herself in the kiss, and the sensations rocking her body. It was as if they were teens, she was so close to climaxing…and they were both still dressed.

"Stanton. *Please.*"

Smoky blue eyes, half-lidded, looked at her. "What do you want, babe?"

"You. All of you."

He bucked against her, his breath as short and gasping as hers. "You've got it."

"I mean…not here, in the dining room."

"Tell me where." He eased them both back onto solid ground, and when her soles hit the floor she still clung to him, afraid her legs would give out. She wanted him but not here.

"The sofa. Is that okay?"

"You've got thirty seconds to undress." His growl made her laugh and she shimmied out of her slacks, her cashmere turtleneck. The cool air in the living room was no match for the heat that he'd started with one simmering glance. "Wait."

She paused, her hands on the sides of her red thong. He stood fully nude at the end of the sofa and it was all she could do to not lie back on the cushions and beg him to take her. But she knew he'd always appreciated watching her take off her underwear, and more than anything she wanted to pleasure him the way he did her. Without reservation and with a level of generosity she hadn't known before.

"You're stunning." His fingers traced the line of her red bra covered in black lace, burning a line along her breasts. When he slid the straps off, she reached for him, but he stopped her hands and placed them on his waist. "If you touch me now, this will be over faster than either of us want."

"I need you, Stanton."

"I know, babe. It's a two-way street with us." He unclasped her bra and dropped it to the side, allowing her breasts to spring free and brush his chest. The thick mat of hair scratched against her nipples, already hard, and would have made the heat between her legs almost unbearable, if it wasn't so delightful.

"Only you know how to make me this hot, babe." She admitted the secret she'd kept for too long.

"No one can possibly enjoy you as much as I do." His teeth grazed her sensitive skin along her throat, down the curve to her shoulder. "Just wait." But she didn't have to wait as he reached between them, down to her apex, and slipped one, two fingers into her.

"Stanton, I can't hold...on..." Her sudden climax rocked her against him, her body refusing to do anything but accept pure pleasure from the man her heart had never let go.

"That's it." He waited for her to come down from the ride before easing them both onto the sofa, where she spread her legs and watched him don a condom. When he looked at her, he wore an expression she wanted to never forget. Of a man who'd searched forever for the right partner, and finally found her.

"Come here, Stanton. It's your turn."

"No 'turns,' babe. Just us."

He entered her in one sure thrust, and she told herself she'd hang on to meet him, to make sure they both orgasmed at the same time. But after only two strokes she was breaking apart again, screaming his name.

Stanton kept thrusting and as she again peaked, he yelled out.

Dominique relished his full weight as he collapsed against her, the sensation of him inside her and their joining the only thing that made perfect sense in the midst of the danger they'd found.

Dominique slept the deepest and longest she had since starting on Charlie's story. As she became aware of her surroundings, she saw that it was dark outside, dawn's first fingers of soft peach light at least an hour away. Lying on her side, facing the wide, paned windows of the guest room that overlooked the lake, she was aware of Stanton's breath fanning her neck, his arm resting around her waist. It was the arm he'd injured by protecting her outside of GGPD. First the bullet had nicked him, and then he'd jammed his shoulder when he'd forced them both down. He'd finally admitted just how sore it was after their third round of lovemaking. His wince as she'd dried him off after their second shower spoke volumes. His waterproof bandage had survived the night, much to her delight, but the bruising and swelling clued her in as to how much pain he must be in. He'd agreed to ibuprofen and an ice pack, hence his ability to sleep soundly. His snores were comforting, and a tear spilled down her cheek. It was insane but true: she'd missed Stanton's snores.

Don't get used to it.

She allowed herself to mentally replay the last eight hours. After they'd had mind-blowing sex in the living room, they'd almost made it to the bedroom before they detoured to the bathroom and the tiled shower. Then later, much later, they'd taken their time in his bed, savoring each and every stroke, kiss and whispered plea.

Well, at least *she* knew she'd savored it all. It seemed Stanton did, too, but she couldn't go there. If she did, it'd be too easy to think they'd be able to pick up where they'd left off, or maybe a few moments before he'd proposed and she'd freaked out. Why hadn't she at least told him all she needed was a break, instead of ending it like that?

Fear, pure and simple. She'd been afraid of the strength of their connection. Since that first time they'd met and he'd convinced her to go for coffee with him, she'd known that Stanton was going to change her life. It had been during an early spring snowstorm and she'd been at GGPD to research a story. Stanton had stopped in to check on Melissa, who'd had a particularly rough time with a case that required her to fire her weapon. Dominique had noticed his physique first—it was impossible to pass up the way his body filled his custom-tailored suits—but once she looked into those brilliant baby blues, the ground under her boots had moved. She remembered the outfit she'd worn, too— short black wool skirt, ribbed tights, her favorite red Hunter rubber boots. It had bothered her that she was in the more practical boots instead of her killer heeled leather ones—that was how badly she'd wanted to impress him. Because he'd impressed the heck out of her. Their romance was storybook. Until long work hours on both their parts, complicated by both of their driven natures, had turned the romance part sour.

The sex, though—that had never been anything but sweet. And hot.

His arm moved, his hand reaching for hers, intertwining their fingers. "Why aren't you sleeping?"

"Neither are you."

"Are you okay?" he asked.

"I'm good."

"Stop."

"Stop what?"

"You're overthinking this. Just enjoy it. We can both use the rest, and—" he shifted and rose up, swearing as he put weight on his bad arm "—it's still dark out. Let's try for another hour."

She turned onto her back and looked at him. "Do you need more ibuprofen? You could piggyback it with Tylenol if the pain's worse."

"I'll live. It didn't wake me up."

"I'm sorry that I did. I suppose it's the strange bed. But I slept like a log until now."

"Your brain never shuts down," he said.

"Neither does yours."

"Shhh." He settled on his back and indicated she should rest her head on his shoulder.

"No, not this side. You're bruised. Here." She got up and quickly rounded the bed, slid under the covers next to him, on his uninjured side. "Your shoulder is a hard pillow."

"Then come here." He helped her snuggle down onto his chest, and she forced her thoughts to a back burner. Stanton was correct. This wasn't the time to rethink anything. As her cheek lay against his bare chest, his hair tickling her skin but in the best way, her body relaxed against him. Her lids grew heavy and the last thing she heard before drifting back to sleep was the sound of his heartbeat under her ear. Slow and steady. Dependable.

For a precious moment, she forgot she was in the crosshairs of a killer.

Chapter 11

Stanton woke later that morning to an empty bed. He looked around the room and saw no signs that Dominique had ever been in here, save for her scent in the sheets. His arm complained as he rolled to sit on the side of his bed. The doc was right; he'd need more meds to keep it from becoming a distraction. But there wasn't anything he could take, or do, to keep him from his main distraction: Dominique.

She'd rocked his world last night. Judging from her reactions to their lovemaking, she was feeling the same. Except she hadn't stayed, even though she'd drifted back to sleep after waking him up with her restlessness before dawn. The sound of the guest shower door closing and running water told him where she was. But it gave no clue as to what she was thinking or feeling. Did she already regret their actions?

His phone buzzed with calendar alerts related to Colton Protection and he allowed a wave of relief to calm him down. At least he had his business to take care of while he waited for Dominique to conduct more police interviews and probably stop at the *Gazette* today. He'd been able to put her off going into her office long enough. Security training told him she didn't need to be anywhere near an obvious place she normally went. It would make her an easier target for the cartel to hit. Yet he also knew that Jimenez shied away from highly visible sites for shootouts. He preferred dark alleys, far from the glare of public opinion. To try to take out Dominique at the local media outlet was plain stupid. Of course, Stanton thought firing outside of the police station wasn't a brilliant move, either. Yet it had happened, and from the texts he had from Troy, it was a confirmed cartel hit.

He called Melissa to see if there was any other news on Jimenez or cartel-related crime.

"Chief Colton."

"It's me. Your brother Stanton." Usually she answered with a warmer greeting. Her curt identification underscored how stressed she was.

"I know. I'm sorry. It's all hands on deck, as I'm sure you caught a whiff of yesterday."

"Anything I need to know for my current assignment?"

"Other than keep Dominique in hiding until this is

all over, which she's not going to agree to? No, nothing I can really talk about yet."

"I'm not asking you to tell me any details, but give me a break, Melissa. If there's more threats against Dominique I have the right to know."

"It doesn't get worse than being in a kingpin's crosshairs, does it?"

Tension practically crackled over their connection, unusual for the Colton siblings. Recrimination flooded his gut. "Hey, sis, I'm sorry. You're in a crappy mess right now and the last thing you need is any pressure from me. I'm sure I'll be in there with you later in the day. Dominique's far from finished with her long line of interview subjects."

"Look, Stanton. I'm trying to get Dominique another interview with the lab assistant who was fired as the other one didn't give her anything, thanks to Internal Affairs. I know why they're not willing to budge, but I'm hoping to get approval for Bonnie to open up to her."

"Let me guess, you have some leverage?" He knew Dominique was stymied by the lack of transparency and he saw her point, and also felt for his sister's position.

Melissa's pained grunt told him all he needed to know. "I'm trying, Stanton, believe me. And I meant what I said to you both yesterday. The sooner we get to the bottom of this the better for all of Grave Gulch, but especially Dominique. I'm open to anything she needs, anyone she wants to interview, to complete her story."

"I know." He wished Melissa would just throw down

a gauntlet and say that Dominique couldn't come back to GGPD or interview any officers or employees until they had Jimenez in custody. But he couldn't ask her to do that, and she wouldn't. Melissa's remonstration over his trying to convince Dominique this story wasn't worth her life proved it.

"I'll see you both later, then? How's it going by the way, out at the lake house?"

"Ah, fine. It's nice to have the place to ourselves."

"How 'nice' are we talking?" Uh-oh. The elder sister that he was never able to get anything past was on the line.

"We'll see you later, Melissa." Before he hit the red "end call" button, he heard his sister's laughter. At least he'd managed to lighten her mood.

Dominique was happy to let Stanton drive them back to town as it allowed her time on her laptop to summarize what she'd learned yesterday and highlight the answers she still sought. The real bonus was not having to look Stanton in the eye. The things they'd done last night!

No. She made herself sit taller in the passenger seat. She was not going to be embarrassed about expressing her sexuality with Stanton or any other man. Not that there'd been another since him. She'd tried to date here and there but had never gotten past the first meetup. Her heart had never let go of Stanton.

"Thanks for agreeing to take me to my office first." She owed him that much.

"I don't want to, and as your expert guard I'd advise against it. But I know you well enough to understand your need to get into the *Gazette* and see your colleagues face-to-face."

"It's more than that. I need to verify some of my sources, and it's best to do it on-site, with all of the tools we have." She also needed to back up the files she'd accumulated so far. It didn't do to trust the cloud when such a powerful cartel was the subject of an exposé. "You can work on Colton Protection stuff in the lounge. You always enjoyed it there before." As soon as she referred to their time together, she wanted to bite her tongue. Stanton had been the perfect gentleman this morning, not teasing her at all about last night. It wasn't like him. He used to love to make her blush, and she was an easy target for his gentle flirting, no matter how much she enjoyed their sex life.

"As long as I have you in my line of sight, I'm cool with it."

"You can't have a straight view of me if I'm in my office." Why did he have to be so unreasonable? Her spaces were safe.

"Then either I work in your office with you, or you enjoy the lounge with me."

The answer was made up for her because immediately upon passing through the building and then the *Gazette*'s second layer of security, Dominique was thronged by her colleagues. High fives, congratulatory greetings and smiles contributed to a festive atmosphere. All were excited over the scoop she'd obtained regarding the Randall Bowe sighting in the park. Stanton took a seat at a small workstation and fired up his laptop.

When the exuberance died down and the other journalists went back to work, Stanton was still on his laptop, looking up to ascertain her presence on a regular basis. Warmth and regret mingled in her center, her affection for him making the reality that they could never be a couple again all the more poignant. He must have sensed her consideration as he looked up from his screen and his brows rose in query.

"I'll work out here with you. Most of the people I need to talk to will be stopping by to grab a cup of coffee, anyway." She plopped down in the workstation across from his, careful to give him lots of space. Thankfully he'd taken a single spot without an extra chair, so it didn't seem odd that she sat at a different table. The last thing she needed was an accidental brush of her thigh against his, or any other body contact. She squeezed her eyes shut, willing the mental images of last night away. They were a treasure she could unlock and examine again when she was alone, after Jimenez was caught. When she no longer required a bodyguard, and Stanton was once again out of her life.

The thought was so sad that she opened her eyes and got right to work. Whatever it took to keep from wondering why it was so painful, when she'd been the one to walk away in the first place.

Stanton's phone lit up with a text from Melissa.

Have Dominique stop by GGPD. I've cleared the interview with the lab assistant.

His first impulse was to fire back, Why don't you tell her yourself? Melissa had Dominique's contact information and he saw this for what it was. His sister wanted him to give Dominique the good news, make him appear as the good guy. Melissa was too busy to be playing matchmaker but he'd learned long ago that some things weren't worth arguing over. Especially when Melissa had her hands full with bad cops and beating back a powerful surge of crime.

"You look…bemused." Dominique placed a mug of coffee next to him.

"Thanks. Actually, I have some good news." His sister might be annoying but he had to admit, it felt good to see Dominique's eyes light up as she continued to look at him. She'd been avoiding him all morning. To be fair, he'd done the same. Mornings after were never easy.

"Oh yeah?"

"Yeah. Melissa said you should stop by GGPD as soon as you can. Internal Affairs has completed the Randall Bowe portion of the internal investigation and the lab assistant is free to discuss everything with you."

"That's great! Not that it shouldn't have happened sooner, of course." He bit back a grin. Typical Dominique, always making certain that he knew she hadn't missed or forgotten an iota of the situation.

"I thought you'd be pleased."

"Melissa had you be the messenger, eh?" She regarded him. "Is she afraid to talk to me directly, or was she trying to give you a friendly shove toward me?"

Surprise gave him pause. "You miss nothing."

"It's my job. Observation." Her cheeks flushed, reminding him of her nipples, dark and hard under his fingers, his tongue. He broke eye contact, needing to mentally regroup. Before he convinced himself that there was a way he could persuade himself and Dominique that they belonged together and could work it all out.

It hadn't worked before, and nothing had changed from what he'd witnessed this morning at the *Grave Gulch Gazette*. Dominique's goal was to win a Pulitzer, and commitment in terms of family and kids wasn't in her wheelhouse. Why couldn't he just accept that?

Nope. Not something he was going to think about. Been there, done that, got the broken heart.

"I want you at the table with me and Bonnie Stadler. And not just because you're my bodyguard." At GGPD again, Melissa had given Dominique the former lab assistant Bonnie Stadler's information. Dominique had scored a meeting at the coffee shop with her and was in no mood to deal with Stanton's suddenly hands-off approach. Since they'd walked into GGPD, he'd expressed his desire to sit in the break room and work.

"You didn't want me with you at the *Gazette*, yet now you do?" His blue eyes were laced with Arctic ice.

"If I wasn't already certain you're such a badass tough guy, I'd swear you're goading me to a fight." She sank into the chair opposite him and looked around to make sure they were alone. It seemed the police station was as overwhelmed as the newspaper, with the constant stream of events thanks to the cartel, the ongoing corruption scandal at GGPD and Randall Bowe's recent sighting. "The interviews go smoother if you're there. Your presence adds—"

"Stability?" Only after she felt her face grow hot did he allow a slow grin to crease his face. Her gaze lingered on his lips, unable to look away. He was a maestro with that mouth. And his hands...

She blinked, shook her head. It didn't matter if he knew that he'd thrown her off balance. Her hormones had been doing their own thing since he'd saved her life. "Call it whatever you want. But there's something else." She looked away, back at him again. "Until they are certain they've caught the corrupt cops, how do we know the lab assistant isn't one of the bad guys? I mean, Randall Bowe's already a definite, so why not his colleague? If I were working against GGPD, being paid off by the cartel, I'd make it look like my boss was all to blame, too."

"Why don't you just bat your eyelashes at me while you're at it, Dominique?" He ground out the words and she allowed herself a chuckle at his expense.

"Since you're in charge of my safety, I figured you'd want to know all the angles."

He gathered his laptop and bag without comment and they proceeded to the exit. Stanton checked the street before motioning for Dominique to walk next to him. They headed for the coffee shop, a few blocks away.

"Are you certain you have an interview?"

"You're the one who told me Melissa arranged it." Doubt crept in, though, her hopes sinking as she acknowledged the possibility that the woman might not show.

"If you wanted to get me alone, all you had to do was ask." His jest calmed her. This was preferable to the awful quiet in the car this morning, when she'd wondered if he was regretting all they'd done last night. She'd figured out that while it might not have been her smartest move, or moves as it were, she would never regret the time with Stanton. The past couple of days had taught her the hard way just how short life was.

"Stanton, I want to come clean with you on something. About last night—"

"Nope, no talking about personal stuff during working hours."

Dominique took his interruption for what it was. Last night was supposed to be a final, better farewell for each other. Not something to rehash. Fine.

They arrived at the café and he held the door for her. When she entered, she spied a woman sitting alone at the counter and walked up to her.

"Excuse me, are you—"

"Bonnie Stadler, the former GGPD lab assistant? Yes. You must be Dominique." The woman had silver hair and bright green eyes that assessed both she and Stanton. Her features matched the photo the *Gazette* had used when her termination was announced.

"Yes, I'm Dominique de la Vega, with the *Grave Gulch Gazette*. This is Stanton Colton, my personal security advisor." She didn't look at Stanton as she was certain he was trying not to laugh. But "bodyguard" sounded overdone inside a friendly cafe.

"Stanton and I met at the GGPD Christmas party last year." Bonnie smiled at him.

Stanton nodded. "We did."

"Let's get our drinks and sit down." Stanton placed their order before walking with them to a table. Dominique and Stanton took stools across from Bonnie, who leaned back against a wall. She looked Dominique in the eyes, her expression grim. "I'm glad I finally have the opportunity to talk to you about everything. I'm sorry I couldn't see you sooner but until the internal investigation committee gave me the okay, my hands were tied."

"I understand." And she did. But now she wanted answers. "Why don't we begin with what you feel Randall did wrong, if you would?"

"Sure. As long as this is off the record? I want to help you get the story but I don't want my name in the paper."

"That's fine." Dominique's patience was wearing thin but she felt Stanton's calm presence and did her best to soak it in.

Bonnie crossed her arms in front of her chest. "My work here was ideal up until about a year ago. I enjoyed working for Randall. He was a generous boss and mentor, and I learned so much from him. As you can see, I'm no spring chicken. I went back to college in my late fifties and got my degree. I wasn't sure I'd ever be able to land such a plum job. It's very satisfying, when we match up evidence to crimes and help nail the bad guys and gals." She paused. "Randall began doing more and more work on his own. At first he said it was because he was having marital problems and needed the extra time away from home. But then

I noticed that I wasn't seeing anything that had to do with the more serious crimes. Randall had processed the evidence and filed his report before I ever set eyes on it. We worked on Drew Orr's case, and Everleigh Emerson's, but I wasn't allowed to so much as read the evidence reports. I thought that was odd, for a man who'd so strongly mentored me previously."

"What kind of evidence are we talking about?"

"The usual. Fingerprints, bullet casings, blood stains, DNA. Mostly we test for fingerprints, the break-downs of batches of heroin—how much fentanyl it's been cut with, if any—and occasional blood types when there's an assault or worse. Anything with DNA or more complicated lab work gets sent out. Still, we could accomplish an impressive amount of work at GGPD, to enable our officers to get their jobs done. And, of course, our work aided the DA when it's time to prosecute the criminal."

"What specifically do you know Randall Bowe did or didn't do?"

"Several things. First, he was a witness in several court cases against drug dealers for this local cartel. In each case, he testified, under oath, that there was no evidence he'd consider valid for use against the deal-ers. It took me a while to put it together, but one night I worked late and needed the file for a heroin OD. I wanted to verify the officer's report that the user who'd died was also a dealer. The officer bagged dozens of bags of heroin. When I opened the file, there was no mention of the drugs. Nothing. As if the officer never filed the evidence. I questioned Randall about it the next morning and he said he'd tested the powder, only to discover it was all baking soda."

"Has that ever happened before?"

"Never. We've had one or two times with fake drugs, but that doesn't happen with *this* cartel. They're slick and here to do one thing—make money. How I finally proved that Randall was lying to me was that I found the evidence the officer had brought in, stuffed in a tea tin, you know the kind you find at specialty stores? Randall's a big tea drinker. I'd had other cases that he'd taken over go bad, in my opinion. So I took it upon myself to search his office when he was out."

"Did you confront him with what you found?"

"No. I was terrified, frankly. I'm not sure if you know, but he'd recently purchased a Lamborghini. Really stupid, if you ask me, because it's a red flag when a government employee all of a sudden affords luxury anything. I figured there was a good chance that he was being paid by the cartel to stifle evidence, make it disappear. I wanted to talk to the officers who brought the evidence in, but I didn't know who to trust anymore. Once someone you've trusted, who has made a good difference in your life, goes bad, it's very upsetting."

"So you reported it."

"I did. I went to Lansing, took a personal day, and reported it. I felt awful, going over Chief Colton's head, even though I was fired." Her eyes darted to where Stanton sat, taking it all in. She knew Melissa was his sister. "Randall disappeared days after I reported him, from what I understand. And it looks as though there could be one or two bad cops who've been helping him, too, from what I've read in the paper. It makes me sick to think I was working next to someone who let a serial killer go free. None of us are safe until Len Davison is caught." Bonnie shook her head. "Tough times for Grave Gulch."

"Can you tell me, Bonnie, if you know anything about Charlie Hamm, about his case?"

"The convict who died in the prison fight a while back?"

"Yes."

"We've had so many cases. But I remember his in particular because one day there wasn't a lot of evidence in his file and the next, a suitcase was there. Randall wouldn't answer my questions about it." As Bonnie spoke, Dominique snuck a look at Stanton. His blue gaze steadied her, and he gave her a slight nod. He thought she was handling this well, on the right track.

"I haven't been able to confirm that Charlie's fingerprint wasn't on the suitcase. He swore it couldn't have been his."

Bonnie nodded. "I agree. Randall Bowe made up what he wanted to for the witness stand. Charlie's wasn't the only case. But I got fired before I could do anything more to help."

Dominique looked at Stanton again, and saw her satisfaction at finding the truth reflected in his gaze.

They really made a good team.

It's only temporary.

Best she remember that.

* * *

The de la Vega home was lit up as Dominique and Stanton walked up to the front door. He'd insisted on coming because he was her bodyguard, yes, but he'd always enjoyed her family.

"You can wait outside if it's going to be too awkward. You know my sister is going to assume we're an item again."

He wanted to remind her that for one blissful night they had been an item again, and a hot one at that. But her stilted mannerisms communicated her insecurity over the situation. Dominique's family was from Colombia originally, and she and her twin, Soledad, were first-generation Americans. Rigo had married an American woman he met when he was serving in the US Navy as an exchange officer, in Jacksonville, Florida. She was from Grave Gulch and he'd promised to bring her back to her hometown as soon as his military stint was over. That had been before Dominique and her twin were born, over thirty years ago. Their mother had passed five years ago, leaving Rigo heartbroken.

"I wouldn't dream of it, and not just because I can't let you out of my sight. I love your family and your dad's great."

"He's paying you."

"Handsomely, I might add." Stanton couldn't help teasing her.

"Okay. Well, I gave you an out."

"You did." And she might not believe it, but he was looking forward to the party.

They walked into the amber glow of family, friends and the most enticing aromas of the meal, catered by a local favorite restaurant if the logo on a delivery van in the driveway was an indication. Rigo's pair of boxer dogs trotted over to greet them.

"Hi, girls." Dominique squatted to pet them, accepting sloppy kisses from Rosa and Rita. Another reason he'd fallen for her way back when. She didn't care about what mattered, like the mess a dog's affection could make. As much attention to detail as she paid to her outfits, and as expertly as she applied her makeup, Dominique was grounded.

Dangerous territory.

"Dominique!" Aunt Gloria walked over, her dark hair worn long like her niece's but with strands of silver that reflected the overhead lighting. Her eyes widened as she recognized him standing behind Dominique. "And Stanton—wonderful to see you again." Gloria hugged him and he hugged her back, feeling as though he was some kind of prodigal son. Which was ridiculous, as he hadn't been the one to walk away. And Aunt Gloria wasn't even Dominique's, or his, mother.

You pushed Dominique away. You let her go.

He mentally bristled. Hadn't he been the one who'd reached out with texts, phone calls? And Dominique had let them all go without one single response. Her silence had given ghosting a whole new meaning for him that included pain, shame and regret. He felt a wet tongue on his hand and looked down at Rosa, whose soft brown eyes were beseeching him, as if to say, "Why did you stop coming 'round?" Rita sat patiently and waited for him to pet Rosa, then accepted his attention.

"Where's Dad?" Dominique scanned the spacious great room where friends and family mingled in several groups.

"Back in the kitchen with your uncles."

Dominique looked at Stanton. "Come on. Let's get it over with." Her grin relieved him. At least she wasn't harboring a grudge about her father any longer, for hiring him without her permission. Maybe Dominique would actually enjoy this time with her family.

They walked around a wall to the kitchen, which overlooked part of the great room and the roaring fireplace. So typical for a de la Vega function, the men and women chatting and enjoying themselves.

"*Mija*. Come here." Rigo held open his arms for Dominique, and Stanton waited while they embraced, nodding at the other men who were mostly Rigo's brothers and close family friends.

"Happy Birthday, Daddy."

"Thank you, but let's not talk about birthdays. I'm too old for this." His grin belied his words and the low rumble of male laughter surrounded them. Rigo's dark eyes sparkled. "Who's this handsome man you've brought to our fiesta?"

"Funny, Dad." Dominique turned and greeted the other men before she returned her attention to Stanton. "I'm going to find my sister. Are you okay with me not staying in here with you?"

"Yes. As long as I can see you." The house was spacious but small enough that he'd be able to keep her in sight range, as long as she stayed on the same floor, as she caught up with Soledad.

"Great." She poured sparkling water into two large red plastic cups and gave him one. "We're both on duty, aren't we?"

"Cheers." He tipped his and as their cups touched he looked into her eyes. There was a light in them that he'd normally attribute to appreciation, but what was she grateful for? It couldn't be him, specifically. That he'd agreed to them coming to the family party, much closer to the center of Grave Gulch?

"Cheers." She smiled and before he realized her intention, leaned up on her tiptoe and smacked his cheek with a very loud, definite kiss. "Don't ever change."

Stunned, he watched her sway as she left the room and walked over to where Soledad stood in front of the fireplace.

A hard grasp on his shoulder by her *tío* Héctor reminded him he wasn't alone. "She sure is a beauty, my niece. What are your intentions, *amigo*?" The group of men again erupted in laughter, but Stanton didn't miss Rigo's more measured look. Like him, the older man seemed to wonder what indeed his plans were for his and Dominique's relationship.

Aw, man, he was so screwed. He'd begun thinking of them as having a relationship again. Not the best place mentally, when she had a big bullseye on her back and a cartel kingpin who wouldn't stop until she was dead.

Chapter 12

"You look tired, sis." Dominique motioned for Soledad to join her on the ledge of the stone-front fireplace. The heat warmed her back, still sore from the attack and then Stanton's heroic save in front of the police station.

Soledad laughed. "I'm always tired by six o'clock. You would be, too, if you got up at two a.m. to bake bread Monday through Saturday. I'm usually getting ready for bed about now."

"I suppose you're right." She didn't want to scare her sister, but her curiosity won out. "Have you noticed anything unusual around our apartment building?" They rented at the same address, their apartments across the hall from one another.

"Like what?" Deep lines appeared between Soledad's brows. "Drug deals?" She knew Dominique was digging up information on the local cartel; Dominique had told her twin all about Charlie Hamm and his poetry.

"No. Strange people, probably men, lurking about?"

Soledad tilted her head slightly, her gaze on their mother's colorful silk rug. "No, not at all. Are you thinking that the kingpin has a stakeout on you?"

"You know I am. I know you told Dad about my story, Soledad. And he hired Stanton to protect me. I meant to call sooner but, well, it's been chaotic."

"I figured you'd be upset that I told Dad, but can you blame me? I'm worried about you. When he told me he'd hired Stanton, I knew you'd be really ticked off. I thought you weren't calling me until you cooled down. I only told him because I care, sis."

"I appreciate that, but I wish you'd talked to me first."

"Like that would have convinced you to let this story go, or to at least stop instigating a cartel leader to place a target on your back?"

"This isn't all about me, Soledad. There are lives at stake, not to mention the justice I'm seeking for Charlie. This cartel is particularly nasty. They'll go after my family if they think it'll make a difference in whether I keep digging. Please be aware of your surroundings until these bad players are caught. I don't want you to take your personal security for granted."

"Trust me, I don't. I'm not the fearless soul between us, remember?" Soledad's query made Dominique smile.

"Of course I do."

"I'm not sure you do. I'm the one who likes to bake

cookies and bread, who made a living out of producing comfort food. You've always been about the adrenaline rush, getting to the truth. Remember when you stuck up for both of us to those three bullies in middle school?"

"Hey, if I hadn't known you were behind me, ready with your baton from drill team, I might not have been so bold." She'd told off all three boys, who'd kept following her and Soledad home from school, to the bus stop, around the school corridors if they stayed after for one of the various clubs they'd enjoyed at the time. Soledad was in the gourmet bakers' club and Dominique found her twelve-year-old kindred spirits in the school paper's office. The memories brought back the scents of that room, from the dusty reams of computer paper stacked against the brick walls, to the dry eraser ink as she'd written on the large whiteboard at one end of the classroom-turned-newsroom. She'd known in her bones that journalism was her calling. No amount of encouragement from well-meaning English teachers who'd insisted her talents might be better used in fiction and its myriad genres mattered. Dominique had answered her soul's calling to find the truth and write about it.

"You're thinking about the school paper, aren't you?" Soledad prompted.

"Of course. Telling those boys to leave us alone was one thing. We scared them for a bit. But what kept them away was the editorial." Dominique had snuck in the bullies' full names, totally against school policy. It had cost her detention for a week straight. "It was all worth it. They never bothered anyone again."

"They didn't." Soledad eyed her. "I get that you're always going to be chasing down justice. It's in your blood. But don't you want more out of life?"

"More?" She tried to keep a cool countenance as her sister seemed intent on her emotional jugular.

"Don't stare at me like a hungry goldfish." Soledad's command sent them both into a fit of giggles, remembering the poor sad creatures they'd won one year at their local parish picnic. They'd come home with the fish swimming in dyed water, pink and green, in fishbowls that fit in their hands. Mom had immediately purchased a large bowl complete with filter, much to Rigo's chagrin.

"They lived for three years. A record."

"Mine lived a day longer." Soledad made Dominique's giggles start all over again. "Back to the subject, sister of mine. I don't know about you, but I've been having serious baby pangs lately."

"What?" Dominique wasn't surprised that Soledad was thinking about starting her own family, but she wasn't in a serious relationship at the moment. "As in, you want a baby no matter what?"

Soledad waved her hand in dismissal. "No, not yet. I mean, I hope I find someone to start a family with. You already have found your soul mate, Dominique. Why aren't you jumping on it?"

Usually they'd have a good laugh over Soledad's choice of wording, as it was a perfect euphemism for sex. Dominique couldn't speak past what felt like a sucker punch to her gut, the snarl of emotion in her throat.

"We—we're—we're not together, Soledad." She hissed her response, not wanting any of their father's guests to hear.

"Come on, Dominique. You two were making eyes at each other in the kitchen over your water, for heaven's sake." Soledad placed her hand on her wrist. "Hey, I'm sorry. You've been through an awful lot these past few days, and I know you haven't told me all of it. Don't think I haven't noticed the bruises still on your throat."

"I told you I ran into trouble. Stanton was there. He saved my life, I realize now. And has again since then, too. Twice."

"That's why I told Dad, sis. If anything ever happened to you…" Soledad's matching dark eyes filled with tears. Dominique shared her sister's concern, because she felt the exact same way about her twin.

"I know. And I'm sorry that I haven't kept you up on all of the story's developments."

"I don't care about the story, this one or any other, as much as I care about you. I want to know what you're thinking, and what you're feeling." Soledad poked her in the chest for emphasis. Right over her heart, a heart that raced at the emotions this conversation had set free. As if unbridled by Stanton last night while they made love, her hormones raced around, and it wasn't solely about sex anymore.

Was this deep longing in her soul, the one she'd ignored for the last two years, not only due to her breakup with Stanton, but in fact an unrecognized-by-her biological clock's incessant ticking? More likely, it was her extreme regret that she hadn't given Stanton another chance. Heard him out, and allowed him to hear her out, after things had settled. Because if she had, they might be at a point now where having kids wouldn't feel so strange. Where they both accepted each other's jobs, and the inherent risks with them. Wasn't that what two mature, loving partners did?

"You look like you've seen a ghost."

"Maybe I have. Of my past, present and future."

Soledad rolled her eyes. "Stop making it so dramatic. It doesn't have to be a twisted Dickens plot. There's nothing more natural than wanting to settle down, have a home, build a family, if that's what is right for you."

"Maybe." She'd focused on her career so much and had thought she'd found the perfect partner in Stanton, before. Before he'd decided that the only relationship they could have would be if she'd quit her job, or at least switched to "safer" stories, and have his babies. But had he ever asked her to quit? Or demanded that he wanted kids? As she reviewed that painful day, all he'd been asking her, and insisting upon, was that they marry. And that yes, he wanted children as soon as possible. But could she have convinced him to wait?

"What? Tell me, sister."

"I know it's not like me, but these past days with Stanton have got me thinking. Maybe it isn't such an awful idea to think we could have made a go of it. And you know how you're always saying you can feel your eggs screaming for a baby daddy?" They both giggled. "You know what I mean. I think mine are, too, but I ignored it before. Shoved it down."

"So you, Dominique de la Vega, are admitting that—*gasp*—your biological clock is ticking?"

"I suppose I am." But it wasn't a purely biological event. It had everything to do with the sexy man standing in her dad's kitchen, laughing and talking with her relatives as though he were part of the family, too.

"What does Stanton think?"

"I haven't mentioned any of this to him, how could I?" At Soledad's mind-meld stare, she relented. "Oh. My. Goodness. I think I may have made a huge mistake with one of the people who meant the most to me." Recrimination reared its nasty head and pried at her peace of mind, what little she had left. "What a mess I've made of things."

"Well, duh. He was stupid to give you an ultimatum about marriage two years ago, and you were equally idiotic to not answer his texts and calls. We've already determined this. That doesn't matter now. My point is, what are you going to do about it today?"

"I, I'm—"

Her phone buzzed and she pulled it out of her red leather cross-body bag. It was from her senior editor.

Hamm witness wants to talk to you on landline in office. Come in ASAP.

She looked at Soledad, who stared at her with expectation. "Spill it, Dominique. What are you going to do about Stanton now?"

"I'm not doing anything but getting to the *Grave Gulch Gazette*. I've got a break in my story."

"We haven't even sung *'Feliz Cumpleaños'* yet. Dad has to blow out his candles. All fifty-nine of them."

"More like put them out with a fire extinguisher." At Soledad's shocked gasp she laughed. "I'm teasing. He's the one who said he's too old for birthdays."

"Fifty-nine isn't old." Soledad stood with her and held out her hand. "Give me your cup. You go and do whatever you have to."

"Thanks, sweetie." She kissed Soledad on the cheek, gave her a big hug and relished the resounding hug back. There was no one who knew her better than her sister.

Except perhaps one man, who stared at her from the kitchen with unmistakable admiration. And maybe something more that flickered in those indigo depths.

Stanton recognized Dominique's straight-spined posture, her purposeful strides toward the kitchen as confirmation that the text he watched her read was important.

Her perfume reached him a split second before she did and his nostrils soaked it up. As if being separated for the last half hour was a lifetime. He stifled a groan, the urge to get out of the house, away from her. Away from a second broken heart. He had a job to complete, and he would. Then they'd be out of each other's lives again.

"What is it?"

"I have to go into the *Gazette* offices." She held up her phone so that he could read the text. His stomach clenched as he realized what this might mean. Besides giving Dominique her story, the witness who lied on the stand and sent Charlie to prison might very well know who attacked her.

"What are you talking about, going into work?" Rigo's rich tenor flowed across the kitchen and he watched the interaction between father and daughter. Dominique blushed under her father's scrutiny. Stanton felt sorry for Rigo; he was about to find out what came first for his daughter and it wasn't going to be a birthday party.

"I do have to go in tonight, briefly." She shot a look at Stanton to see if he was going to rat her out. He stayed quiet, wondering how she could justify blowing off her father's celebration. "But not until later. I'm here until the cake is served, Daddy." She walked over to Rigo and gave him a hug. "Nothing's more important than family."

Stanton watched in dumbfounded silence. Where was the Dominique who'd stormed out of his apartment after he'd begged her to stay and start a family with him? Realization dawned and it wasn't welcome. One thing being in security taught him was that denial never kept anybody safe, including him. It was time he admitted the real reason he and Dominique hadn't worked out, despite their incredible chemistry and solid friendship.

It wasn't that Dominique didn't want to settle down; she just didn't want to do it with *him*.

"You didn't have any cake." Dominique chided him as they left the house. The cold sting of the early spring night cut through his coat and he shoved black leather driving gloves on.

"Sugar messes with my senses." Not unlike Dominique, but he wasn't having sweet thoughts about her at the moment. And he was telling the truth. He had a terrific sweet tooth and didn't know when to stop when he started. So he mostly didn't start.

"Fair enough. I have to say, though, that it was the best chocolate cake Soledad's ever made. She's finally gotten the cocoa proportions down to a science. It took her since she opened the bakery, and she wouldn't sell chocolate cake there until she got it right." Her admiration for her twin was evident. Like a hot knife searing his gut, right through to his heart.

She didn't want a family with you. Why hadn't he figured this out, seen this, before?

"Stanton, what's wrong? You don't agree with me going into the *Gazette* this late?"

"You're going to do whatever you have to for your story. You always have."

"Ouch. That sounds personal."

"Nothing personal going on here. I'm protecting you and you're choosing to engage in risky behavior."

She stopped in front of the passenger door and faced him. Their breath hung in heavy clouds between them, and he saw her shiver. Dang his arms for wanting to hug her to him, warm her up. His job was to keep her alive, not make her comfortable.

"Something's been bothering you since before Dad blew out his birthday candles. What is it?"

"It's occurred to me that I've read you wrong all

along." He couldn't stop his harsh words if he wanted to. "It wasn't that you didn't want to settle down or have a family. It was me. I wasn't the one for you."

Her eyes widened and her mouth gaped open. He'd struck an honest chord, apparently.

"Stanton, that's not true in the least. But this isn't where we're going to have this conversation. And not now, when we're both under a lot of pressure."

"You act as if we'll have things to talk about after the kingpin is captured, after the threat against you is neutralized."

"You never know, we might." Her chin jutted out and her arms were folded across her chest, the way she always held them when he'd angered her.

"I don't know a lot, but one thing I do know, Dominique. When my contract is up with you, so is our time together." The momentary relief he felt at jabbing out at her, inflicting her with the hellish pain he was in, was short-lived. The flicker of confusion across her expression morphed into hurt, and then her icy mask was firmly in place.

"Whatever. Let's go. The sooner I get answers, the more quickly you'll be free from having to spend your time with me." She reached for the door handle.

Explosions rent the night air and he acted on instinct, grabbing her and throwing them both to the ground. A sharp pain ran through his shoulder, his arm, but it was muffled by the adrenaline that immediately began pumping through his blood.

"Stay down."

"Stanton, it's not—"

"We need to get out of here." Fear sliced his heart. He'd been so wrapped up in his hurt, feeling her loss over again, that he'd not been paying attention to their surroundings as he should. He eased off her, onto his knees, and reached for her hand to help her.

"Stanton, no." She sat on the ground, looking up at him. Her hand grasped his. "It's fireworks. My family always shoots them off for birthdays, remember?"

He stared at her, dumbfounded. Laughter and whoops from the back of the house reached them and mortification rushed over him. An uncomfortable heat crawled up his neck.

"I, ah, yeah, I forgot." He shouldn't keep holding her hand, but it was his anchor to reality. He'd allowed himself to be caught in between his feelings for Dominique and the valid fear that she might get hit by Jimenez no matter how well he did his job.

"You okay, Stanton? I'm usually the one who's wound tight." They stood up together, and he couldn't help thinking this was more like her protecting him.

"I'm good. Let's get you to your office."

"I'm going to be stuck here for at least the next few hours. The security guard is on duty, so why don't you rest in the lounge? There's a sofa in there."

"Only if you'll come in with your laptop and work there." Did she really think he'd let his guard down? He might have made a fool of himself with her family's fireworks display, but he wasn't abdicating his duty. Whether Rigo had paid him or not, this was where he belonged.

Protecting Dominique.

"Fine." Her sigh let him know she was as tired as he was of the constant tension between them. Making love the other night had eased it for a bit, but there would always be a level of give-and-take between them.

Once settled in the lounge area, he watched her call numerous people, sometimes by texting first.

"Still no answer from the witness?"

She shook her head. "No. My boss was right to have me come in, as the witness is only going to talk on our office landline. I get it. But he's not been easy to connect with, that's for certain. It took me months to track him down and then convince him to meet with me this week. And you know how that turned out." She pointed at her throat as if he'd need a reminder at how close that jerk had come to strangling her.

"Who else do you want to talk to?"

She pursed her lips in concentration, scrolled on her laptop. "This is becoming so much bigger than Charlie Hamm's story, isn't it? There's Len Davison, serial killer, who targets older men as they walk their dogs. Bowe destroyed evidence against him and blamed Bonnie, his assistant at the time, firing her. The drug cartel wanted to frame Charlie, to keep the heat off of them. Now they're after me. The other person I need to verify statements with, besides Johnny Blanchard, is Charlie's lawyer. His lawyer was less than helpful, frankly, and I blame his incompetence for Charlie's conviction as much as the false evidence and lying witness."

"Has his attorney ever answered any of your calls?"

"No, but maybe I'll get lucky tonight. Catch him off

guard with an evening call." She dialed the phone and put it on speaker. They were alone in the lounge area, the few other reporters working the night shift at their desks, coming in sporadically for hot beverages or to heat up food in the microwave.

"Hello?" A wary greeting.

"Mr. Chambers? This is Dominique de la Vega, from the *Grave Gulch Gazette*."

"I know who you are. I only picked up to tell you in person to stop harassing me. I've got nothing for you."

"I'm sorry, but I have some questions about Charlie's case."

"Don't we all? But the truth, Ms. de la Vega? There are no questions as far as I'm concerned. Charlie was the target of the Jimenez cartel. Yeah, I know all about them, does that surprise you? I've had to protect my family from the cartel, trust me. I suggest you keep yourself safe, because they're ruthless."

"Are you saying you might not have given Charlie's case all of the required efforts because of pressure from the cartel?"

"Heck no. I did what I could for Charlie. But the GGPD lab's director, that Randall Bowe character they just sighted in Grave Gulch Park, he's responsible for Charlie's imprisonment. Him and that darn witness, Blanchard. They made sure Charlie got put away for a long time. And when that wasn't enough, when it was clear Charlie's case was going to be reopened, they had him killed."

Dominique's face paled, then red rushed into her cheeks. "Why do you think that, Mr. Chambers?"

"I don't think it, I know it. Do I have evidence? No. Darn cartel knows the law as well as I do, leaves no crumbs, no traces that would link them to any of the myriad crimes they've committed in this town. Murder's the least of it, if you ask me."

Stanton heard the attorney's frustration, but also wished the man would understand he was speaking to an ally in Dominique.

"All I'm asking, Mr. Chambers, is that we meet and I interview you for the story I'm working on. You of all people will understand that I'm seeking justice for Char—"

"Justice was not served and it won't be until they arrest and prosecute Randall Bowe! Add in the cartel and its entire group of thugs, especially its kingpin. I'm out. I did what I could do for Charlie. He's dead, may he rest in peace. I've accepted that and I'm working on cases where I can still make a difference. I suggest you do the same with the stories you choose to pursue." He ended the connection. Dominique grimaced, but not before Stanton saw the frustrated disappointment in her eyes. His chest ached for her.

"Want a cup of tea? I'm buying." He rose and went to the beverage counter, turned on the coffee maker that took pods of tea, too.

"Sure. Earl Grey." She typed on her laptop with aplomb, as if a nasty, embittered defense attorney hadn't just cussed her out and slammed the phone in her ear.

"What are you writing?"

"He may not be on the record, and I can't use any

quotes, but I always keep notes about my conversations and interactions with possible interviewees. You'd be surprised how many of them come around once the bad guys are behind bars and they know they're safe."

"He didn't sound like he was going to change his mind."

"Maybe not, but he has a family to protect. I can't blame him." She paused. "I've been thinking."

Oh boy. Here it came. She was going to lay it on him about their lovemaking, which neither had addressed. He mentally scrambled for an emotionally detached response. Still stinging from overreacting to the fireworks, he needed to demonstrate he had it together.

"Oh?" He pressed the button and waited for her mug to fill.

"I was stupid to show up at my dad's tonight. Family is very important to me, and it would have hurt to miss his party, but honestly, the cartel could have tracked me there and innocent people could have been hurt, or worse."

"I took all precautions to ensure you were not followed."

"I know, but it's a matter of time. I don't think I should go back to the lake house, either. If anything happened to your parents, I'd never forgive myself."

"They're out of town."

"Still…" She blew her hair out of her eyes as she stared at her screen. Was she using it as a shield to keep from looking directly at him? He wouldn't blame her. Whenever their gazes locked, it usually led to either quarreling or being in bed. Neither of which served them at present.

Not that he wouldn't enjoy making love to her again. Dang it, this was going to hurt when it was over. Losing her all over again.

The portable phone unit that was connected to the paper's landline lit up and she hit the speaker function again. "Dominique de la Vega."

"It's Johnny Blanchard." The witness Dominique had sought, had been attacked for, whom he'd taken a bullet graze for.

"Mr. Blanchard, thank you for getting back to me. I'm sorry we haven't been able to connect." Dominique's voice reflected none of the excitement he saw in her alert posture, the way her fingers reached for her cell phone to record the interchange and then flew across her keyboard as she took notes.

"You have no idea. You almost got me killed over this. I want to help you out, but I can't risk coming into the paper, or even into Grave Gulch." His voice was muffled, almost a whisper, and Stanton's hackles were up. If he were alone, wouldn't he be able to speak more clearly?

"Can you tell me where you are?"

"I'm working under an alias at an event place up north. I used to do this before, before…"

"You don't have to explain. Can you tell me where, exactly, and I'll meet you?"

"It's not going to be that simple, Ms. de la Vega. How do I know you won't be followed by them, and bring them to me? I'm safe up here."

"I'm working with the top in the business regarding security. My bodyguard takes all precautions to ensure we're not followed. You can trust me on this."

The static of the connection echoed in the lounge area as Blanchard vacillated.

"You can't bring the cops, whatever you do. Or any kind of personal protection. It'll be a tip-off, if I'm being watched by my former boss. I can't risk it."

"I understand. When were you looking at meeting?"

"I have to work an event on Saturday. It's actually two weddings, one in the morning and one in the afternoon. I think we'll have a better chance of not being targeted, if they're watching us, at such a big public venue." Blanchard gave the information as easily as someone discussing the weather.

"That makes sense to me, but can you give me the address? I have a lot going on with this story and will have to rearrange my schedule." Stanton admired Dominique's ability to sound equally casual, yet continue to pressure him for some answers.

"I'll give you the address at midnight, Friday." He saw her suck in a breath. That would give them only an hour or two of leeway, if this event site was as far "north" as he suspected.

"If you change your mind—"

"I won't. And call me Johnny. We both have too much riding on this to be so formal, Dominique." Before Stanton could let himself get riled by the man's flippant tone with her, he disconnected. Dominique sat still, as if processing what Blanchard had said.

"It's a setup, Dominique."

"Maybe. But maybe not. We can ask GGPD to help us out here, can't we? I don't want to alert the local authorities, wherever this resort is. Besides, there wouldn't be enough time to inform them, and then have the kind of backup we're going to need."

He shook his head. "I don't like this." He hesitated before dropping another information bomb on her. "I heard you on not wanting to involve either of our families in this anymore than needed. Before you suggest it, we can't go to either of our apartments. The cartel's already been checking on both, I'm certain." He set the hot mug of tea next to her laptop, careful to avoid any situation where they'd have skin-to-skin contact. The air was filled with the electricity of the danger they faced. The lethal situation that Dominique was contemplating putting them both in.

"Why don't we go to a hotel? Two adjoining rooms, of course." She blushed and he had a shock of satisfaction for a few seconds, realizing that she was as affected as he was by their being together again.

"I can't trust that. There could be a lookout in every hotel between here and wherever Blanchard is, especially if it's a setup." He saw the realization soak in as the lines between her brows deepened and her skin paled. The reach of the cartel seemed indomitable. "I do know of a place that's safe, further north."

Chapter 13

"We can go to my parents' cabin."

"The cabin, as in almost five hours away?" Dominique stared at him. "How do you expect me to work there? Do they even have Wi-Fi?"

"Yes, *that* cabin. It's most likely an hour, two at most, from where Blanchard claims to be working. The wedding venues he's talking about are clustered along the lakeshore. I'll surveil it before you can go anywhere near it, Dominique. I'm almost certain this is a setup, but I know you won't let go of it unless we give it a try. We're going to have to have backup from local police, and it'll take time to coordinate it. We'll head up there tonight, and then have all day tomorrow before you meet with him on Saturday."

She contemplated her options as she looked into

his vivid eyes. No games, no harsh walls, just Stanton being real with her.

"You're certain the cabin is wired? That it's not a dial-up connection?" She watched the insistence in his eyes meld into laughter.

"Yes, positive. And if it fails, you can use my phone as your hot spot. On my dime."

Stanton and the words "hot spot" were a dangerous combination, so she shifted her attention to the newsfeed exclusive to the *Gazette*. It scrolled on a large monitor mounted in the corner of the lounge room, next to two other monitors that displayed various news outlets and the local police scanner's audio feed. A name caught her attention.

"Stanton, there's been a Len Davison sighting on the outskirts of town." She heard the catch in her voice. It was in the same area they had departed earlier— where her family lived. "I'm calling Troy. Or should I call Melissa?"

"Try Troy first. Melissa's going to be swamped if this is a legit report." His attention was on the monitors, too. As much as she loathed a threat to her family, she experienced some relief to have Stanton's focus elsewhere. Because whenever he looked at her for more than a blink, she internally combusted amid all the conflicting emotions she had for him. For them. For a future with him.

Troy answered on the first try, and she wasted no time getting to the point.

"Is my family safe, Troy?"

"No one's safe if this guy's around. His pattern is to

hit next month, though, so there's that. But he's shown a definite preference to kill fifty-something men. Does that match anyone close to you? Your dad?"

"Yes. My father just turned fifty-nine tonight, as a matter of fact. He walks his two boxer dogs in Grave Gulch Park regularly, morning and evening, unless there's horrible weather." Rigo, Rosa and Rita were practically fixtures there, so consistent was her dad.

"I'd suggest you tell him to knock off the walks, especially to Grave Gulch Park, for a bit. If we're lucky we'll apprehend Davison before he strikes again, but it's not worth the risk." Troy was convincing.

"Will do. Thank you, Troy. Also, Troy? Stanton's going to be calling you soon. We're going to need some backup from the local police up north for a witness I need to interview. Can you handle the liaison?" Troy's audible groan sounded over the speaker.

"I'll give you a call sometime tonight," Stanton interjected, looking at Dominique with chagrin. "I'm not in favor of it, cuz, trust me. But I'm not going to stop this intrepid journalist from doing her job."

"Copy that. Both of you stay safe. Good luck talking to your father, Dominique."

"Thanks."

They disconnected and she began to gather her things.

"Are you through here?" Stanton's disbelief reflected in the pitch of his voice.

"Not in the least, but if we're going to stop at my father's, and make it up to your family cabin before we both collapse from exhaustion, we need to get a move on it, don't we?" She couldn't look at him, or he'd read what she had to hide from him. Her absolute need for him, and the fact that she'd never gotten over him. It was more than the hot sex, the stolen kisses over the past several days.

What she had with Stanton was meant to last a lifetime. Before she could analyze it, she had to make sure they survived the next forty-eight hours.

"I know you're not keen on me doing the interview, but I find it hard to believe that Johnny's setting me up at this point. We haven't been targeted since the shooting outside of GGPD. I think the increased presence of the officers on the streets and around Grave Gulch has made a difference, don't you?"

Stanton's teeth ground together and he fought to keep from shouting that he wasn't willing to risk losing her, no matter what. If he wasn't driving them to the cabin, and they didn't have a solid three more hours ahead of them on the dark, slick roads, he'd pull over and do whatever it took to convince her to change her mind.

"It's foolish to assume you're not being set up. And let me be clear—Johnny isn't the one doing the planning, the scheming. It's Jimenez. He was able to scare Johnny off your original interview, remember?"

"Your sarcasm isn't going to help us." She turned from him and he peripherally saw the glow of her phone screen as she checked for messages. "My father's agreed to lay low until Davison is caught. Thank you for stopping by there again. It's added a lot of time to your driving. Any chance you'd let me spell you?"

"Nope." Her safety was his main, his only, mission. It had been since the day they'd met. Since he'd fallen for her. And now, fallen again.

You never fell out of love with her.

No, he hadn't.

"What's so serious that you're sighing and moping over there?"

"What's not serious, Dominique? You're the target of a major kingpin who kills as easily as he sips his morning coffee. Your family's from Colombia. Didn't your father ever talk about why he left in the first place?"

"When did he tell *you*?"

"We've had our conversations over the past couple of years." Rigo had confessed to getting out of his native country to seek a more stable, safer life in the US. When Rigo and his family left Colombia, it had been torn apart by vying cartels. As he'd described it to Stanton, it had been a literal war zone.

"I'm glad he trusts you, he should. He's always tried to protect Soledad and me from the harsh truth of his childhood. I suppose it's like a family who has a war veteran. We didn't talk about it unless Dad brought it up. Did he tell you that's how he lost his father and brother? Only he, my three uncles and his mother made it out."

"Your father's a man of integrity and he'll do anything for his family. Proof is how much he's paying me."

"That's not even funny."

"Humor's not intended. I'm serious. He promised to pay me double the usual amount." A hefty sum, as Colton Protection's reputation and stalwart record allowed for the high price tags. Stanton received the most of any of the agents not because it was his business but because he had the most experience.

"Dad's always respected you."

"And I him." This was getting uncomfortably close to an intimate conversation. They were going to have a hard enough time keeping themselves detached from each other while in the small but modern cabin for the next two nights.

"I honestly thought he wasn't going to agree to stop walking the dogs in the park. If you hadn't backed me up, I think he'd be there now."

"Rigo's proud, and tough, but he's not stupid." The description gave him pause. Was he proud, tough and not stupid? Had Dominique been attracted to him because he was just like her father?

Dominique laughed. "No, Dad's definitely not unintelligent. You're a lot like him, in fact."

He groaned. "Stop."

"No, not in a bad way. I don't have some kind of daddy issue, if that's what you're thinking. You're not, are you? After all we've been through?"

"I think it's best to not think about anything that involves us, especially now. We've got to come up with how we're going to safely have you interview Johnny, and it has to be timed with law enforcement's takedown of the cartel and Jimenez. Otherwise none of this, your hard work, your wish to get justice for Charlie Hamm, absolutely nothing will have mattered."

"Because I'll be dead."

Over his dead body.

Stanton was quiet for much of the drive, and she kept telling herself it was because he was intent on making certain they hadn't been followed. They were in a car that an agent had brought to her father's when they'd gone to warn him off walking the dogs in public for the foreseeable future. Stanton had insisted that all precautions be taken, including assuming that his vehicle had been made and there was a GPS device hidden on it.

Dominique hadn't admitted it to him yet, but she was a little embarrassed that she hadn't thought of all the ways the cartel could track them. She wasn't a cop, and she appreciated being able to leave those concerns to the experts. But still, she should have had more awareness.

Distraction had warred with her sense of purpose. Her focus on the story was paramount, but ever since her discussion with Soledad at Dad's party, she couldn't shake her sense of failure. She'd neglected to realize what mattered to her most until it was too late. Her career still mattered and writing the truth was definitely her calling. But so was being with the one man who made her heart open, who helped her be the best she could be, even when he was scared witless about her activities.

You blew it.

She had indeed blown it to smithereens, hadn't she?

Running from her deepest emotions, and the one man safe enough to share them with.

"We're almost there." His calm countenance usually soothed her but in light of her epiphany all it elicited was sadness. It was too easy to imagine he'd always be here, at her side. Looking out for her.

"Great." He had to be exhausted with five hours of driving behind him. It was past midnight and now less than twenty-four hours until Johnny would tell them where he was. Stanton had called Troy on the drive, and Troy verified he spoke to several local law enforcement agencies in the north part of the state, and all were on standby until Johnny identified the resort. FBI, DEA and the state troopers were being informed and in turn releasing all information pertaining to the cartel as it occurred.

She couldn't ask for more. But her heart wanted it all.

The last hour they'd passed zero other vehicles as Stanton had exited the highway and taken them through back roads to the secluded family cabin. The road had become barely wide enough for their car, with tree trunks on either side, giving the impression that the forest was swallowing them up.

"Here we are." The cabin seemed to come out of nowhere, and she let out her breath. It had been a while since she'd been here with him. That last time, it had felt like a honeymoon as they'd spent a long autumn weekend alone in the rustic retreat. He shut off the engine and they both turned on the flashlight function of their phones to get out and gather their few bags. Not for the first time, Dominique was grateful for the go bag she kept in her locker at the paper. She'd replenished it a few weeks ago, her sixth sense telling her that she was going to get very busy with the Charlie Hamm story. Of course, she'd had no idea how busy, or how much her life could change in a matter of less than a week.

They trudged through damp leaves to the porch, where Stanton waved for her to put her bags down. "I'll bring them all in." He unlocked the door and let them in, flicked on the lights. The cedar scent of the building instantly brought memories rushing back, including the long nights in front of the now-cold wood-burning stove.

"I'll start a fire." She relished having a task that had nothing to do with the danger that shrouded them.

"Go ahead. Do you remember how to use this?" It was a wood pellet stove and besides being a cleaner burn, was simple to operate.

"I do." Just as she remembered how he'd taught her, and then once satisfied the heat level was where he wanted it, he'd turned to her and taught her about heat levels she'd never experienced with another man.

Stop it.

She filled the stove with the pre-sized briquettes and used the long matches to ignite them. Blue flames licked up the insides of the piping hot walls and she swung the door closed, latched the hinge. The window on the door allowed her to watch the flames take hold of the pellets, and heat began to emanate. Sounds of bags being dropped on the floor, Stanton's steps, the wind through the trees, all melded into background noise as she stared at the flames and tried to be anywhere but in the middle of a life-threatening investigation, having only now figured out that she'd let the one who mattered most get away.

Stanton told himself that he wasn't going to go anywhere near Dominique. They were both exhausted and had no idea what the next two days would have in store. Although he had a sinking feeling that the entire pursuit of her story could go very, very badly if he didn't do his job right.

She sat in front of the fire, cross-legged, as he'd watched her do before. Dominique was good at meditating, at allowing herself to zone out when she needed to. He had a pang of envy as he watched her. Quickly replaced by the burning need to touch her. Hold her.

To make love to her, if only one more time.

He kicked off his shoes and walked toward her, the warmth from the stove already significant. She didn't move as he sat down on the floor beside her.

This is a bad idea.

He was tired of listening to his mind, to that place that still had some integrity left. All he wanted was to be able to show the woman that mattered most to him what it was like to be made love to by the one man who loved her most. No matter the cost, because in truth, tonight was all they had.

She turned to face him and watched him. He was lost in her gaze, their eyes locked together as they'd been since he could remember.

"You know what's funny?" His voice caught, and he didn't think he'd ever felt as vulnerable.

Dominique reached out and ran her fingers on his cheek, smoothed back the hair that had fallen on his forehead. "That we're still awake?" Her tender smile tugged on their connection, the thread that ran through him, right to his center. Her hands grasped his and they intertwined their fingers, all the while never breaking eye contact.

"That, yeah." He cleared his throat. "I was about to say something a little more profound."

Her laughter was pure, without the weight of the past days. "It's just like me to stomp on your seriousness, isn't it? Or to jump in, thinking I already know it all? Go ahead, tell me."

But now he was...nervous? It wasn't a usual feeling for him. "I've been thinking that I can't remember a time when we weren't together."

"Um, what about the last two years?"

"Have we really been apart, though? Sure, we didn't see one another and you avoided me at every event we ran into each other at, but it hasn't broken this." He carried their hands to his heart, and then hers. Her pupils dilated in the amber glow of the woodstove, her lips parted as if she needed more air. If she was like him, her heart was pounding in her ears, too.

"No, it hasn't. We definitely have a connection. But..." She kept looking at him, blinking, her eyes reflecting tears. "What are we going to do about it? What can we do about it? We're not compatible."

"I'd say we've done exceptionally well through...

let's see, an attack—" he hated bringing that up again, worried that the memory triggered the pain she'd already survived "—being shot at twice, and the worst thing of all."

Her brows rose and she leaned in. "What?"

"Fireworks."

Her gasp of surprise turned into a laugh, until the air between them electrified. They were no more than a whisper apart.

"We have done very well." She agreed. But did that mean she'd been having some of the same thoughts he had? "But we've also been under a lot of pressure. I don't know, Stanton. We're a good team, and we work together like lifelong partners. I mean, career-wise."

"And I mean *all*-wise. I made a big mistake when I pushed you on a solid commitment. Love is an action, and you were right there, every night, no matter how far my jobs took me. Those two weeks I was in Syria—"

"Protecting a hellcat actor on the movie shoot from Hades." She grinned. Her voice on the other end of the line after every day, while he'd been guarding the inconsolable diva who'd insisted on partying each night after her shoot, wearing the entire crew out, had been his saving grace.

"I'm sorry I tried to make you agree to something you're not cut out for." He'd been an ass, plain and simple.

"Oh, Stanton, I was awful to you. It's not that I'm not cut out for family. All during my father's party, all I kept seeing was how it would be if we had a child, who would they look like. Would you be holding him or her or would I?"

The last of his restraint broke. "Dominique, I can't promise you anything, not before you get this story. Not until we know all the cartel players are behind bars."

She placed her finger on his lips. "You're not the one who needs to be apologizing, and we're going to get this story and help GGPD get the bad guys."

"I'm glad we had this talk." He grinned, the elation in his chest almost too much to bear. "We both need rest now."

"Not on your life." She placed her hands on his shoulders. "How's your arm?"

"My arm? It's fine. Why?"

"Because we're going to be up for a while, and the way I want you, you're going to need your arm." She closed the inches between their mouths and when her lips touched his, he let himself be the man he was always meant to be. With Dominique.

Relief buoyed the constant desire she had for Stanton as the kiss deepened from a physical seal of their mutual regrets and hopes for the future, to an expression of the searing passion they'd never been able to let go of. His lips molded to hers as his hands held her face like a precious piece of glass art, his fingers reaching to her nape and his thumbs stroking her jawline. Heat rained over her skin, each caress heightened by the warmth from the woodstove. She ran her fingers through his hair, pulled him closer, unable to get close enough.

It'll never be enough.

With Stanton, it was true. She could never get enough. But there was an awful lot of satisfaction between her need and how she knew she'd always want him.

"Babe." He broke from her lips, dragged his mouth down the side of her throat. When his hands slipped under her top, she reached down and lifted it over her head. Stanton unfastened her bra and her breasts were free for his appreciation and her pleasure as he cupped one in each hand, played with her nipples.

"Please, Stanton." She nipped his earlobe, clung to his shoulders as the waves of her desire increased.

"Lie down." He helped her onto her back on the fluffy rug, and she shimmied out of her pants. She went to remove her panties but he beat her to it, slowly taking off the silky pair with excruciating deliberation.

"Babe, now, I can't take this." She sat back up and helped him out of his button-down shirt, eased the sleeves from his arms. Kissing his bandaged upper arm, she noticed bruising that wasn't there yesterday. "Your arm, Stanton…this has to hurt."

"Not as much as I'm going to if we don't make love." He stood and quickly chucked his pants, giving her a beautiful view of his glorious nudity, before he rejoined her on the floor. "We can use the sofa or go to the bedroom."

"This is way more fun. Unless your arm—"

"The heck with my arm." His mouth was on hers again, and the kiss was one she'd always remembered. She savored each and every kiss, tongue stroke, the scent of Stanton as he drove her to the place she only visited with him. Pure freedom from all that ever worried her, freedom to enjoy the delight of being with the one man she loved more than any other. Even his pause to retrieve a condom seemed part of the dance of their sexual reunion, the few seconds just enough for her to position herself to welcome him fully into her.

They joined like the seasoned partners they were, his thrusts met by her hips with vigor and timing that bespoke of how well they knew one another. Just as she thought she'd never be able to relieve the insistent heat and tension that he caused, she broke apart and he shuddered with a force she could only attribute to love. Nothing less. No one else, only Stanton.

Chapter 14

Dominique woke in the cabin's main bedroom under piles of quilts the next morning. The warmth that had allowed her to slumber so peacefully was gone. She reached her hand across the bed, under the sheets, to confirm what she knew—Stanton had left. The numbers on her phone told her it was almost seven. Two hours later than she usually rose. Sitting up, she stretched and yawned before padding to the window. The first glow of sunrise hit the surrounding woods, and she thought it would be nice to allow this image to stoke the hope in her heart.

Her body was pleasantly sore, and she grabbed her clothes, neatly folded on the nightstand, conveniently next to a small handgun that she knew wasn't there by accident. Stanton's work. She never worried about how she stored her clothes when she was camping or here in the cabin, and weapons weren't something she bothered with. Except Stanton had insisted she learn how to fire a weapon and they'd gone to a firing range when they'd dated. The last time they'd been out here in these woods, they'd done target practice with his family's shotguns. She acknowledged for the millionth time that Stanton never stopped doing his job. He was protecting her, even as he folded and neatly stacked the outfit she'd pulled out of her overnight bag and flung over the wooden rocker at the foot of the bed last night. The room had touches of Italia Colton everywhere, from the brightly hued quilts and bedding, to the fluffy towels in the comfortable bathroom, larger than normal for a cabin. Even though it had been years, this log house felt like a familiar pair of socks to her. Warm, supportive, secure.

A gunshot sounded and fear threw cold reality over her post-sex reverie.

"Stanton?" She shouted for him as she grabbed the weapon and scrambled to throw on her clothes. The shower would wait. Her hands shook as she pulled on her underwear and pants.

"Get down!" His voice thundered from the outer room and she complied, making certain she was out of view from the two windows in the room. "Stay away from the windows and take the revolver from the nightstand."

"I am!" Didn't he realize he'd taught her well? Her shirt on, she shoved into a thick sweater and pulled jeans over her leggings. If she had to run outside, she'd have to do it without her coat, still in the car.

More shots sounded, followed by deep voices. She froze in place, wondering if this was about to be her last minutes on earth. When she heard the front door open, she cried out and crawled forward. No way was she going to allow Stanton to launch himself into a gunfight against the cartel without her help.

Once at the bedroom's threshold, she stood and ran into the living room. The sight of Stanton in the cabin's front doorframe gave her momentary relief. He was still alive. But he wouldn't be for long if he stayed where he was, so vulnerable to any shot.

She trembled in place as he spoke to their killers.

"Yeah, we're here for a quick getaway. My girlfriend and I needed out of the city, ya know?" His voice was remarkably steady.

"Sorry to bother you, man. We were tracking a buck but scared him off." A deeper, gruff voice. It sounded sincere, but how could they know who this was?

"There's no hunting on private property. This stretches all the way down to the public grounds."

"Yeah, we didn't see the signs until we were up on your cabin. It won't happen again."

"Thanks."

She allowed herself to catch her breath, all the while poised to step up and fire at anyone who threatened Stanton. But it sounded like hunters who'd gotten lost. It could be a ruse by the cartel, but she immediately dismissed it. If they were found here, criminals would shoot first, come up with excuses later.

The searing pain in her chest took a bit to figure out. It was her heart, anticipating how she'd feel if anything ever happened to Stanton. Hoping against hope that he'd not get killed while standing out there, guarding her. How had she ever thought she could be with a man who faced life and death every day?

After what felt like hours, Stanton came back into the cabin.

His face, drawn and pale, made her already racing pulse stop in its tracks, before ramping up again. Maybe she'd been wrong to assume the interlopers weren't dangerous.

"What?"

"It was a man and his teenage daughter, hunting. He's teaching her how to track prey."

"Do you believe them?" She didn't think a father-and-daughter pair fit the description of cartel hit men, but anything was possible.

He closed his eyes, his way of giving himself space to think. When he opened them, their brightness was startling against the backdrop of the log walls. "Yes. I told them that they needed to keep their hunting to public lands. Our property backs up to state grounds, so it's an innocent enough mistake. They're not the first hunters or hikers to make it."

"But usually you don't have the worry of assassins stalking you." She went to him and wrapped her arms around his waist. "I'm so sorry you've been drawn into this."

"I haven't been drawn into anything. This was my choice, to take this particular job, remember?" He hugged her back, but then gently let go. She followed suit, unable to figure out where his heart was at. "We need to figure out our plan of attack. The midnight phone call is going to leave us with enough time to get in place, but only if we have several ways we want to work it lined up."

So that was that. Stanton wanted to focus on why they were here in the first place, and it was a harsh reminder that he wasn't here to work on their relationship.

Neither are you.

No, she was here to get the story. Clear Charlie's name. Maybe help out Johnny Blanchard if she could, if he was able to help law enforcement pinpoint Jimenez's location. It was the absolute pits that she'd figured out, too late, that she and Stanton might have been able to make a go of it. She'd had her chance to tell him how she really felt, her regrets included. The heat of their passion last night wasn't the right time, and it appeared that he thought she'd been clearing the air for them to have another round of lovemaking. It was time to accept that she'd messed up, and let it go. Before the distraction got them both killed.

"Look, Stanton, I'm sending Troy up there along with two other officers, and I think I can get the DEA to cough up one or two agents. But there aren't any guarantees. Isn't there some way you can convince Dominique that she's got as much as she's going to get for her story? She's got the solid facts now about Bowe's involvement and how the evidence against

Charlie was planted. I can't overlook that this Johnny Blanchard meetup appears to be a big setup." Stanton listened to his sister via wireless earbuds as he paced the cabin's front porch, using his binoculars to continually scan the woods for any suspicious movement. Dominique remained inside, working on the information she'd already collected, culling it into salient prose. She never mentioned it, but he had to wonder how much of the pressure she put on herself was from her editor at the *Gazette*. It angered him that her boss might encourage her to risk her life for an article, no matter how important.

What really upset him, though, was that he'd not been able to figure out a way to convince her that she needed to call off the meetup with Johnny Blanchard. He'd already lied under oath on a witness stand. Why would she ever trust a perjurer?

"You know her, Melissa. I hate to say it, but she's just like you. Once she's made her mind up, she's going to follow through. And she actually had a good point, about whether the meeting with Blanchard is for real or not. This is an awfully complicated ruse for a setup. The cartels like to keep it simple. A more straightforward manner would have been to threaten Dominique's family if she didn't lay off the Charlie Hamm lead."

"Well, they did threaten her, and tried to kill her, three times. But you're right—this cartel in particular is noted for its brutality. Luring a reporter who's writing a story about an already dead prisoner and reformed drug dealer isn't something I'd expect from Jimenez."

"So you admit there's at least a chance it's not a setup?" He rested his binoculars on his chest, where his heart remained steady only because of years of training and surveillance experience.

"The chance that it's legit isn't great enough to keep me from sending backup." Her frustration plucked at his conscience. His sister worked harder now than he ever had, and she wore the town's safety around her neck without complaint. "There's always the long shot that Jimenez will show, and we'll nab him. That would solve a lot of problems for Grave Gulch. I found the clothing items you asked for, by the way, and I'll have an officer drop them before you and Dominique leave the cabin for wherever the meetup ends up being. Once we know where and which resort, the logistics will be a little easier."

"Thanks for doing this for me." The depth of his gratitude surprised him, until he remembered his true motive. He knew he couldn't live without Dominique. The last two years had been filled with an awful lot of desolation without her. Three near misses in as many days had brought him to his mental and emotional knees. He surrendered. The only way out of this was to keep them both alive to hopefully work things out after Dominique got her story.

"It's not for you, Stanton, even though I don't like the idea of you being involved in this one bit. It's for our native city, and for future generations. If we don't care enough to clean it up, then who?"

Melissa disconnected and he was left alone in the warming air with what he'd been trying to ignore all day. There wasn't going to be a reprieve; the meeting with Blanchard was going down, and whether or not it was a setup, he had to prepare as if it was.

He'd done some research of his own on all of the event venues in the area and narrowed it to two possibilities. Both were hosting weddings this weekend, two per day. It was unlikely Blanchard would use his real name when he was supposedly on the run from the cartel, but Stanton had inquired, to be thorough. No Blanchard on either resort's payroll. But he'd gained some intel that would reassure him that Dominique was being as safe as she could be, in case the cartel had found her. No doubt the cartel had both her and Stanton's profiles memorized, was on the lookout for them. They'd be identified the minute they stepped out of their vehicle at whichever resort.

Unless he and Dominique didn't look like themselves. He had a solid idea, and Melissa seemed to support it. First he had to convince her of his plan.

Johnny Blanchard's hand shook as he dialed the number on his cell phone. His nerves were shot. Maybe with the extra bucks he'd get for helping the cartel land the reporter chick he'd get himself a small place up here, far away from Jimenez.

The connection happened faster than he expected and he almost dropped his cigarette.

"Why didn't you call sooner? Did they take the bait?" It wasn't Leo, the thug Johnny usually dealt with. It was Jimenez himself on the line, his voice reaching through the phone, as if by sheer force of will he could crush Johnny with his words.

"Yes, yes, jefe, no worries. Hook, line and sinker, I'm telling you." He puffed on his cigarette as he stood on the concrete platform outside the resort's kitchen. "They'll be here exactly when I tell them to. And your niece's wedding will go off without a hitch later this afternoon, too." He knew it had better or he'd be fish bait at the bottom of the lake that the resort so magnificently overlooked.

"I want them at the bottom of the lake before my niece ever says 'I do.'"

"No problem. I'm telling them to show up in the middle of the first wedding, to give the cover of the crowd. Three hundred people will be admiring the grounds and the wedding couple. The last people they'll notice are me and the reporter."

"Don't forget her bodyguard."

"You said Leo will take him out first."

"Leo's not coming. He ran into a snag."

Johnny's blood ran cold and he fought to keep from hyperventilating. *Snag* was Pablo Jimenez's pet word for *dead*. As in, he'd had Leo killed. Or offed him on his own. *Oh, crap.* Not Leo. Leo was Jimenez's longest-running employee. If he'd been killed by the kingpin, no one was safe. Including a weasel who'd lied on the stand. Maybe he could run now, get away before the darn reporter and her bodyguard showed up.

"Don't think about it, Blanchard. I've got eyes on you twenty-four seven. You'll never survive if you try to run. After we take care of the reporter and her boy toy, there's a big promotion for you." Jimenez was practically psychic, with the resources he had. Johnny looked around at where the building's roof began, searching for security cameras.

"Yes, sir. I'm your man."

"You'd better be. Or you'll be nobody's anything."

After Jimenez disconnected, Johnny couldn't stop his mind from racing, his pulse from hammering, his breath from getting so shallow he sank down on his haunches and began to tug at his hair.

He saw Jimenez's plan so clearly now. He wasn't only going to have de la Vega and her bodyguard killed, he was going to make a three-for-one deal. Johnny knew he was in Jimenez's crosshairs, too.

"You have got to be kidding. I think the lack of sleep is getting to you." Dominique stood up from the kitchen table where she'd been working on her laptop and began pacing in the small kitchen. It was past one in the morning. Blanchard had called and unwittingly verified one of the two resorts Stanton had already figured it was. And now he was asking her to think of going to the interview in some kind of disguise, just in case it was a setup. "I've never had to pretend I'm anyone but me. It's bordering on unethical, since I already have the interview set and Johnny Blanchard's counting on me to show up, at whatever time he gives me."

"He's not going to dictate our arrival time. That would be insanity." Stanton was at his breaking point with her, she could tell from the hard glint in his eyes. He'd agreed to support her through the end, to get the story, but he wasn't going to budge on any of his safety precautions.

"I know you're right, but let me get my head wrapped around this. I suppose it would be okay to try to not look like my usual self. Are you thinking wigs, different kinds of clothing? Or maybe we can look like we're hikers who wander in to use the facilities? That's not so uncommon." She'd used various restrooms as needed when she'd hiked along the lake's edge.

"I'm thinking we should fit in with the kind of event they're staging. A wedding."

"Oh, so you're saying show up as if we're guests of the bride and groom. Crash either, or both, of the weddings." She nodded. "Yeah, I can do that. That makes sense."

"Not guests."

"Not guests?" Puzzlement and the late hour reflected in her impatient tone.

A knock at the door had them both freeze in place, until Stanton remembered Melissa's promise. "It's okay. It's an officer Melissa sent." He went to the door, and after verifying who it was, opened it. A man in civilian clothes with silvering temples walked in, and looked at them one at a time. "Ms. de la Vega, I'm Brett Shea. My K-9 partner, Ember, is in my vehicle. You may remember me from that story you did on the opioid crisis a couple of years back."

"Of course I remember you. Please call me Dominique, Detective Shea."

"And call me Brett." He nodded at her before he turned back to Stanton. "Here's what you asked for."

He handed a large, hanging garment bag to Stanton, and an even larger hanging bag to Dominique. She grasped the bag and gasped.

"What kind of clothing weighs this much?" She looked at Stanton, then Brett.

"A wedding dress," Stanton answered. "It's the best way for us to go in without question, without drawing attention to you."

"That makes no sense. The bride always gets all of the attention at a wedding."

"Yes, but it's not what Jimenez will be expecting. They'll assume we're coming either dressed as guests or waitstaff. We found out the timing of the two weddings and if we arrive just ahead of the second wedding party, it'll be assumed we're the next couple getting hitched." His gaze was unwavering and she'd no doubt he'd gone over all of the different scenarios in his head, and had picked what he thought was best. She trusted Stanton's security instincts, as she knew he trusted her reporter's hunches.

But a wedding gown?

Dominique's gut twisted, but it wasn't over dressing as a make-believe bride to get to the last yet most important interview for her story. It was from the painful stab of disappointment that it wasn't a real dress—her dress, for pledging to love for the rest of her life the man looking at her with complete confidence.

Dominique sat next to Stanton in the back seat of Colton Protection's largest SUV as they rode to the wedding venue. Detective Brett Shea was dressed in a black suit and drove, to give a more realistic impression that they were a genuine bride and groom, driven by a professional chauffeur. Brett's K-9 partner Ember sat in the cargo area of the vehicle, her black Lab features appearing calm and sweet, but Dominique knew the dog would help take down any criminal she was instructed to. She was so grateful for Melissa's support and made a mental note to take the GGPD chief out for a nice dinner when this all settled down.

Please, let it settle down. Because the alternative was unthinkable. But also too real, too close, to ignore. She and Stanton might not come out of today alive.

She couldn't look at Stanton, because all it did was send her stomach into flips, ratcheting the anxiety that she was already working overtime to tamp down. Stanton wore a tuxedo as well as he wore his custom suits; he swore they helped him do his job better because they allowed for more physical movement as needed. It was as if she'd conjured this event in some twisted way, when she'd admitted to Soledad that she'd been thinking more about what it would be like to be with Stanton forever. To marry him, be his wife. Have their babies, little mini Stantons.

Wearing the frothy white dress, which fit her remarkably well for a borrowed item out of one of the GGPD officer's closets, must have triggered some kind of subconscious thought stream of ridiculousness. Thinking about being with Stanton forever was one thing, but to picture that their children would be exactly like him, or her, was beyond a dream. It was a certain definition of insanity.

His hand covered hers and he squeezed. "It's going to work out, Dom. Trust me."

Unable to not look at him any longer, she took him in. He was still outrageously handsome, the crisp white shirt and black tie complementing his skin and the purposeful scruff at his jaw. His eyes sparkled with focus.

"I do trust you. It's myself I'm worried about. What if we can't find Blanchard?" The plan was to corner the lying witness while he worked this afternoon, during the preparations for the second ceremony. Blanchard had insisted they arrive at four o'clock, in between the two weddings and a full two hours before the second ceremony was scheduled. He'd told them to meet him near the pier that stretched out into Lake Michigan. Because the resort was in a cove of sorts, it didn't have the concerns of rough waters that other buildings that hugged the shoreline did. Instead, they were going to corner him in the resort's commercial kitchen.

"You'll do what you need to. And don't hesitate to use your weapon." His reminder of the handgun holstered to her thigh in lieu of the traditional garter made her smile.

"We've never done anything the easy way, have we?" She couldn't help but grin and was delighted when he smiled back.

"No. No, we don't." He squeezed her hand again and then let go, turning his gaze to his window. "How far out are we, Brett?"

"Another ten minutes."

It was time for them to focus on their plan of action.

* * *

The first wedding party was nowhere in sight when they pulled in front of the employee entrance. The DEA agent working with them today was already inside the venue, posing as a photographer, taking pre-event shots. The same agent had ascertained that a man matching the description of Johnny Blanchard was indeed working as a dishwasher in the large commercial kitchen. As of now, there was no hint of other cartel members on the premises. No dark figures skulking about, no whisper of drugs available for a good price.

"We can wait here as long as you need us to, Stanton." Brett turned to look at each of them. "Dominique, I hope like heck you get the truth out of this lying scumbag. We've all been following your reports back at GGPD, and while I have to say I wasn't thrilled when you first exposed the corruption going on in our lab with Randall Bowe, I'm positive we're on the same side. Whatever you two need, I'm here."

"Thank you. That means a lot." Dominique fought back tears. It was one thing for Melissa, who knew her well, to support her efforts, but for a seasoned veteran like Brett to back her spoke volumes.

"Now, go get him."

Chapter 15

Only after they were certain no one would see them entering this back way did they leave the safety of the SUV. They walked into the resort's back entrance holding hands, each rolling a small suitcase provided by GGPD to help with their disguise. It was all about appearing like the about-to-be-married couple that they weren't. Stanton was humbled by the grasp of Dominique's hand in his. *"I trust you."* It weighed heavy, the gift of her complete confidence. And he vowed to meet it, to get them out of here alive.

Stanton had gone over every inch of the plan that Melissa gave him to follow, including the intel they were being fed from the DEA as their assigned agent, David Gonzalez, uncovered more about Johnny Blanchard and Pablo Jimenez. There were zero indications that any of the cartel were present at the resort yet, with the only guests confirmed present with the first wedding party. The second wedding's party and guests would begin arriving in an hour, as per usual resort protocol.

He hadn't worked as long as he had in the security industry to ignore the one thing his most influential trainer had told him. *Always trust your gut, and don't give up until you figure out the source of your unease.* Something was bothering him and it began with Blanchard's insistence on speaking to Dominique on the resort's pier. He'd checked out photos of the long wooden structure and it didn't look like an obvious choice for what was supposed to be a private meeting.

Go over your checklist.

His professional routine tried to take over but he couldn't stop staring at Dominique in the wedding gown. It was nothing like her taste. He'd always imagined she'd wear a very simple dress, if they ever took vows. Her figure was all the decoration any outfit worn by her needed. And though this wasn't her style, the over-the-top, celebratory design showcased her beauty. And his secret desire that one day, she'd really be his bride. Or maybe it wasn't such a secret, after all he'd revealed it to her last night. The dress belonged to one of the officers who'd married in the last year; she'd gotten divorced six months ago and told Melissa that she was happy to see it used for a "better cause." He'd grinned when Melissa texted him that tidbit, and passed it on to Dominique in an effort to lighten the energy flowing between them in the cabin as they worked and prepared. Dominique hadn't done more than offer a shadow of her usual smile, preoccupied by their plans.

"Stop looking at me." She hissed out of the side of her mouth as they made their way down a corridor, past employee locker rooms, and wound up in front of the catering kitchen. Thank goodness for the DEA agent who'd emailed and texted the resort's floor plan, complete with all of the employee offices. He'd tracked Blanchard to the kitchen, and the plan was to walk through the large space together, acting as if they wanted to see their cake early. It was confirmed that cakes had already been delivered for both weddings, so it wouldn't seem that unusual.

"I can't help it. You're so…foamy." He swallowed a chuckle.

She tugged the yards of a veil to the side, showing her annoyance with the overdone dress, and frowned. "The word is *frothy*, and dang it, I just got my lipstick on the veil." A large smear of crimson stood out among the sea of pearl white netting.

"Good thing it's a loaner, and the previous wearer doesn't care what happens to it." Warmth struck in his chest, and if it wouldn't be a risk to her life, he'd suggest they disappear into an empty space and enjoy a bridal kiss or two.

"Stanton, there's so much I want to say." Tears reflected in her eyes, and the heat in his chest bloomed into all-on protective mode.

"We'll talk later, after you get the rest of your story." He tugged on her hands, willing her to stay steady, focused on the plan. He used his finger to catch the tear running down her cheek. Keeping her alive was all that mattered. They could sort anything else out later, couldn't they?

She nodded, sniffed, swiped at her eyes. "Of course." Her chin jutted out and she let go of his hands. "Yes, let's get on with it."

"Do you have your phone on its record setting?"

"Yes, and—" she pressed the screen "—we're connected, right?"

His phone vibrated with her call and he answered it, leaving the line open. "Yes."

"Are your earbuds in?" She was teasing because he hadn't suited up his audio yet. He retrieved them from his trouser pocket, also checking to see that his weapon was holstered. He set the tiny speakers in place.

"They are now. Ready?"

"Ready."

She began to turn toward the kitchen entry but he couldn't let her go in yet. His arms reached out and he looked up and down the corridor to verify they were safe before he planted a searing kiss on her lips. If anyone did see them, they'd assume it was wedding-day magic.

Her lips were so soft, her tongue, her body willing as she clung to him. He forced himself to pull away before they got lost in the moment, lost in each other, lost in the bond they'd have no matter what the future held for them.

"You've got this, Dom."

"Thanks."

A quick wink was her parting gesture before she

disappeared into the kitchen and he began the hardest part of the entire plan: the waiting.

The kitchen's high noise level startled Dominique after the quiet of the corridor. The doors she'd entered through must have some kind of noise buffering. Pots and pans clanged and voices rose over the cacophony as a woman she assumed was the head chef issued rapid-fire directions to her sous-chef and other workers. They were at the far end of the large space, underneath a humongous rack of cookware, and hadn't noticed her yet. Scents of sautéing vegetables and butter hung heavy, and like the decibels, the temperature of the room was higher than in the corridor, making her perspire as if it was a summer day and not early spring in Northern Michigan.

Several other workers were scattered at various workstations, including two women who were fussing over the wedding cake, adding last-minute decorations. Blanchard was reportedly the dishwasher, and she saw one man working at the large stainless steel machine, pulling out clean dishes and stacking them on serving carts, then pushing the carts into a precise line closer to the long, spotless island where all manners of chopping, tossing and mixing were going on.

She sucked in a deep breath and headed for him. Her phone felt heavy in the pocket she'd cut a hole in and wired the microphone through. The device was taped inside the dress's bodice. Since it was white, it was practically invisible against the padded fabric. As she approached the dishwasher, the man she hoped was Blanchard, the noise quieted a bit, urging her to move faster. The last thing she wanted was the full attention of everyone present—Blanchard would never talk to her then.

"Excuse me, are you Johnny Blanchard?"

The man twisted so quickly to face her that he dropped the stack of white porcelain plates he'd been holding. As the sounds of ceramic crashing against the hard, tiled floor echoed around them, he stared at Dominique with eyes widened in shock. His skin visibly paled as his lips trembled.

"Who are you?" His voice shook.

"Mr. Blanchard?" She needed him to verify before she continued.

He looked away toward the chef's table, and gave a quick wave. "Sorry, I'll get it cleaned up. No worries, we have lots more dishes."

"Johnny?" She was sure this was her man, as his unique voice matched the phone calls.

"Yes, it's me. Johnny Blanchard. Who are you?"

"Dominique de la Vega. *Grave Gulch Gazette.*" She added the last in case she'd scared his memory away.

She shrugged, looking down at the wedding dress. "I'm sorry for the surprise but I had to make sure this wasn't a setup."

"Sure, I get it, but I can't break away right now." He walked over to where a broom and dustpan hung on a far wall and brought it back. "And now I have this mess to clean up."

She wasn't going to apologize for his skittishness. "We can do the interview right here as you work, if that's okay with you. Everyone here will think I'm the bride, checking in on things, right? Why don't you take me over to the cake after you're done sweeping? Pretend to help me get a peek at it."

"I think it's best we don't talk right here." He was so shaky as he swept up the broken dishes that her hackles went up.

"Why is that?"

"I'm due for a break now, anyway. We can go for a smoke and I'll tell you all you want to know."

"Mind if I wait here with you?"

"I guess not." His frown contradicted the words but she knew that she had to keep pressing him. She'd lost interviews before because of nervous sources who'd changed their minds at the last minute. The stakes were too high to lose Johnny Blanchard, now that they had him. "You're welcome to go wait for me on the loading platform. Door's over there. But I can't tell you anything, not anymore. If you're smart, you'll get out of here." He pointed to the exit.

"You can tell me everything I need to know now. Did you lie on the witness stand for the Jimenez cartel? Did Pablo Jimenez pay you to perjure yourself?"

He stared at her with wild-looking eyes for a solid second before his gaze scuttled away.

"Not here. Outside."

She and Stanton had anticipated this, and she knew she'd be safe on the platform as the DEA agent was nearby. Troy and the other officers had also surrounded the resort at critical points. Stanton would hear this exchange and have everyone move to the best vantage. But he'd told her to always give it five minutes whenever she could, to ensure the agents and officers were in place.

"Okay, I'll go out there, but since I don't have a coat, please hurry. We'll have to make the interview a quick one." Hopefully this would encourage him to spill it all. Less time to consider his words.

"Go ahead, I'll be right there." He nodded at the door as he carried a dustpan full of porcelain pieces to a large trash receptacle.

She stepped around the remaining mess and smiled at the gawking cooks and cake decorators as she made her best attempt at being the happy, about-to-be-married bride. It was surprisingly easy, acting the part.

Because you know it's not all an act.

Yeah, she wished it was really happening for her. With Stanton. And as soon as this was behind them, they'd talk. He'd said it, and she wanted to.

As she stepped outside, the early spring wind hit her skin first, followed by the scent of Lake Michigan. The pale blue sky made the water appear like a sapphire, broken only by white caps frothed up by the high winds. Her voluminous skirt felt like a scrap of fabric for all the protection it offered against the weather. She ignored her shivers and spoke aloud, knowing Stanton could hear her and would relay all to the others.

"I'm on the loading dock platform. The dishwasher confirmed he's Johnny Blanchard and he looks just like the witness sketches the newspaper printed during Charlie Hamm's trial and he has the same voice as the man I've spoken to in numerous phone calls. I believe it's him. I identified myself to Blanchard. He has a smoke break coming up and agreed to speak to me then. All that banging and crashing you may have heard—I surprised the heck out of him and he dropped several dishes that he was moving. So far no one's questioned me as to my identity." She scanned the surrounding grounds, from the parking area to the rocky beach to the water, but saw no agents or officers. It wasn't a reason for concern; they were all trained to blend in. Still, it would have been nice to see a familiar face.

And then she did. She spotted Stanton's unmistakable profile near a grove of trees to the right of the resort. It gave him a perfect line of sight to her. Confidence buoyed her and she turned when she heard the door swing open, ready to get this last crucial interview over. To get what she'd fought for over the last year. Justice for Charlie Hamm.

Johnny Blanchard walked out but wouldn't make eye contact with her. Her nape hairs rose, and the shudder that racked her body had zero to do with the outside temperature. Following behind Blanchard was a shorter man in a tuxedo. She wanted to believe it was a legit member of the wedding party, but the man's face was stamped with determination and…satisfaction.

Charlie stepped to one side and the man approached her, closing the distance in three steps. But not before she saw the knife blade in his hand.

"Finally we meet, Dominique de la Vega. Allow me to introduce myself. I'm Pablo Jimenez. I believe you've been upset with how I conduct my business?"

He smiled broadly, his teeth accentuating his dark looks, but the smile wasn't jovial. It was the leer of imminent death.

Never had Dominique regretted not telling Stanton she still loved him more.

Stanton knew the figure on the cement platform with Dominique and Blanchard a split second before he spoke, because he matched the physical descriptions of the kingpin. He saw the flash of metal, knew that the bastard had chosen now, this resort so far removed from Grave Gulch, to make his appearance. To prove his point that no one was out of his reach.

"The man identifies himself as Pablo Jimenez, and he is holding a weapon to her midsection, a knife blade approximately six inches long." As he fed the other agents the information, he fought to stay in the moment, to ignore the existential, psychic pain ripping through him. He'd made a huge mistake by not staying in the corridor, but he'd wanted to be in place as soon as he'd heard she was going outside. If he'd come through the kitchen he would have seen Jimenez and stopped him before he ever stepped on that platform.

"I can't get a clear shot of him or Blanchard, not without risking hitting Dominique." Troy's grim assessment enraged Stanton. "Neither can David." Troy was working closely with the DEA agent, too.

"Someone has to be able to take them down. This guy's unstable. He could drive that blade in at any point."

"If Jimenez wanted her dead, he'd have already

stabbed her." David's voice was calm, controlled. Because *he* wasn't in love with the woman dressed in a bridal gown. "Let it play out. He's making sure there aren't any law enforcement agents in the area. He thinks we'll react right away."

David was right: Stanton knew it in his bones. But as he watched Dominique, clearly agitated, arguing with Jimenez, he couldn't help but see everything that ever mattered to him being snatched away.

Dominique.

Why hadn't he told Dominique that he still loved her, that he wasn't going to take no for an answer this time? That he'd live with her, they didn't have to get married, it could be on her terms? Why had he been so obtuse?

Steady is as steady does. He had to rein in his emotions or he'd lose her…forever.

"If you try to make a move or give me any reason to think that you're here with anyone but that stupid bodyguard who I see is near that tree over there, I'm going to slice out your heart and hand it to your father. Wrapped in a copy of the *Grave Gulch Gazette*, of course."

Dominique stared at the man whose criminal machinations had cost so many lives, and the one she was here to avenge, Charlie Hamm's. Johnny Blanchard was standing next to her in silence like the spineless, lying jerk that he was. And she knew Blanchard wasn't her threat. Jimenez held all the power, total control, over whether she lived or died.

"You're a backstabbing, evil little snake." She spat at Johnny Blanchard, who remained in place in such a resolute manner she was certain it was to block any attempt at a shot to his or Jimenez's head.

"You're like all the rest. You don't understand who's running the show." Blanchard snarled at her, his rotting teeth revealing he wasn't only a lying witness but probably one of Jimenez's users. Johnny's newfound confidence sickened her.

"Do you understand what he's telling you, Dominique? I have all the power. Whether you live or die. Understand?" Jimenez said her name as if they'd known each other for a lifetime. She hated it, hated all he stood for.

"I do." Teeth clenched against her shudders, she refused to engage him further.

"You must understand that it's hard for me to trust people at their word these days. If you are lying, or do anything I don't tell you to, I'm going to have your bodyguard's head blown off. I have dozens of my men surrounding this hotel. There's no way out. You must come with me."

She mentally heard Stanton's voice screaming at her to not go anywhere, not with Blanchard or Jimenez or anyone. But Jimenez threatened Stanton's life, leaving her no choice. Plus, the tip of his knife was pressing against her ribs through the bodice. The way Jimenez was leaning into her, she'd be surprised if her skin hadn't been pierced. At least she wasn't feeling anything deeper.

"Where are we going?" She spoke for the mic. Stan-

ton and the others would be able to at least follow them.
Maybe, if they were lucky, someone would get there
ahead of them.

"Oh, I can't say, sweetheart. How do I know you're
not wired?" He viciously pulled at her bodice, yanking her up onto her tiptoes as peered down inside at
her bare skin, her breasts. She held her breath. If he
saw the mic on the underside—

"Nice view, *querida*, but better for you that you're
not mic'ed up." He pressed her bodice back against her
chest, hard, knocking her backward a few steps before
Jimenez grabbed her and pulled her back to standing.
She glared at him as the imprint of his hand made her
want to scream, to kick, to rage. Amazing how a small
piece of stainless steel aimed at her liver could keep
her from acting.

"I'm the one you want. Leave the rest out." She
didn't want to draw attention to Stanton, not knowing
how much Jimenez knew.

The slap came hard, across her mouth. She tasted
blood.

"No one tells me what to do." He motioned at
Blanchard. "Frisk her. Now!"

She endured the humiliation of being felt up her
front by the slimy man.

"Not her top, you fool. Her legs. Make sure she
doesn't have a weapon." Jimenez's forehead shone with
perspiration, his tone impatient. Great. Not only was she
facing a psychopathic drug kingpin, but he was getting
annoyed by his minion. Blanchard's calloused, dirty
fingers scaled her legs under the billowing skirt, and

she held her breath as he found the holster and retrieved the handgun with a satisfied smirk. She fought to not give one back to both of them, as Blanchard hadn't noticed the phone in the concealed pocket. Probably didn't realize such a fancy dress could have pockets.

A car moved in her peripheral vision and Jimenez turned her around to face forward. A black SUV with blacked-out windows stopped at the bottom of the platform's stairs.

"Get in the car." He pressed the knife into the crucial space above the small of her back, right over her kidneys. The man had a thing for vital organs.

Every instinct warred with what she had to do if she was to have a chance to keep Stanton alive. Getting in the vehicle was all but a warrant for her death, but she couldn't risk Stanton's life, too. Getting into Jimenez's SUV was her only choice. She had complete faith that Stanton would use every available resource to save her.

As she was stuffed into the back of the SUV's hatchback, she felt the weight of the phone on her thigh and risked a look back to where Stanton had been. One last connection to help her through.

He was gone.

Stanton was on his last shred of sanity. His only reprieve was the fact that both Troy and David had vehicles and were following Jimenez's. The DEA agent was lagging behind because he'd been positioned inside, and Stanton had to wait for Troy to run out of where he'd hidden and get his car. The other officers were scrambling to follow, and they all relied on Dominique's phone's information. The SUV she'd been taken in was out of sight, through the copse of trees that lined portions of the property. It felt like years when Troy pulled up to where Stanton had concealed himself. He jumped into the passenger seat. Troy floored it before Stanton got the door closed.

"We can't lose her." He watched the map on his phone. He and Dominique had synced GPS systems. She was a blinking dot about a mile away on the drive that circumvented the resort. "Stay on this road. He's a mile ahead of us, driving around the grounds on the access road. What the hell is he doing?"

"We're good. You've still got comms with her, right?" Troy expertly drove at top speed along the graveled path.

"She still has her phone but can't talk or they'll know. Wait…she's texting!" He stared at the jumping dots, willing words to form.

Locked in back of car. Blacked out back here. Impossible to see where I'm going or what they're doing. Partition between me and them. Heard gunshot. Think he killed Blanchard.

Exultation urged him to not give up, to keep the belief they'd get through this. That somehow he'd help her, because he sure hadn't done her any favors by not being in the kitchen when she'd needed him.

Are you okay? He'd seen the blade dip into her dress and prayed it hadn't broken her skin or worse.

I'm good. I lo—

Her text cut off and he switched to the map. "They've stopped. They're at the resort's beach—here, turn right—and the location looks like, like…" His heart stopped for several beats, and he struggled to breathe. He didn't want any of his organs to work, not if what he was seeing was true. The pulsing red dot indicated that Jimenez had driven onto the resort's infamous pier, used for romantic wedding shots.

"What is it?" Troy's professional edge cut through Stanton's fear.

"It looks like she's in the middle of the lake. In the water." Alone with Pablo Jimenez. The man who'd put a hit out on her was going to make good on the threat himself.

Dominique felt the car stop. She prepared for the back hatch to open. She was on her back, her legs poised. When it lifted, she waited for Jimenez to move. When his hands reached forward under the hatch she reared into a back arch and kicked at him with all her might. One of her feet landed in his face but his surprised grunt of pain held no satisfaction for her, not as long as she had to fight for her life. She hadn't been able to finish the text to Stanton, because the car had stopped and she wasn't about to let Jimenez haul her out like a sack of potatoes.

Using his momentary confusion, she slid out and righted herself, and ran for her life. One step, two, three—

She came to a dead halt as something stopped her midstride, so violently she fell flat down, her hands catching her. Splinters dug into her palms as she realized he'd stepped on the long skirt, trapping her. The dock was under her hands, her knees, water surging around in the bay that the venue used for photo ops. Was this how it was going to end for her? Gutted and tossed off the pier?

Two boots were on either side of her as the kingpin crouched over her. She was on her stomach, on her elbows. She could buck up, try to hit him in the privates with her head—

"Turn. Over." The cold steel of a different weapon— a gun—at her temple. And he still had that knife, because he flashed it in front of her eyes. "Now!" he growled and she slowly, methodically, got to all fours, trying to figure out how to get on her feet. She could dive off the pier, hope his aim was awful and that she'd be pulled out of the icy depths in time. The sounds of slamming doors reached her and she knew that at least she wasn't alone. But she never wanted Stanton to witness her death at the hands of this cruel, sick man. As she attempted to stand, though, her hair was painfully pulled as Jimenez flipped her over onto her back. She was vulnerable, staring up at him.

Astride her, Jimenez leaned in and she felt his breath on her face. He had a weapon pointed between her eyes and a knife at her rib cage, and in a moment of horrifying clarity she understood what he was doing. If Stanton or the other officers shot at him, he'd collapse atop her, stabbing her to death, even if he didn't fire a bullet in her brain before he gasped his last.

"If you're going to kill me, at least tell me why you did it."

"Why does anyone do anything? Grave Gulch is mine, my area. Charlie Hamm was like all the other dealers who got a case of the guilts over what they'd done. So he tried to turn my best dealers around. That was his first mistake. He should have shut up and been glad he'd only gotten years."

"So you paid Blanchard to lie on the stand about Hamm?"

"Of course I did."

"Where's Blanchard now?"

"I didn't find him useful any longer. Much like you." The barrel pressed deeper in her skull and she knew he wouldn't be able to crouch like this forever.

"You'll never get away with it. You're going to be caught."

"No, *querida*. You can't see it, but there's a skimmer craft awaiting me at the end of this pier. I'll be in Canada sipping on cerveza for lunch, before your body is cold. Before the fish finish you off."

She let him talk, and in the one instant he glanced up and looked down the pier, presumably at his escape boat, she made the move of her life as she lifted her leg up and kicked him as hard as she could in his privates. At the same time, she pushed at his arm, moving the knife blade the precious inches that allowed her to twist to the side without getting stabbed.

Caught by surprise, he teetered on one foot, still

holding the gun and knife, one in each hand. Dominique shoved against his chest with all her might, prepared to be dragged into the lake with him. But a gunshot rang out, and she saw his shoulder jerk. The knife blade was so sharp it cut through her skirt in a perfect arc, and took yards of fabric with Jimenez as he plunged into the lake. She scrambled to her feet and ran back toward the beach, toward the man at the end of the pier who ran toward her, gun in hand.

Stanton.

"Get down!" Stanton yelled, his relief that Jimenez had been hit and that Dominique had broken free short-lived as the man surfaced and leveled his weapon on her. Stanton stopped, fired his second bullet for the day.

Gunfire rent the air, throwing chunks of the wooden pier airborne. Stanton ran. There was no way to be certain that the fire was friendly, and there was nothing he could do if they were surrounded by cartel shooters. He had to get to Dominique.

Dominique wasn't going to stop for anything, either, as she barreled toward him.

More gunfire, but this time he saw Jimenez fall backward, clutching the hand that had held the gun. Pounding steps behind him, the other officers moving in to apprehend the kingpin. The splash when Jimenez hit the water, the same water he'd planned to dump Dominique's body in.

Dominique.

He stopped in his tracks, allowed it to sink in that she wasn't dead. She'd made it.

No thanks to you.

He'd put her life at risk.

"Stanton!" His name, spoken by her, the sweetest gift. He held up his hands to stop her; he didn't deserve to hold her ever again. But when she wrapped her arms around him, his own mirrored hers and he held as tight as he could without crushing her.

"Dom."

"Oh my heavens, I thought I'd never get to see you again." She sobbed against his chest and he sank his face into her tangled locks, breathed in the scent of her. He wasn't worthy of her but he couldn't stop from surrendering to the embrace.

"You made it, babe."

She pulled back. "No, Stanton, *we* made it."

Stanton's eyes shuttered the moment she said *we*. His body tensed, and the warmth she'd clung to disappeared when he took a step back. He shrugged out of his jacket and helped her into it. Good thing, as she was shaking all over. A combination of cold, shock and relief. It was impossible to pinpoint any one emotion. Except the one singular feeling she had for Stanton.

"Stanton, I tried to text you." Maybe he hadn't seen it. She had to tell him.

He held up his hand. "Don't. You've been through so much. You're a hero, Dominique. You helped bring down someone who's been Grave Gulch's scourge. And you rescued yourself."

"Now wait one minute, Stanton Colton. I wouldn't have known how to do any of those defensive moves without the training you gave me. And if I hadn't had you to fight for, to come back to, I don't know…" She couldn't finish as sobs broke through again, tears spilled, whipped away by the lake wind.

Flashing lights caught her glance and she saw two EMT units arriving, along with several police cruisers. "Holy cannoli, I had no idea so many LEA were here." She looked at him. "Did you know?"

"No. They weren't part of the original plan, but Troy and the DEA agent called them in two hours ago when intel revealed Jimenez might be here. But no one has a recent photo of him and didn't know who to look for."

"Wait—so Troy knew Jimenez was here? Did he tell you?"

"No. He couldn't."

"So I didn't have to throw my back out? There were snipers all around?"

"No sharpshooter was going to risk the shot while Jimenez had both the gun and knife on you." His face contorted in pain and she knew it wasn't physical. Her heart, their heart—because it was one, she didn't doubt it any longer—hurt.

"Stanton, I'm okay, we're okay. Look." She held up her arms, turned around, her one leg bare where Jimenez's knife had cut through the skirt. But he wasn't looking, he was letting go of her hands, making way for the EMTs jogging up to them. "Stanton, wait!" Desperation clawed through her shock, through the adrenaline coursing into her body. "We are not ending it this way."

Stanton stepped one foot closer, held a hand up to halt the EMT. "Give us a minute, will you?"

"Ah, sir, we've got to tend to her."

He turned back to her. "You made it out okay, and that's all I was assigned to do."

"But—but we aren't done, Stanton. Your job may be over, sure. Hasn't this taught us about what's most important?"

"What's most important is that you're safe and alive. And my job here is finished."

Pain wracked her and it wasn't from the assault by Jimenez. This was one-hundred percent heartbreak. "Is there nothing I can say to change your mind?"

He didn't answer, instead stepping back and nodding to the EMTs to move in. Tears streamed down her cheeks, their warmth zero comfort as she was forced to see reality. Nothing had changed between her and Stanton. Not as far as he was concerned.

"Ma'am, come with us. Are you able to walk?" The young woman in an EMT uniform placed a space blanket around her and Dominique realized how very, very cold she was. Her heart felt as if it was freezing inside her chest, which seemed empty as the one thing that had kept her going walked away, toward the blue flashing lights. It shouldn't have surprised her. He'd said that when the assignment was over, he'd walk away. For once she wished Stanton wasn't a man of his word, so damn stoic. That he'd have realized he, too, was still in love with her. Which clearly he wasn't, because a man in love fought for his soul mate.

"Ma'am, you okay?" Dominique blinked, looked at

the EMT, whose face was stamped with concern. "It's warm in the truck."

"Okay." She let the EMT walk her to the emergency vehicle, too numb to do anything but comply. She'd used up her defiance against Jimenez, and it had saved her life. But she'd lost her heart, the one man she'd ever loved.

As the EMTs took her vitals and hooked her up to a saline drip "as a precaution against shock," she watched Jimenez as he was wheeled by on a stretcher, his shoulder and arms wrapped in bandages and an oxygen mask on his ugly face. Her mind tried to connect the dots; she'd gotten him to confess, had proven Charlie Hamm's innocence. He'd go away for life with the almost certain conviction the DA would obtain with the evidence she'd been instrumental in uncovering. The *Gazette* might get that Pulitzer after all. But no matter what her thoughts revealed, nothing mattered to her heart. Broken, shattered, hollow, lost.

Without Stanton at her side, her joy was extinguished.

Chapter 16

Two weeks passed with no word from Stanton. After the shock at all that had happened wore off, Dominique had thrown herself into the story. The initial overview had made headlines but now she was writing the deeper parts, including how she'd gone undercover to sneak into the resort. Of course that hadn't gone so well, but at least it had worked out in the end. She'd been interviewed by several television news outlets, and her reporting skills had garnered accolades she'd only ever dreamed of.

Just as stubborn was her belief, deep down, that somehow, someday, Stanton would get over his pride over how the takedown hadn't gone quite the way he'd planned. She acknowledged that it had to have been difficult to see her in such a vulnerable position, but she'd survived. They'd survived. Why couldn't he see that?

"I'm so impressed with all you've accomplished here, Dominique." Melissa sat back in her desk chair. They'd spent the last two hours going over statements and checking facts. "And I appreciate that you agree we're on the same team."

"Of course we are. Have you had any luck figuring out if there are more corrupt people at GGPD?"

Melissa shook her head. "I have my suspicions but it's slow going. Nothing worse than a corrupt cop, I'll tell you."

"I'm sorry you're dealing with this."

"You sound like Stanton." Melissa must have seen the shadow pass over her face. "Speaking of my brother, what's going on with you two? He's tight-lipped with me."

"Nothing's going on. He was so upset with himself that I was ever in danger with Jimenez. I haven't been able to break through his wall, and he hasn't spoken to me since the resort takedown."

Melissa sighed. "My brother can be an ass. This is all his pride. He'll come around, Dominique. I've no doubt you're the love of his life. My only question is, is he yours?"

"I'm sorry, but I can't comment on an ongoing investigation." She winked and Melissa laughed. They promised to get together for lunch soon and Dominique left the station. It was a perfect spring day with bright blue skies and a hint of warmth in the breeze that came off the lake. She couldn't help smiling to herself at Melissa's observations.

The tables had turned on her communications with Stanton. Unlike when she'd walked away from him two years ago, this time she was the one texting and calling him, leaving messages that went unanswered. Her one consolation was that he hadn't blocked her.

Soledad had cared for her the first few days she'd been back in her apartment, and she appreciated it but they all knew the only person she wanted at her side was unable to be there, away licking his emotional wounds. Her father had promised to continue to avoid walking his boxer dogs in Grave Gulch Park, to her relief. Her twin had been a huge support and texted her frequently to keep her chin up and have faith that Stanton would be back.

All of these thoughts whirled in her mind as she left GGPD and walked to meet Desiree Colton to get the sketch artist's story on spotting Randall Bowe. The colorful playground equipment caught her eye and she headed toward a bench where she saw the woman with a tiny tot, her son, Danny. Dominique's heart constricted as she recalled Desiree's son had been kidnapped back in January.

"Desiree, hey!" Dominique stood in front of the mother and child, smiling at Danny's cherubic smile. The boy's tiny hands clutched a plastic dinosaur to his chest as he leaned against his mom, his gaze looking up at Dominique in question. If she ever had a child, she'd never want them to go through what he had. Desiree's eyes were bright and hopeful but the lines around them highlighted the hell she'd lived through.

"Hi, Dominique. Here, have a seat."

"Mommy, I want swing."

"Honey, play with your dinosaur here on the ground for a bit, then I promise I'll push you." Desiree hugged her son and guided him to a spot next to her feet.

The toddler plopped down and began to push the plastic beast through the wood chips, making growling noises.

"Godzilla has nothing on that dinosaur."

Desiree smiled. "He loves it. Ever since…January, he hasn't let go of it."

"I'm so sorry for all you've been through, and I promise this won't take long. Thank you so much for agreeing to meet with me."

"I would have sooner, but I had to have Chief's go-ahead." Desiree's expression was apologetic.

"I understand." She pulled out her notebook and reread her notes.

Desiree's phone sounded and she fumbled in a large combo tote/diaper bag. "I can never find my phone when I want to."

"I get it." Dominique wrote down a couple of quick questions she wanted answered, but was interrupted by a high-pitched scream.

"Mooooommmmyyy!" Danny was halfway across the playground, tucked under the arm of a woman in a straw hat, yelling for Desiree. His chubby hands reached toward them on the bench.

"Danny!" Desiree yelled as she shot like a rocket

from the bench and ran to him. The woman carrying Danny looked over her shoulder, spotted Desiree coming after them, and dropped the child as if he were nothing more than a pillow. The woman took off and disappeared through the trees at the end of the park. Shock and panic pulsated through Dominique as the unbelievable scene played out. Her hands shook and she remembered she had her phone, she could get help.

Dominique verified that Desiree had Danny in her arms before she pulled out her phone and dialed Melissa's number. She reported the attempted kidnapping to Melissa, and when Desiree and Danny returned, handed the phone to Desiree. "It's Chief Colton."

Desiree's hand shook and she wasn't letting go of Danny. Dominique guided her to the bench and helped her sit down.

"Chief. It was this same woman I've seen before. I've actually seen her, in that hat and sunglasses, at this playground the last few days. It could have been Hannah." Dominique knew Everleigh's grandmother Hannah had kidnapped Danny once before. "I can't deal with this. Do you think Danny's being—" She cut herself off, obviously aware of Danny's innocent ears. Desiree was clearly concerned that Danny was being targeted, that this attempt wasn't random.

Dominique seethed with frustration and anger that Danny had been almost taken again. Desiree and he had been through enough. As soon as the call ended, Desiree's eyes filled with tears.

"You're okay? Danny's okay, aren't you, buddy?" Dominique did what she'd want Soledad to do if she was in the same situation. "Are they sending out a unit?"

Desiree nodded. "They'll be here any second. Thank God." She hugged her son to her, her grief at almost losing him a second time palpable.

"I'll stay here until an officer arrives. And we'll do the interview another time."

"Oh no, we won't. These awful people have had enough hold over all of us for too long." Desiree looked at her with steely determination. "What do you want to know about Randall Bowe?"

Stanton went over his intended words, the phrases he'd memorized, again as he drove out to the de la Vega house. Thankfully, Rigo had agreed to his plan. He didn't risk telling Soledad every detail as she'd tell Dominique in a Michigan minute, and this was one time he wanted to truly surprise her. It was the least he could do after all he'd put her through.

It'd be easy to back out, to hide behind the truth that he'd let her down and was too protective to ever be comfortable with what she did for a living. But she, and he—*they*—deserved more. Their love deserved every iota of effort and work, no matter how difficult. Because love like this came about once in a lifetime, and he was tired of living his life without her.

He hoped she would still have him. She'd kept up a constant stream of encouraging texts and voice mails over the past fourteen days. It was difficult to not respond, but he wanted—no, needed—for her to see that he'd changed, too. He would have her any way she agreed to be with him.

Nerves made his palms slick on the steering wheel, so unlike him. Yet it was nothing compared to how he'd perspired in abject fear as Dominique had lain vulnerable on that pier, under the threat of vile Jimenez.

Let. It. Go. If he allowed the memories of that day to rule his actions, he'd never forgive himself.

Pulling into the de la Vegas' driveway felt like coming home. They were as much his family as his own and had been since he had first dated Dominique. Her car was already in the driveway, but if their plans were on track, she had no idea that anyone was here.

The hands that waved at him and gave him a thumbs-up through the garage windows made him smile. The family was all hiding, waiting for his signal to burst back into their own home.

He walked to the porch and rang the bell.

Running behind. Be there within the hour.

Dominique stared at Soledad's text, annoyance at her twin flaring. She fired back her own.

What do you mean you're running late? Where is everyone else?

She thought that it was going to be family pizza night, but when she'd arrived at her father's home, no one else was here. Even Rosa and Rita were nowhere to be found.

The doorbell rang and she paused. It was past delivery time, and it was a Saturday night, so it wasn't the postal service. Maybe her dad had ordered the pizza since everyone seemed to be late, and hoped someone would be here to get it.

When she looked through the door's side windowpanes, she paused. The profile was one she'd memorized, one every inch of her being recognized.

Stanton.

Opening the door, she looked him over from head to toe.

"Where's the pizza?"

"No pizza. But I have these." He brought out from behind his back the largest bouquet of red roses that she'd ever seen and handed them to her. "Can I come in?"

"I don't know. Is this going to be an easy conversation, or a difficult one?"

"It all depends on you, Dom." His eyes were brighter than usual and her breath caught.

"Stanton, please don't get upset."

"I'm not upset, babe. I'm in love. And I'm lost. I'm nothing without you."

She moved aside. "Come in, then." The roses were heavy in her arms, arms that only wanted to hold Stanton, and never let him go. But they gave her shaking hands something to grasp as she watched him enter the house and close the door, walk the few steps to where she stood in the foyer.

"Did you get my texts? My voice mails?"

He nodded, his gaze never leaving her face. As if

he was memorizing every millimeter of it. Hope blossomed under her rib cage but she stood still, wanting him to have his chance to say what he wanted to say, to know she wasn't going anywhere. Never again.

"I did. And I read them, and listened to them, at least a hundred times each."

"Why didn't you reply?" She sounded like the breathless woman in love that she was.

"I had to get things right in my head. It was my fault that you were alone with Jimenez and Blanchard at the resort. I know what you're going to say, and you know what? It doesn't matter. I still got to you in time, because I helped you learn all those spectacular defensive maneuvers. See? I listen to you, I do. Always. Between you knowing how to handle yourself and me shooting, along with everyone that was there that day, we got through it. We make a great team, Dominique. I'm in love with you, always have been, always will be. And I'll be next to you in any way, shape or form that you'll take me. It's your call, Dom. No more wedding bell pressure from me."

"What if I *want* to marry you?"

His head did that tiny tilt that melted her heart. "Do you?"

She nodded. "I do. If I'd been more mature the first time you asked, I would have stayed, worked things out with you back then. But you're right, I was so into my job that I was missing everything. My family, a life outside of work, and most important, you. Being with you, working together these past weeks, has taught me that I can have both. I can be with you and be me. In fact, I'm the best me when I'm with you. I'm in love with you, too, Stanton. I love you and I'm here, whenever you want to marry me. If you still do."

He took the few steps needed to be face-to-face, and leaning over the roses, kissed her with such reverence that her stomach quaked as her heart blossomed. When he lifted his mouth from hers, he grinned.

"What is it, Stanton?"

"Give me the roses first." He opened his arms and she handed him back the humongous bouquet, which he placed on the living room sofa. But instead of walking back to her, he turned toward the kitchen.

"Okay, everyone, come on out!"

The garage door opened and Dominique watched in delight as her sister and dad, aunts and uncles, along with the dogs, poured through the door, filling the kitchen and living room. Frank and Italia Colton followed, as did Melissa and her fiancé Antonio, Clarke and Everleigh, and Travis and Tatiana, plus the rest of the Colton family. Stanton smiled at everyone. "Now remember the plan, everyone."

He turned back toward her and walked to where she still stood in the foyer, as surprised as she was awestruck at what she knew he had taken planning. And thinking. And most of all, love.

Stanton's eyes glittered and he took her hands in his. "I was hoping you'd say what you did about marrying me." He pulled something out of his trouser pocket and sank to his knee. "Will you marry me, Dominique de la Vega?"

"Yes, Stanton Colton. Yes!"

He placed a stunning white diamond on her left ring finger in one swift move, and before she could admire it he was on his feet, pulling her into his arms. Where she belonged.

The family cheered and clapped, wiped joyful tears from their cheeks as Dominique and Stanton sealed their commitment with a kiss.

Dominique knew this was what mattered most. Family, love and Stanton.

* * * * *

Check out the previous books in the
Coltons of Grave Gulch series:

Colton's Dangerous Liaison *by Regan Black*
Colton's Killer Pursuit *by Tara Taylor Quinn*
Colton's Nursery Hideout *by Dana Nussio*

And don't miss Book Five

Guarding Colton's Child *by Lara Lacombe*

Available in May 2021 from
Harlequin Romantic Suspense!

WE HOPE YOU ENJOYED
THIS BOOK FROM

HARLEQUIN
ROMANTIC SUSPENSE

Danger. Passion. Drama.

These heart-racing page-turners will keep you guessing to the very end. Experience the thrill of unexpected plot twists and irresistible chemistry.

4 NEW BOOKS AVAILABLE EVERY MONTH!

He thought she deserved the full truth.

And I can't give it to her here and now.

"It's a complicated situation," he stated, hearing how
weak that sounded even as he said it.

"Like Lockley?" Norah replied.

"She's a different animal completely."

The voices started up again, and Norah at last relented.

"Okay, I believe you need my help, and I'm willing to
hear you out," she said. "Let's go."

Jacob didn't let himself give in to the thick relief.
There was genuinely no time now. He spun on his heel
and led Norah back through the slightly rank parking lot.
When they reached his car, though, she stopped again.

"What are we doing?" she asked as he reached for the
door handle.

"I'd rather go over the details at my place. If you don't mind."

"You don't live here?" she asked, sounding confused.

"Here?" he echoed.

"I guess I just inferred…" She gave her head a small shake. "I'm guessing it's complicated? Again?"

He lifted his hat and scraped a hand over his hair. "You might say."

He gave the handle a tug, but Norah didn't move.

"Changing your mind?" he asked, his tone far lighter than his mind.

"No. But I need you to give me the keys," she said. "I want to drive. You can navigate."

"I thought you believed me."

"I believe you," she said mildly. "But that doesn't mean I come even close to trusting you."

Jacob nodded again, then held out the keys. As she took them, though, and he moved around to the passenger side, he realized that her words dug at him in a surprisingly forceful way. It wasn't that he didn't understand. He wouldn't have trusted himself, either, if the roles were reversed. Hell. It'd be a foolish move. It made perfect sense. But that didn't mean Jacob had to like it.

Don't miss
The Negotiator *by Melinda Di Lorenzo,*
available May 2021 wherever
Harlequin Romantic Suspense
books and ebooks are sold.

Harlequin.com

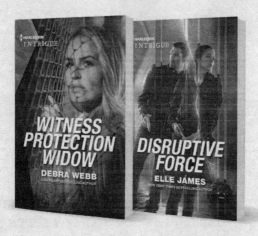

Love Harlequin romance?

DISCOVER.

Be the first to find out about promotions, news and exclusive content!

Facebook.com/HarlequinBooks

Twitter.com/HarlequinBooks

Instagram.com/HarlequinBooks

Pinterest.com/HarlequinBooks

YouTube.com/HarlequinBooks

ReaderService.com

EXPLORE.

Sign up for the Harlequin e-newsletter and download a free book from any series at **TryHarlequin.com**

CONNECT.

Join our Harlequin community to share your thoughts and connect with other romance readers!
Facebook.com/groups/HarlequinConnection

HSOCIAL2021